TWILIGHT PLEASURES

"I tried to fight it, but . . ." Cupping her face in his palms, he kissed her lightly, his tongue sweeping over her lower lip, dipping inside to caress her own.

Gasping with pleasure, she melted against him, her arms twining around his neck. All thought of right or wrong fled her mind as he kissed her again, one hand stroking her back, her hair, as his other hand drew her closer. Lost in his touch, enflamed by his kisses, she couldn't think, could scarcely breathe. There was only Micah.

His scent surrounded her.

His kisses intoxicated her.

She shivered with anticipation when his tongue stroked the sensitive skin beneath her ear.

He was going to bite her . . .

Other titles available by Amanda Ashley

Published by Kensington Publishing Corporation

TWILIGHT DREAMS

AMANDA ASHLEY

ZEBRA BOOKS
KENSINGTON PUBLISHING CORP.
http://www.kensingtonbooks.com

ZEBRA BOOKS are published by

Kensington Publishing Corp.
119 West 40th Street
New York, NY 10018

All Kensington titles, imprints, and distributed lines are available at special quantity discounts for bulk purchases for sales promotion, premiums, fund-raising, educational, or institutional use.

Special book excerpts or customized printings can also be created to fit specific needs. For details, write or phone the office of the Kensington Sales Manager: Attn.: Sales Department. Kensington Publishing Corp., 119 West 40th Street, New York, NY 10018. Phone: 1-800-221-2647.

First Printing: September 2016
ISBN-13: 978-1-4201-4248-8
ISBN-10: 1-4201-4248-8

eISBN-13: 978-1-4201-4249-5
eISBN-10: 1-4201-4249-6

10 9 8 7 6 5 4 3 2 1

Printed in the United States of America

For all those who make my life bright
Especially my husband, without whom I wouldn't have
William, John, and Dave
Julie and Marty
Ashley, Amanda, Wade, and Will,
McKayla, Luke, Marissa, Abbey, and Aly
Brandon, Skylynn, and Everley
David and Tim
Love you guys!!!!!

Prologue

Micah Ravenwood strolled through the dark streets of Morgan Creek. The town belonged to master vampire Rylan Saintcrow. Only a few years ago, Morgan Creek had been a haven for a coven of the Undead, what Micah had come to think of as a sort of roach motel for humans. People wandered in, but once they crossed the bridge, they were trapped.

Several years ago, Saintcrow had freed the captives. The vampires had scattered, and Saintcrow and his newly turned bride had gone off on an extended honeymoon. Three of the women who'd had nowhere else to go had elected to stay. To Micah's surprise, he had fallen in love with one of them. Shirley was the sweetest, kindest, most generous soul he had ever known.

With her health failing, he had begged her time and again to let him bring her across, but she always refused. Tonight had been no different.

"People aren't meant to live forever," she had replied with a wistful smile. "I'm ready to go home."

Micah smiled faintly as he turned up the winding path to his lair. As always, Shirl had left a light burning in the front window for him. It was a gesture that never failed to amuse him. He had no need for lights, but it was Shirl's way of saying she loved him.

He paused to glance at the house. Large and square and made of gray stone, with turrets at the corners, the place reminded him of an old English fortress or, more fitting, perhaps, considering the inhabitants, Dracula's castle. Thick iron bars covered the front door and the windows. Once Saintcrow's lair, Micah had taken it over when Rylan and Kadie left town.

After turning off the lamp, Micah made his way through the dark house, up the stairs to one of the turret rooms, then down the narrow staircase to his lair, located in the bowels of the huge old mansion. Shirley had her own house, but she spent her nights here, with him.

Eager to see her, he quickened his pace as he traversed the dark corridor, only to slow as he neared the door. The air carried the unmistakable scent of death. He paused, hoping he was wrong, but his preternatural senses detected no heartbeat coming from the room beyond. Knowing what lay on the other side of the door, he waited several moments before stepping into the room.

Shirley lay on her side, one hand pillowed beneath her cheek, a faint smile on her lips.

Micah knelt beside the bed, the sting of tears in his eyes as he brushed a wisp of fine gray hair from her brow. "Dammit, Shirl, why didn't you let me bring you over?"

He had been a young vampire, newly turned, when they'd met. Despite the difference in their ages—she had protested she was old enough to be his mother—the affection between them had grown deeper, stronger. She had been his rock, his tether to a world that was no longer his. She had comforted him when the realization of what he'd become had grown too heavy to bear, soothed him when the lust for blood threatened to drive him insane. She had taught him patience, made him laugh, mothered him when he needed mothering, loved him unconditionally in spite of the vast gulf between them. And now she was gone.

He lost track of time as he sat beside her, their shared memories unfolding like a movie through his mind.

In the hour before dawn, he bathed her, dressed her in her favorite white skirt and pink sweater, then left the house.

She had chosen a casket only weeks ago—a plain pine box. Unbeknownst to her, he had taken it back and bought the best casket money could buy. The outside was pale blue with solid gold handles, the inside lined in white silk. Nothing but the best for his best girl.

It waited for him in the garage. With his preternatural strength, he hoisted it onto his back and carried it to the old cemetery. Setting it aside, he found a shovel. Tears stung his eyes as he quickly dug the grave and eased the coffin into the hole.

After brushing the dirt from his hands, he returned to his lair. Lifting Shirley gently into his arms, he carried her quickly to the cemetery. He hugged her close for a long moment, reluctant to let her go.

"I'll miss you," he murmured. "Thank you for making the last four years bearable."

Settling her inside the casket, he smoothed her hair, then kissed her withered cheek. "Rest well, sweetheart."

Fresh tears stung his eyes as he closed the casket.

It took only moments to fill the grave.

"Dammit, Shirl," he murmured as he smoothed the dirt over her resting place, "you should have accepted the

Dark Gift. You'd have been strong again. You wouldn't have grown older, your pain would have been gone. We could have explored the world together, just the two of us."

Leaving the cemetery, he imagined Shirley strolling down the golden streets of heaven, happy to be reunited with Rosemary and Donna. He imagined the three old friends laughing together, all the aches and pains and grief of mortality forgotten.

Hands shoved deep into his pockets, he went back to the mansion, the rooms now as empty as his heart. Never again, he thought. Never again would he let himself care for a mortal female. Never again would he put himself through the hell of watching a woman he loved wither and die.

Next time he fell in love—if there was a next time—it would be with a vampire.

Chapter One

One year later
Southern California

Micah sat at the long ebony bar inside The Lair. He had been coming here long enough to recognize most of the patrons—women looking for a one-night stand, men looking for a woman—any woman—to ease their loneliness for a night or two. He had been in Southern California less than two weeks and had already reached the conclusion that coming to the City of Angels had been a mistake. He had been wandering from one goth hangout to another in hopes of finding a lady vampire, someone to take his mind off his loss, his loneliness, but if there were any vampires here, he hadn't been able to find them. The state seemed to be filled with nothing but movie stars, wannabe movie stars, surfers, and beach bunnies.

He was about to leave the club when he saw her—a young woman who stood an inch or two over five feet. Long blond hair fell in soft waves over her shoulders. Even in the dim light, he noticed her eyes. They were an unusual shade of blue, almost turquoise. Contact lenses, perhaps? A gray sweater and a pair of blue jeans caressed a petite but perfect figure. He guessed her to be in her mid-twenties.

She glanced around the bar, obviously looking for someone. To Micah's surprise, she lifted a hand in greeting when she saw him at the bar and hurried toward him.

"Joseph Burke?" she said, smiling. "Sorry I'm late. I'm Holly Parrish."

"Pleased to meet you, Miss Parrish. Can I buy you a drink?"

"A vodka martini, please," she said, taking the stool beside his.

Micah relayed her order and asked for another glass of wine for himself. "Holly," he murmured. "I'm guessing you were a Christmas baby."

"Good guess." She smiled that enchanting smile again. "Mr. Gladstone is very anxious to have you on our team, Mr. Burke. He's prepared to pay you twice what Lindor-Beakman is offering, along with the usual perks, of course—a company car, a three-week vacation, and the best health insurance on the market."

Micah sipped his wine. "I must admit, it sounds like a very generous offer."

She nodded. "You won't find a better one." Lifting her glass, she took a swallow.

His gaze moved to her throat, his nostrils filling with the warm, rich scent of her blood, the flowery fragrance that clung to her hair and skin, her perfume. The faint, musky scent of woman. She might be short and petite, he mused, but she was all female.

Setting her glass aside, she licked her lips. "So, if you're willing to accept Mr. Gladstone's offer, we can close the deal right now. I have the necessary papers in my bag."

"I'd be more than happy to accept, Miss Parrish, if I was Joseph Burke."

She blinked at him. "Excuse me?"

"I'm not Joseph Burke. My name is Micah Raven-wood."

"But . . . you . . . why didn't you stop me . . . ? You . . . you let me sit here and make a fool of myself."

"Sorry," he said, smiling, "but I was very much enjoying your company."

Holly stared at him. She hadn't paid any attention to his looks before. She was here on business, nothing else. Now, she wondered if there was something wrong with her, that she could sit next to such a handsome man and not even notice. Perhaps she needed glasses. Or a vacation! Micah Ravenwood was beyond handsome, with hair so dark a brown it was almost black. His eyes, too, were dark brown, with a hint of mystery. And his mouth . . . well-defined, sensual. She looked away when she realized she was staring. But who could blame her?

Suddenly uncomfortable, she mumbled her thanks for the drink, grabbed her bag, and slid off the stool, eager to put him and this night behind her.

"I'd love to buy you another round, Holly."

His voice, deep and dark and as rich as Irish whiskey, stopped her in her tracks.

Holly glanced at the door and then at her watch. She would wait for Mr. Burke for another fifteen or twenty minutes, and then she was going home to soak in a hot bubble bath. Whiling away the time with Micah Ravenwood certainly wouldn't be a hardship. It had been months since she'd been out with a man. What harm could there be in having one more drink with the most handsome guy she had ever met? So, she'd made a fool of herself. After tonight, she would never see him again. And sharing a drink with him sounded so much better than spending another Friday night alone in her empty apartment.

"You're not married, are you?" she asked.

"No, ma'am."

"Then I accept your offer," she said, returning to her stool.

He signaled the bartender for two more of the same. "So, who or what are Lindor-Beakman?"

"You must be new in California."

"Sort of. I haven't been here for several years."

"Oh. Well, they're a rather well-known investment firm, and our biggest competitor."

Micah nodded. "If I'm ever in the mood to invest, I'll be sure to call you first."

"I'd appreciate that."

"So, what do you do when you're not stalking clients?"

Holly shrugged. "The same things as anybody else. Take in a movie. Read a book. Go for a walk along the beach."

Micah glanced around. "This seems like an odd place to do business."

"I thought so, too," she said with a grimace. "I know it's all just make-believe, but seriously, why would anyone want to be a vampire?"

"Staying young and living forever might be considered a perk by some."

"Maybe. But if vampires existed, which, thankfully, they don't, no one would want that lifestyle. I mean, all the books say they can't go outside in the sun and they can't enjoy a good meal, and then there's the whole blood thing," she said, grimacing. "All that aside, what's the point of living forever if you can't have a family?"

"I guess you want a lot of kids."

"Dozens," she said, grinning.

He lifted one brow. "Dozens?"

"I'm an only child. I always wanted brothers and sisters. I don't intend to let any kids I might have grow up without siblings."

"That's an unusual outlook these days, when people are marrying later and limiting their families to one or two."

"I guess so. What about you?"

"What about me?"

"Do you want a big family?"

"I never thought about it," he lied. He had come from a loving family. Once, he'd hoped to have a wife and children of his own. That was no longer possible. He sipped his wine, but it tasted sour on his tongue. "So, who's the lucky man who's going to father all those kids?"

"I don't know," she said, somewhat wistfully. "I haven't met him yet."

His gaze met hers. "Maybe you're not looking in the right place."

His voice moved over her like silk, making her think of tangled sheets and warm summer nights. Clearing her throat, Holly said, "Well, to tell you the truth, I don't have a lot of time to look. I work all week, spend Saturdays cleaning my apartment, picking up my dry cleaning, doing the laundry. . . ." She shook her head. "By the time Saturday night rolls around, all I want to do is veg out in front of the TV."

"So, what if I asked you to do all those things on Sunday instead, and go out with me tomorrow night?"

Holly lifted her glass and took a long swallow. Her first instinct was to say no. Other than his name, she didn't know anything about Micah Ravenwood. He could be a rapist or a child molester or a con man. These days, only an idiot hooked up with a stranger she met in a bar, especially a bar filled with Dracula wannabes.

"I could show you my ID if that'll help you make up your mind."

"What would that prove? Those things can be easily faked these days."

He nodded. "True enough. Can I call you sometime?"

"I guess so." Taking a pen from her bag, she wrote her cell number on a cocktail napkin.

"Thanks, sunshine." Rising, he took her hand in his and kissed it. "Good luck with the real Joseph Burke."

Holly stared after Micah Ravenwood, stunned by the tingle of electricity she had experienced when his lips brushed against her skin. Nothing like that had ever happened before. But then Micah Ravenwood was like no man she had ever met. She couldn't quite put her finger on what it was that set him apart. Oh, he was handsome as sin, his voice as seductive as a warm fire on a winter night, but it was more than that.

Bemused, she finished her drink, wondering if he would call her and what she would say if he did.

She was about to leave the club when her cell phone rang. Joseph Burke, no doubt, calling to apologize for missing their meeting, or, worse, Mr. Gladstone wanting to know how the meeting went.

She felt a sudden prickle of anticipation when she picked up the phone. "Hello?"

"So, how about that date?"

It was Micah. She would recognize that deep, mesmerizing, sexy-as-hell voice anywhere. "What did you have in mind, Mr. Ravenwood?"

"I'm willing to do anything you want."

That voice. It made her think of a dozen things she would like him to do, none of them likely to happen with a man she had just met, sexy voice or not. Taking a deep, calming breath, she said, "There's a movie I've been wanting to see."

"Fine by me. Should I pick you up?"

"How about if I meet you there?"

He laughed softly, obviously amused by her prudence. "Just tell me when and where."

"Tomorrow night, at seven, in front of the theater on Main Street."

"I'll be there. Sweet dreams, sunshine."

Even over the phone, the sound of his voice sent a shiver of pleasure spiraling through her. She was smiling when she ended the call.

Holly thought about Micah on the drive home and while taking a shower, eating dinner, brushing her teeth, lying in bed. Who was he? What did he do for a living? How could she have forgotten to ask?

Was she making a mistake, going out with a man she knew nothing about just because he was incredibly handsome and had a whiskey-rough voice she could listen to all day long?

Holly shook off her fears. She had pepper spray in her bag. She knew a little karate. She would be surrounded by people in the theater.

She was worrying for nothing.

Smiling at the thought of seeing him again, she closed her eyes. No house cleaning tomorrow. She needed a haircut and a manicure.

And a new outfit. For a new man.

Chapter Two

Holly smiled when she saw Micah waiting outside the theater on Saturday night. Clad in black slacks, a black shirt open at the throat, and a black leather jacket, he looked handsome and mysterious and just a little dangerous. He whistled softly when he saw her, which made the hours she had spent shopping for a new outfit and having her hair and nails done worth every minute. And every dollar.

He paid for their tickets and followed her into the lobby. "Do you want popcorn?" he asked. "Ice cream? Candy?"

"Popcorn, of course. It's not a movie without popcorn. And a soda, please."

"So, how was your day?" he asked as they took their place in the concession line.

"Busy." Holly couldn't help sneaking glances at his profile while they waited in line, noting, as she did so, that several other women were also admiring him.

His gaze moved over her. "I can see you didn't spend the day cleaning house."

"You're very observant," she said dryly.

"Well, you look great." She wore a pair of crisp white slacks and a blue silk blouse that made her eyes sparkle like sapphires.

"So do you. Sort of like James Dean."

Micah chuckled. "That's me. Rebel without a cause."

"Are you a rebel?"

"I can be." He paid for the refreshments, trying not to grimace as the scent of butter and salt stung his nostrils.

Although the theater was crowded, they managed to find two seats in the last row. Micah handed her the popcorn, glad to be rid of it, then set the soda in the cup holder between them.

He hadn't paid much attention to the title of the movie when he bought the tickets, and now couldn't help grinning when he realized it was a horror film and that the monster was a vampire.

Leaning toward her, he whispered, "I never would have figured you for a horror buff."

"Why not?"

"You just don't seem like the type."

"Well, if you get scared, just let me know and I'll hold your hand."

"Really?" He flashed her a wicked grin. "Then I'll get scared."

Micah settled back in his seat as the theater went dark. After a number of trailers, the movie started. It was your typical monster movie, with the vampire being the villain, and not a suave, charming type either, but a ruthless killer who ripped out hearts and savaged throats. A team of vampire hunters chased him across the country, with the leader of the slayers predictably falling in love with the heroine. Of course, the vampire loved her, too, but he never had a chance.

About halfway through the movie, Micah reached for Holly's hand, whispering, "Okay, I'm scared now."

Holly looked at him and shook her head, but she didn't pull away.

The movie ended with the vampire hunter saving the heroine from the nasty vampire by driving a stake into the monster's heart, then setting him on fire.

Micah grimaced as the vampire went up in flames. There were few things he feared, but death by fire was one of them.

They remained seated during the credits, waiting for the crowd to disperse.

"So, did you like the movie?" Holly asked.

"It was all right," he said with a shrug. "But it would have been nice if they'd let the vampire get the girl."

"Seriously? He was a killer, a monster. He didn't deserve a happy ending."

"Maybe not, but he loved the girl, too."

"Well, he had a funny way of showing it. Carrying her off to his lair and keeping her prisoner."

"True, but she wouldn't have stayed with him otherwise. Besides, given the chance, she might have made him change his evil ways."

"Quite the optimist, aren't you?"

"Not really," he muttered. "Are you ready to go?"

She nodded and they left the theater.

"Would you like to go out for a drink or get something to eat?" Micah asked.

"I guess so. There's a nice club just down the street."

"Great."

"What do you do for a living?" Holly asked as they strolled down the sidewalk. "You never told me."

"I'm sort of between jobs at the moment."

"What do you do when you're working?"

"I was a computer programmer in a little town called Morgan Creek." The lie rolled easily off his tongue.

"I've never heard of the place. Where is it?"

"Wyoming. It's a ghost town now."

"What happened?"

Good question, he thought. Unfortunately, he couldn't tell her the whole truth, so he settled for part of it. "Business fell off. When the owner left town, only a few people stayed behind. But now they're all gone, too."

"That's so sad. I hate to hear about a business failing, but a whole town?" She shook her head.

"I hated to leave, but . . ." He made a vague gesture with his hand. "Things happen."

"We're here." Holly paused in front of a large, redbrick building. A bright green neon sign in the shape of a guitar made the place hard to miss. The words CALIFORNIA COWBOY blinked off and on over the entrance.

Micah held the door open for Holly, then followed her inside. "So the girl likes horror films *and* country music," he mused. "I find that an intriguing combination."

"You don't like country?"

"Hey, what's not to like? Sad songs about cheating hearts and lost love . . ." He swore under his breath. Shirley had loved country music. They had spent many a night sitting on her front porch, listening to Lady Antebellum and Toby Keith and her favorite, Garth Brooks.

"Micah? Are you all right?"

"Yeah, fine. There's an empty booth in the back. Come on."

After ordering drinks, Micah asked Holly to dance.

She fit in his arms as if she had been made for him. He twirled her around the floor, keenly aware of her curvy little body brushing against his, of the attraction that sparked between them. Did she feel it, too? How could she not?

He was thinking of stealing a kiss when an unmistakable scent wafted through the air. Looking toward the entrance, Micah felt all his preternatural senses go on alert.

Taking Holly by the hand, he led her off the floor.

"Is something wrong?" she asked as he hurried her back to their booth.

"Our drinks arrived," he replied, his attention focused on the man and the woman who had just entered the club. The woman was a vampire. He wasn't sure what the man was. Not a vampire. Not entirely human.

Holly followed his gaze toward the couple standing just inside the door. "Do you know them?"

"Never seen them before," he replied. But he didn't like the looks of either one. An odd tang that reminded Micah of smoke and something he couldn't quite put his finger on clung to the man. It smelled like death.

Micah watched the vampire and her companion glide across the room to the bar. The woman had been turned in her early twenties. She was tall and thin to the point of looking anorexic, although being one of the Undead made that technically impossible. She had hair so fine, so pale in color, it was almost invisible. The man was shorter, with spiked brown hair and an ugly scar along the left side of his neck. They sat side by side, their heads close together. Micah frowned when he heard the woman mention Saint-crow's name.

"Holly, would you excuse me for a minute? I need to make a phone call."

"Is something wrong?"

"No, I just need to check in with an old friend of mine. I'll be right back."

Micah left the club by the back door. In the parking lot,

he pulled his cell phone from his pocket and punched in Rylan Saintcrow's number.

The master vampire answered on the first ring. "Micah, where the hell are you?"

"California. Where are you?"

"In Morgan Creek. We got here late last night."

"Everything okay?" Micah asked. "I thought you'd be gone another year or so."

"Yeah, well, Kadie got tired of traveling so we came home for a while. What's up?"

"I'm in a country bar. . . ." Micah grimaced at the sound of Saintcrow snickering. "There's a couple here. The woman's a vampire. Tall, skinny, pale blond hair. Looks like a refugee from a Nazi death camp."

"Leticia Braga," Saintcrow said, all amusement gone from his voice.

"You know her, then?"

"Yeah, I know her. She's poison."

"As bad as Lilith?" Micah asked. Lilith had turned him into a vampire against his will, thereby putting an end to his hopes of becoming an actor. Turned him and abandoned him. He had met Saintcrow soon after. The master vampire had taken Micah under his wing and taught him what he needed to know to survive his new lifestyle.

"Worse."

"I get the feeling there's something you're not telling me."

"She's been hunting me for a long time."

"How long?"

"About two hundred years, give or take a few."

"Why?"

"We had a little disagreement."

"Little?" Micah snorted. "Must have been some hellacious argument, to last over two centuries." Of course, for a vampire, a couple hundred years wasn't all that long.

"Yeah," Saintcrow said dryly, "it was. Maybe someday I'll tell you about it."

"Sounds like a good story. Is she as old as you are?"

"Not even close," Saintcrow said. "Is she alone?"

"No, there's man with her."

"Built like a bull? Short dark hair, smells like smoke and wormwood?"

Wormwood, that was it, Micah thought. "I take it you know him, too." No surprise, there. When you'd lived as long as Saintcrow—who had been turned during the Crusades—you were bound to have run into a lot of people, both alive and Undead.

"All I know is what I've heard," Saintcrow replied. "His name's Mahlon. He's Braga's bodyguard."

A vampire with a bodyguard. That was a new one. "What is he?"

"I don't really know for sure. Some say he's a demon summoned by a witch. Some say he's a Djinn. Others say he's human but immortal."

"Is that even possible?"

"I don't know, but I'd steer clear of both of them if I were you."

"Yeah, that sounds like good advice."

There was a moment of silence before Saintcrow said, "I'm sorry about Shirley."

Micah swallowed hard. "Thanks." He wasn't surprised that Saintcrow knew about her passing. The man had always seemed to know everything that happened in Morgan Creek, whether he was there or not. "How's Kadie doing?"

"Prettier and sweeter every day."

Micah groaned. "Sorry I asked."

"How long are you planning to stay in California?"

"I'm not sure."

"Well, if you want to come back here, you know you're more than welcome."

"Thanks." Micah ended the call. He stood in the shadows a moment, his thoughts on what Saintcrow had said about the strangers in the bar, the deep affection in his voice when he spoke of Kadie. Micah had hoped he and Shirley would have the kind of relationship Saintcrow and Kadie enjoyed, but it was not to be. Micah would never admit it to anyone else, but it had hurt, knowing that Shirley hadn't loved him enough to accept the Dark Gift.

With a shake of his head, he slipped his phone into his jacket pocket. Shirley was gone and he couldn't bring her back.

Micah scanned the room when he returned to the bar. The vampire and her companion were nowhere to be seen, but the man's stink lingered in the air. Why had they come here? A country bar hardly seemed like the kind of place the Braga woman would hang out. He grinned inwardly as he walked toward the booth where Holly waited. It wasn't the kind of place he normally frequented, either.

Totally besotted, Holly smiled at Micah as he guided her around the dance floor. She feared her infatuation with him had more to do with the amount of alcohol she had consumed than anything else. But there was no denying he was gorgeous and sexy and a fantastic dancer.

She offered no protest when he brushed a kiss across her lips. Quite the opposite. She twined her arms around his neck and, heedless of the crowd on the dance floor, kissed him long and hard. And, oh my, could that man kiss. Never in her life had she experienced anything like it. His lips were cool and firm as he took control, his tongue sweeping across her lips, dipping inside. Every nerve and fiber in her being responded to his touch, and she clung to him as if he were the only solid thing in a world suddenly spinning out of control. If his kisses affected her like this, what would it be like to . . . She quickly put the brakes on that train of thought. She had just met the man! She shivered as he kissed his way along the side her neck. What was he doing to her?

She was breathless when he lifted his head, his dark eyes burning into hers with a need that frightened her even as it unleashed a host of restless butterflies in the pit of her stomach.

She blinked up at him. "That was . . . amazing."

Micah swallowed hard, all his senses screaming at him to take her outside, wrap her in his arms, and bury his fangs in her throat. To drink and drink, until he was sated with the taste of her.

Forcing what he hoped was an indulgent laugh, he said, "Holly, love, I think you've had too much to drink."

"Who, me?"

"Yes, you." He escorted her back to their booth, collected her purse, and guided her toward the exit.

Outside, he turned away from her and took several deep breaths. He wasn't like Saintcrow, who'd had centuries to learn to control his hunger. Sometimes the need to feed was overwhelming. It burned through his veins like liquid fire, the pain growing ever stronger and more excruciating until he surrendered to the relentless craving.

Holly claimed she was "feeling just fine" by the time they reached the parking lot, but Micah refused to let her get behind the wheel.

After settling her in the passenger seat and fastening her seat belt, he asked for her address and drove her home. Walked her to her door. Kissed her good-night.

It was a much more chaste kiss than the one they had shared on the dance floor.

"What about your car?" she asked, fumbling with her keys.

Covering her hand with his, he guided the key into the lock and opened the door. "Don't worry about me. I'll pick it up later. Sweet dreams, sunshine."

He waited until she was inside; then, whistling softly, he strolled down the walkway to the street. Holly stared after him until he was out of sight, then closed and locked the door.

While getting ready for bed, she was embarrassed to recall how shamelessly she had flirted with him, the way she had pressed herself against him while they were dancing. The way she had kissed him, as if she had known him for ages instead of hours. She blamed one too many vodka martinis for making her so bold. Always a good excuse, she thought. She was just lucky he was a nice guy, too nice to take advantage of her. But she couldn't stop wondering what it would be like to be in his arms, to hear his whiskey-rough voice whispering love words in her ear, to feel his hands caressing her . . . "Holly, enough!"

After changing into her nightgown and brushing her teeth, she slipped into bed and closed her eyes.

Micah's image immediately sprang to mind. Tall and handsome, mesmerizing dark brown eyes, a voice that seemed to reach deep inside her soul.

With a sigh, she flopped over on her stomach. Sadly, he hadn't said anything about seeing her again.

Chapter Three

"You never told me there was someone after you," Kadie remarked when Saintcrow ended his call with Micah.

"Eavesdropping, were you?"

She shrugged. One of the perks of being a vampire was supernatural hearing. He could have been in another room or outside the house, and she would still have been able to hear every word.

"It's old news," Saintcrow said, slipping his arm around her shoulders. Ancient news, he mused, blocking his thoughts so she couldn't read them. He wasn't worried about Braga, but Mahlon . . . Mahlon worried him. Braga's bodyguard wasn't a vampire, but he was more than a mere mortal. It was said he watched over her while she rested during the day. Being human—or part-human—Mahlon could cross thresholds uninvited. Solid as a tank and as strong as a bull, he was a formidable foe. At Braga's behest, he had, on numerous occasions, found vampires she considered her enemy and destroyed them while they were trapped in the daylight sleep of their kind.

"Do you think Micah will come back here?" Kadie

asked. When he didn't answer, she nudged him in the ribs. "Rylan?"

"I don't know. Probably. It's the only home he has."

"The town is so different now," she said. "Empty. Dead, even—you should pardon the expression."

During their absence, and with Saintcrow's permission, Shirley and her friends, Rosemary and Donna, had brought the town to life. They had redecorated the restaurant, renovated some of the older buildings, and demolished others. Micah had overseen the work. Saintcrow had paid the bills. The houses in the residential area had previously been inhabited by mortals whose sole purpose had been to supply the resident vampires with blood.

Kadie had been one of them, an unwilling victim, until Rylan claimed her for his own. There had been a time, not so long ago, when she couldn't imagine wanting to live with a vampire. Now she couldn't imagine living without him.

With the passing of Shirley and her friends, Morgan Creek had again become a ghost town.

"Do you want to leave?" Saintcrow asked.

"No. It's good to be back." She had met him here, sparred with him, fallen in love with him. "It's just different, that's all."

She closed her eyes as he leaned in for a kiss. Five years as his wife hadn't lessened her desire for him. Or his for her. If anything, their need for each other had grown stronger, deeper. He was the sexiest man she had ever known, wickedly handsome, an incredible lover.

Kadie snuggled against him when he broke the kiss, his phone call with Micah niggling at the back of her mind. What if Leticia Braga came here? "You told me not to worry," she said at last, "but you're worried about her, aren't you?"

Saintcrow didn't have to ask who she meant. He pushed a lock of hair behind her ear. "Forget about Braga."

"I can't. What's between the two of you, anyway?"

"I destroyed one of her fledglings a long time ago. She's never forgiven me." He cursed softly, then muttered, "Damn her hide, I guess she never will."

He couldn't blame Braga for wanting vengeance against him. Braga had been very much in love with the fledgling he had killed.

Cupping Kadie's face in his palms, he kissed her lightly, and then more deeply, as she wrapped her arms around him. If someone destroyed his woman, he would hunt the guilty party from one end of the earth to the other, no matter how long it took, until he had avenged her death.

Chapter Four

Leticia Braga tossed her prey aside, then wiped her mouth on the clean, white handkerchief Mahlon handed her. "Get rid of him."

"As always," Mahlon said.

"I thought I smelled Saintcrow," she remarked, tossing the soiled cloth into the gutter. "Back in that country bar."

Mahlon draped the dead man's body over his shoulder. "You must be mistaken. He wasn't there."

She glared at him. "You doubt me?"

"No, mistress," he said quickly.

"I'm not blind. I know he wasn't there," she snapped. "I'll meet you at home."

With a curt nod, Mahlon deposited the body in the trunk of his car and closed the lid.

Leticia watched him drive away, the dead man already forgotten as she returned to the club in search of another victim. Saintcrow's scent, faint as it was, lingered in the air. How was that possible when he hadn't been there?

She circled the room, pausing at a booth near the back when she detected the scent of yet another of the Undead. She had been so excited at the prospect of confronting

Saintcrow earlier that she hadn't noticed there had been another vampire in the club.

Frowning, she found an empty barstool, her thoughts churning. Of course! That vampire had been in contact with Saintcrow at some point, or shared the same space. All she had to do was locate the other vampire.

He would lead her to Rylan Saintcrow, and Gavin's death would be avenged at last.

Gavin. As always, pain speared through her very being when she thought of him. He had been an artist and a poet, the most gentle, caring man she had ever known. They had met by accident late one night. She had been hunting for prey when she'd found him lying in a filthy gutter outside of London. At first, she had thought him dead, but then, ever so faintly, she'd heard the stutter of his heartbeat, the quiet hush of his breathing. The scent of his blood had drawn her to his side. She had been about to bury her fangs in his throat when she saw his eyes watching her. Never, in all her years, had she seen eyes like his—large and innocent, as gray as the breast of a dove. She had loved him from that moment. Taken him into her heart and her home. Bandaged his wounds. She had learned later that he had been attacked by ruffians who had robbed him and left him for dead.

In the days that followed, she had learned everything there was to know about him. She had told him of her life growing up in the slums of her native Portugal. Told him everything except the truth of what she was.

Of course, with the passage of time, he had started to wonder why she never changed, never grew older, never joined him at meals, never went walking with him in the morning. Inevitably, the day came when she had to tell him the truth.

"Gavin, my love, I can answer all your questions with one word. Vampire."

He had stared at her as if seeing her for the first time. And then, to her amazement, he had thrown back his head and laughed.

At first, she thought it was because he didn't believe her. But then, to her further astonishment, he had pulled her into his arms and kissed her. "How wonderful!" he had exclaimed. "Now we can be together forever, just as we always dreamed!"

She had turned him that night.

But, all too soon, Saintcrow had put an end to her dreams of forever.

And for that, he would die.

Chapter Five

Holly slept late and woke feeling wonderful. Smiling, she stretched her arms over her head. She'd had the most wonderful dream about Micah last night . . . the most wonderful and the most erotic, she thought, as a sudden rush of heat suffused her cheeks.

She lifted her fingers to her lips. Even now, it was hard to believe his kisses, his caresses, hadn't been real. But of course they weren't, because, in her dream, he had bitten her while they made love. That was an odd turn of events, she thought, but perhaps her subconscious had conjured a vampire because she had met him in a goth club.

Frowning, she sat up. Not for the first time, she wondered why the real Joseph Burke had chosen to meet in such a bizarre place. Was he into role-playing, as were so many others these days? Or was he one of those people who—like her father—believed vampires existed? Her father was truly convinced his best friend had been killed by one.

Thinking about vampires reminded her of her cousin, Ethan. They had gone to school together, been on the high school debate team. Ethan had believed in vampires, too. So much so, that he'd carried a wooden stake and holy water in his backpack. Vampires.

She shuddered at the mere idea, though she couldn't help thinking that, with his thick dark hair and smoldering eyes, Micah would make a perfect vampire.

She shook the foolish idea aside, wondering what had happened to Mr. Burke. If he had been detained or he'd had a last-minute change of plans, the least he could have done was pick up a phone and let her know. She made a mental note to call him first thing Monday morning.

Sighing, she went into the kitchen, her thoughts again turning to Micah. Too bad she would never see him again. Even if she wanted to, she had no idea where to find him. He didn't even live in Southern California. Did he live in that ghost town he'd mentioned? The one in Wyoming? Morgan something? Cove? County? No, Creek. Morgan Creek.

Curious, she went to her laptop to do a Google search. She found links for Morgan Creek Productions, Morgan Creek Golf Course, Morgan Creek Vineyards . . . the list went on and on.

After wasting an hour searching the Web, she shut her laptop. There was no sense trying to track down a man she hardly knew, she decided, as she changed into a pair of shorts and a T-shirt. She had a house to clean, laundry to wash, and a dozen other chores that she had neglected so she could go out with a handsome, sexy stranger.

After a day spent working harder than Cinderella ever had, Holly was ready for a shower, a quick dinner, and a well-deserved reward for all of her hard work—something chocolate and decadent.

Half an hour later, she put on a movie, then sat cross-legged on the sofa, a large bowl of chocolate ice cream topped with hot fudge, a mountain of whipped cream, and a handful of cherries, cradled in her lap.

She had just scraped the last bit of fudge from the bottom of the bowl when the doorbell rang.

Setting the dish aside, she went to the door. "Who is it?"

"Micah."

Micah! She felt herself blush furiously as erotic images from her dream tumbled through her mind. "What are you doing here? I mean, I wasn't expecting you." That was an understatement, she thought, glancing at her skimpy nighty and pink bunny slippers.

"Yeah, well, I wasn't expecting to be here."

She frowned, thinking he didn't sound very happy about it.

Biting down on her lower lip, she opened the door a crack. "I'm really not dressed for company."

He shrugged. "I was gonna call, but then I decided, what the heck, I'd take a chance and see if you were home. And here you are."

She hesitated a moment, then said, "Well, as long as you're here, give me a few minutes to get presentable."

"Sure." With his preternatural hearing, Micah followed her progress through the house, heard the water come on as she brushed her teeth, the whisper of cloth over flesh as she changed her clothes, the quick tattoo of her bare feet on the tile floor as she hurried to open the door.

"Come in," she invited, flashing a tentative smile.

Micah felt a rush of preternatural power as he crossed

the threshold. Most mortals had no idea that thresholds held the power to repel his kind.

"Nice place," he said, glancing around. The walls were off-white, the furniture eclectic. Several family photos were scattered on the mantel; a couple of expensive-looking paintings adorned the walls. An arched doorway led to a small kitchen; two other doors were closed.

"Thank you. It was my grandmother's house," Holly said. "She passed away a few months ago." She gestured at the sofa. "Please, sit down."

Micah settled himself on the couch.

Holly sat at the other end, her legs curled beneath her. "Can I get you anything? Coffee? Soda? I don't keep anything stronger in the house. Oh! Unless you'd like a glass of wine? I found a bottle of Merlot in the cupboard."

"Wine sounds good. Thanks."

Micah blew out a breath as he watched her leave the room. He never should have come here. It was one thing to spend time with her at that country bar or in a movie theater surrounded by people. Another thing entirely to be alone with her in a small space. There were no distractions here—just Holly, the fragrance of her hair, her skin.

The steady beat of her heart.

The enticing scent of her life's blood.

She returned a few minutes later carrying two crystal goblets. "I don't know how good this is," she said, offering him one of the glasses. "I'm not much of a connoisseur."

Micah took a sip. He had never cared much for wine until he'd learned it was the only thing other than blood he could keep down. "It's good."

"So," Holly said, resuming her seat, "how was your day?"

"Quiet." He hated the dreamless sleep of his kind, the helpless vulnerability. "How was yours?"

"I spent most of it catching up on my chores and getting ready for work."

Micah nodded. He missed working, missed feeling useful. He had been on the verge of getting his first film role when Lilith turned him. Since Shirley had passed away, he had been at loose ends. Without her, his nights had been long and empty, his future bleak. He had no purpose, no real companionship, no driving force in his life other than his need for blood. Clearing his throat, he asked, "Where's your family?"

"They live in Sacramento. My dad's a high-powered investment broker."

"Wasn't he upset when you went to work for the competition?"

"A little, but I wanted to succeed or fail on my own merits, you know? I didn't want any special treatment because my dad owned the firm."

Micah nodded. "Was your mother a stay-at-home mom?"

"No, she's my dad's secretary."

Micah grinned. "No kidding?"

Holly laughed. "Mom's always talking about retiring, but I think she's worried that he'll hire some cute young thing to take her place, even though he's forever telling her no one could ever replace her. My dad's a workaholic, but Mom finally talked him into taking a long-overdue vacation."

"Where'd they go?"

"Australia, New Zealand, Fiji."

Micah draped one arm along the back of the sofa and stretched his legs out in front of him. "They sound happy together."

"Sometimes I envy them. I know that's terrible, but I can't help it. They complete each other, if you know what I mean."

Thinking of Saintcrow and Kadie, Micah nodded. He couldn't imagine one of them without the other. He had loved Shirley, but there had always been an invisible gulf between them, one that she had refused to cross.

Holly pressed a hand to her heart as Micah's gaze caressed her face, making it suddenly hard to breathe. To think. There was only the heat in his eyes. Time seemed to stand still as he took the glass from her hand and set it aside, along with his own. Never taking his gaze from hers, he slowly drew her closer, then cupped her face in his hands.

"I'd like to feel that way about someone," he murmured, and kissed her, ever so gently.

Holly's toes curled, her eyelids fluttering down as his lips moved over hers, evoking feelings and sensations that bordered on euphoric. If this was a movie, violins would be playing and fireworks would be exploding in the background, she thought as he wrapped his arms around her.

No one had ever kissed her the way he did, as if she were made of spun glass and might shatter. His hands skated lightly up and down her spine, sending little shivers of delight racing through her. She moaned softly, her hands sliding under his shirt, reveling in the touch of his cool, bare skin beneath her palms.

His arms tightened around her as his kisses grew deeper. Her heart ratcheted up a notch when his tongue met hers. He whispered her name, and her mind filled with images of the two of them locked in an intimate embrace. The world faded away, and there was only Micah caressing her, kissing her, the heat of his tongue on her skin. One minute, she was lost in a sea of sensation. The next, she was alone on the sofa.

Opening her eyes, she saw him standing near the window with his back toward her, his hands tightly clenched at his sides. "What's wrong?" she asked breathlessly.

"I need to go."

"Go?" Dazed, she could only stare at him. "Now?"

He groaned low in his throat.

And then he was out the door.

Outside, Micah drew several deep breaths. He hadn't been intimate with a woman since Shirley passed away. Maybe that explained why he'd forgotten that his physical desire and his unholy hunger were almost inseparably entwined. Kissing Holly, inhaling her warm, womanly scent, feeling her hands moving over him, had aroused more than his passion. It had taken all of his hard-won self-control to keep from sinking his fangs into her throat and tasting her sweetness. He couldn't begin to imagine how horrified she would have been to discover the man holding her in his arms wasn't a man at all, but a vampire.

Hands shoved deep in the pockets of his jeans, Micah strolled down the sidewalk, heading for that corner of the town inhabited by transients and those who earned their living by questionable means. Every city, town, and village in the country had such a place—a part of the community that was shunned by decent, law-abiding citizens.

For a hungry vampire, it was the perfect hunting ground.

He was nearing his destination when he caught Leticia Braga's scent on the wind. Knowing he was no match for her, Micah quickly turned and headed in the opposite direction. As far as he knew, he had been the only vampire in town until Braga showed up. If she was planning to stay, maybe he'd be smart to make himself scarce. He had only been a vampire a little over five years. If push came to shove, his chances of defeating Braga one-on-one were slim to none.

When Micah was well away from the seedy part of town, he slowed. It was getting late. Few businesses were still open. Most of the townspeople were locked safely inside their homes.

He paused in front of a house now and then, listening to the conversation and the laughter of the mortals inside. He recalled the nights he had spent with his own family, constantly squabbling with his four younger sisters—Angela, Delia, Rosa, and Sofia. Saturday afternoons playing touch football with his four older brothers—Sergio, Enzo, Mario, and Paolo; nights spent sprawled on the floor eating popcorn while watching TV. Normal, ordinary days and nights spent with the people he loved. People who loved him. How far away those days seemed now.

Save for his two youngest sisters, Rosa and Sofia, all his siblings were married with kids of their own. He phoned his parents and the rest of his family from time to time, but it was getting harder and harder to explain why he missed so many holidays. He made it home for his nieces' and nephews' birthdays when he could, always showing up after sunset. He tried to make an appearance during the holidays, constantly making excuses for why he couldn't be home on Christmas morning, why he couldn't be there for sunrise services on Easter Sunday or watch his nieces and nephews hunt for Easter eggs.

Shaking off both his memories and his worries, he hunted the dark streets, searching for prey, his hunger growing stronger with every passing moment. Five years a vampire and he still didn't feel like he was in complete control of his hellish thirst. Sometimes he doubted if he would ever control it. He wondered how Kadie managed it. Of course, she had Saintcrow to help her over the rough spots. And having been turned by a master vampire, she was stronger than most.

Not for the first time, Micah damned Lilith for turning him and then leaving him to figure things out for himself. He didn't know what he would have done if Saintcrow hadn't come along. Hell, he probably wouldn't have survived as long as he had. It had been Saintcrow who'd assured him that he could satisfy his thirst without taking a life. Still, there were times when the urge to drink his prey dry was almost overpowering.

He was about to go to bed hungry when a middle-aged man, obviously drunk, emerged from the shadows and staggered toward him. The man was none too clean, smelled like he hadn't washed in days, and reeked of tobacco and cheap wine, but this was no time to be choosy.

When he had first been turned, Micah had been careful to prey only on those who looked clean, healthy, and sober. But Saintcrow had assured him that, to a vampire, blood was blood. He didn't have to worry about drinking tainted blood. None of it could hurt him. It varied in taste and smell from person to person, but in the end, it was all just blood.

Micah took the man quickly, drank only what he needed, and left him propped against the side of a building, little the worse for wear.

He was making his way to his lair when he caught Leticia Braga's scent again. Dissolving into mist, Micah hastened away.

Braga was supposed to be hunting Saintcrow.

So, why the hell was she following him?

Chapter Six

Holly spent most of the night tossing and turning, her mind and her dreams filled with images of Micah. He was the sexiest, strangest man she had ever met. Try as she might, she could think of no reason why he would leave so abruptly. One minute they were in each other's arms exchanging kisses so hot she thought she might go up in flames, and the next he was out the door without a backward glance.

Holly racked her brain, trying to recall if she had said or done anything to make him angry or hurt his feelings, but she couldn't think of a thing.

She was still fretting over it when her alarm went off.

Rising, she went out on the front porch to get the newspaper. She scanned the headlines while eating a bowl of oatmeal swimming in butter and brown sugar. She paused, spoon in hand, when she read the lead article on the second page.

BODY OF PROMINENT BUSINESSMAN FOUND
BY LOCAL HIKERS, DRAINED OF BLOOD.

Holly felt sick to her stomach as she read the story, which stated that Joseph Burke's body had been found by bikers early Saturday morning on a sandy stretch of land three miles out of town. Bite marks on the victim's neck and a heavy loss of blood led police to believe he had been attacked by a wild animal, possibly a rabid wolf, though they were waiting on results from the coroner. Burke had last been seen Thursday night at popular goth hangout The Lair. Police were asking anyone with information to contact them immediately.

Holly pushed the bowl aside, her appetite gone. No wonder Burke hadn't shown up for their meeting Friday night. She glanced at the story again, her gaze drawn to the words, *bite marks on his neck . . . possibly from a wild animal.* She shuddered.

There were no wolves in the city, rabid or otherwise.

Bite marks on his neck . . . last seen at The Lair, a popular hangout for the goth crowd.

And wannabe vampires.

If she didn't know better, she'd think Joseph Burke had found a real one.

Holly had a difficult time concentrating at work Monday morning. Soon after she arrived, she met with Mr. Gladstone, who had also read the article about Mr. Burke's death in the paper. Apparently, so had everyone else in the company. It was all the talk in the cafeteria, with varying opinions on how he'd died, most of them absurd.

"Maybe it was a drug deal gone bad," her friend Coy suggested.

"And they tried to make it look like a vampire bit him?" asked Lynn, who worked in the accounting department. There was no missing the sarcasm in her voice.

"Well, it certainly wasn't a wild animal attack," Coy retorted, "unless there's a lion or a tiger running loose in the city."

"Lions and tigers eat their kills," Mr. Keith from Legal ventured. "They don't drain them of blood."

He should know, Holly thought, since he had gone big-game hunting when he was a young man. "So, you're saying it was a vampire?" Holly asked skeptically. "A real vampire attacked Burke?"

"Have you got a better explanation?" Coy asked.

Holly shook her head.

She was glad to see the day come to an end. She had just shut down her computer and was about to leave when her cell phone rang.

"Hello."

"Holly? It's me, Micah."

"What do you want?" she asked, her voice frosty.

"Listen, I'm sorry about last night. I was wondering if you'd give me a chance to make it up to you."

"I don't know."

"I can't blame you for being upset, but I'd really like to see you again. How about Friday night?"

"I'll think about it."

"All right, sunshine. I'll call you in a few days."

Holly felt the ice around her heart melt a little, but how could she help it, the way that sexy voice of his caressed the word *sunshine*?

"Holly?"

"Fine. I'll talk to you then."

Micah slid his phone into his back pocket. He supposed Holly had every right to be annoyed with him. After a quick make-out session on her sofa, he had left her hot and bothered with no explanation, but then, he could hardly tell her that, had he stayed longer, her health—hell, her life—might have been in danger.

Or that the scent of her blood had been driving him dangerously close to the edge of his self-control.

Or that he had left her to go in search of prey.

None of those options had been remotely feasible, he thought wryly.

Not then.

And not now.

Of course, there was always the truth, but that didn't seem like a smart move, either, especially since news of Joseph Burke's recent demise had been splashed across every paper and blog in Southern California. The press might claim Burke had been attacked by a wild animal, but Burke had been killed by a vampire. Of that, Micah had little doubt. And since he hadn't done it, he figured Leticia Braga was the culprit.

Shoving his hands deep into the pockets of his jeans, Micah strolled down the sidewalk, his thoughts fragmented. He wondered what his odds were of getting another date with Holly, why Braga had been following him the other night, and how Saintcrow and Kadie were getting along back in Morgan Creek.

Feeling suddenly homesick, he pulled out his phone and punched in his parents' number.

"Micah!"

"Hi, Mom. How's it going?"

"Oh, you know, same as always. I'm worried about Sofia."

"Is she still in goth mode?" Sofia was obsessed with vampires. She read every book she could find on the subject, both fiction and nonfiction. She watched every movie, had posters of Dracula on her bedroom walls. Her favorite color was black.

"It isn't funny, Mikey. She's acting moody and withdrawn. All she does is sit in her room with the doors closed and listen to music."

"Ma, that's what teenagers do, remember? It's just a phase. Stop worrying. She'll get over it." He sure as hell hoped so, Micah thought, because the more Sofia learned about the Undead, the more likely she was to start noticing the similarities between the vampires she read about and her own brother.

"I hope you're right," his mother said, sighing. "Where are you? Are you coming home?"

"I'm in California."

"I guess that means we won't be seeing you any time soon. How's the acting business?"

"Slow, Ma." He hated lying to her, but having the family think he was still trying to break into show business was his best excuse for not moving back home. "How's Dad?" His father hadn't been in the best of health the last time he'd seen him.

"He's feeling much better. His doctor put him on some new medication, and it's working wonders. Katy's starting school next year—can you believe it? And Todd broke his arm climbing over the neighbor's fence, and . . ."

Micah closed his eyes, his yearning for home swelling within him as his mother continued to bring him up-to-date on the rest of his nieces and nephews.

He was depressed as hell when he said good-bye.

A thought took him to Holly's house. Standing out of sight in the shadows, he closed his eyes and opened his senses.

She was in the kitchen. From the sound of it, she was

washing dishes. He caught the lingering scents of fried chicken and gravy and, overall, the scent of Holly herself.

The scent of her skin sparked his desire.

The scent of her blood pricked his thirst.

So easy, he thought, so easy to call her to him, to mesmerize her with a glance, to bend his head to the soft curve of her throat and drink. . . . Humans were repulsed by the thought of drinking blood, but he was no longer human. For him, blood was as necessary as food and drink to mortals. No two humans tasted quite the same. Some were sweet, some bitter, some intoxicating, some repellent. For his kind, humans were, quite simply, a vampire buffet.

He took a deep breath, drawing the scent of her blood deep into his lungs. She would be sweet, he thought. Sweet and satisfying as no other.

He padded silently to the front door, the tips of his fangs brushing his tongue as he climbed the porch steps and rang the bell.

He was thirsty.

And tonight, she was prey.

He muttered a vile oath. What the hell was he doing?

He was gone before she reached the door.

Holly frowned. She could have sworn she heard the doorbell, but there was no one on the porch, no one on the sidewalk. She stood there a moment, arms wrapped around her middle. Someone had been there. She was sure of it.

Overcome by a sudden, nameless fear, she darted back inside, closed the door, and turned the deadbolt, the newspaper account of Joseph Burke's death unfolding in her mind . . . *bite marks on his neck . . . vampire.*

Breathing heavily, she stood with her back to the door,

and then she laughed. She had to stop watching horror movies. She was letting her imagination get the best of her. There was no such thing as vampires. Or werewolves. Or zombies.

Just a foolish girl who had seen one too many Dracula movies.

During the next two days, Holly's heart skipped a beat every time her phone rang. It didn't matter that it was never Micah, or that she told herself she was still mad at him. Her foolish heart kept hoping. He continued to invade her dreams.

By Thursday evening, she had convinced herself that he had changed his mind, he was never calling, and she didn't care. It became her mantra—*I don't care. I don't care.*

She was relaxing in a hot bubble bath later that night when her cell phone rang.

"Let it ring," she muttered irritably. "I don't care."

But the caller was persistent and the phone just kept ringing. Scrambling out of the tub, she stubbed her toe on a chair in her dash to find her phone. "Yes, hello?"

"Miss Parrish?"

"Mr. Gladstone. Is something wrong?"

"I'm sorry to bother you at home. I just wanted to let you know that the meeting scheduled for eight tomorrow morning has been canceled, and that I'll be out of the office until Monday."

"Thanks for letting me know, sir."

"You might want to call Maddux and make sure he's received the updated contracts."

"Yes, sir."

"Have a good weekend."

"You, too. Good night."

Holly tossed her phone on the sofa, grimaced when she saw the trail of bubbles and wet tracks leading from the bathroom to the coffee table.

Muttering, "This is all your fault, Micah Ravenwood," she grabbed a towel and mopped up the mess.

She was headed back to the bathroom when the phone rang again. Thinking Mr. Gladstone had forgotten to tell her something, she picked it up. "Hello?"

"Hey, sunshine, did I catch you at a bad time?"

"No, why?" *Unless you consider being wet and naked and dripping all over the floor a bad time.*

"You sound like you're out of breath."

"Well, if I am, it's your fault."

"Mine? I'm not even there."

"Forget it."

"You sound a little out of sorts. Maybe I should call back?"

Holly took a deep, calming breath. "No, I'm fine."

"So, did you decide to forgive me for my churlish behavior?"

"Churlish?" she repeated, laughing. "I don't think I've ever heard anyone use that word."

"I've missed you, sunshine."

She bit down on her lower lip to keep from telling him she had missed him, too.

"So, are we on for Friday night?" he asked.

"I guess so."

"What time should I pick you up?"

"I don't know. What are we going to do?"

"There's another scary movie at the multiplex."

"No more scary movies for me. I think I'd rather go out for dinner and dancing."

"Fine by me. I'll pick you up at eight and take you anywhere you want to go."

"Anywhere?"

"Just name it."

"All right. I'll let you know tomorrow night."

"See you then. Sweet dreams, Holly."

"Good night, Micah."

Smiling, she pressed the phone to her heart.

Tomorrow.

She would see him tomorrow.

Chapter Seven

Friday after work, Holly paid a quick visit to her favorite boutique, where she bought a new black bra, panties, and a floor-length black dress that fit like a second skin.

At home, she took a long shower and shaved her legs. After she washed and dried her hair, she polished her nails in front of the TV, willing herself to relax while her nails dried.

She didn't know why she was so nervous. She had gone out with Micah before, but tonight she felt like a high school girl dating the captain of the football team for the first time. She was all aflutter as she slipped into her new underwear, and then into her dress.

Her heart jumped into her throat when the doorbell rang. He was here!

She took a deep, calming breath, forced herself to walk slowly to the door and pause a moment before she opened it. "Hi."

"Wow, girl, you look good enough to eat."

Holly's cheeks warmed at his words, pleased beyond measure by the admiration in his beautiful dark eyes.

"Are you sure we have to go out?" he asked, his voice husky.

"What would you rather do?"

Sliding his arm around her waist, Micah drew her body against his. She leaned into him, her scent surrounding him, the beat of her heart like sweet music to his ears. "Do you have to ask?"

She stared up at him, speechless, sorely tempted to forget dinner and surrender to the naked wanting in his eyes.

Micah brushed a kiss across the top of her head, then drew back as his hunger roared to life with a vengeance. "Get your coat," he said, giving her hand a squeeze. "I promised you dinner and dancing, and I'm a man of my word."

The restaurant was small and intimate. Holly ordered lobster. Micah ordered the same, thinking, as he did so, that it was a waste of good money, since he couldn't eat it.

But the wine was outstanding.

They made small talk for several minutes, then Holly said, "Do you believe in vampires?"

"What the devil brought that up?"

"Remember the man I mistook you for the night we met? Joseph Burke? He was murdered."

"Yeah, I read about that. Too bad."

"The papers said he'd been bitten. On the neck."

"So you think a vampire killed him?"

"It sounds silly when you say it out loud, doesn't it?"

Micah shrugged. "You know the old saying—if it bleeds, it leads. Reporters will print anything to sell more papers."

"I guess so. Oh, my," she exclaimed as the waitress

brought their meal. "I've never seen lobsters that big." She glanced at Micah. "Have you?"

"No." Catching her gaze with his, he spoke to her mind, implanting the memory of the two of them enjoying the meal together.

She might have remarked on the lobster's size, but Micah noticed there was nothing left when, with a sigh of contentment, she pushed her plate aside and declared she couldn't eat another bite.

After Micah paid the check, he drove to the nightclub Holly suggested. Located in the heart of the city, Gabriella's turned out to be a small intimate club, with subdued lighting and soft music.

Micah whistled softly as a hostess led them to a high-backed booth that offered privacy from prying eyes. "If I didn't know better, Miss Parrish, I'd think you were trying to seduce me."

"I'm not . . . I mean . . ." Feeling herself blush, Holly was grateful for the dim light that hid her heated cheeks.

"Hey, I'm not complaining," Micah said. "Would you care to dance?"

"Well," she said, smiling up at him, "that is why we came."

Hand in hand, they made their way to the dance area, which was like nothing Micah had ever seen before. Tiny twinkling lights outlined the boundary of the floor while the floor itself, lit from beneath, was a sea of constantly changing colors.

Micah drew Holly into his arms, noting yet again how well they fit together. She followed his lead as if they had danced together all their lives.

Holly gazed up at Micah. He had the most incredible eyes. Bedroom eyes, she thought, and felt her cheeks grow hotter. He was an amazing dancer, so light on his feet she found herself looking down to see if he was indeed touching the floor. The way he looked at her, the way he held her, made her feel like the most beautiful woman in the place. His eyes . . . she couldn't seem to look away. Confusion filled her as his voice sounded in her mind, whispering soft, soothing words that made the room and everything in it slip away until there was only the two of them dancing in a red haze to music she could no longer hear.

"Holly, would you like another drink?"

"What?" She blinked up at him, surprised to find they were back in their booth. She stared at the empty glass in front of her. She didn't remember ordering anything.

"A drink, Holly. Do you want another martini?" Her face was a trifle pale. He hadn't intended to take more than a sip of her blood. Had he taken too much? Or was she just extra sensitive to a vampire's bite?

"No, I don't think so." Had she only had one? She felt light-headed, disoriented.

"I think I'd better take you . . ." The words died in Micah's throat when he caught Leticia Braga's scent. Peering over the back of the booth, he saw the vampire and her bodyguard standing near the entrance, scanning the room.

Braga's gaze settled on Micah. She spoke to Mahlon, and they split up, moving toward Micah from opposite sides.

"Dammit!"

Wondering what had Micah so upset, Holly looked over the back of the booth. She didn't see anything out of the ordinary other than a very large man and a scary-looking woman. "Micah . . . ?"

"Not now." *Shit.* He didn't know why Braga was after

him, but he didn't intend to stick around to find out. Or leave Holly behind and at the vampire's mercy.

Muttering, "Hang on," he grabbed Holly's purse, wrapped his arms around her, and closed his eyes.

Holly let out a muffled shriek as his preternatural power engulfed her.

A moment later, they stood on the bridge at the entrance of Morgan Creek.

Looking dazed and confused, Holly stared up at Micah. "What just happened? Where are we?"

Micah considered how best to answer her question, but before he could decide between the hard truth or a lie, Rylan Saintcrow materialized in front of them.

Holly stared at Saintcrow, all the color draining from her face. And then she fainted.

"Pretty girl," Saintcrow remarked as Micah caught Holly in his arms.

"Yeah."

"So, what brings the two of you to town?"

"Leticia Braga."

"She's here?" Saintcrow asked, a faint note of worry evident in his voice.

"No. We were in a club in L.A., minding our own business, when she came in with her bodyguard. She was looking for me."

"Go on."

"I wasn't about to stand and fight, not with Holly there. I couldn't leave her behind, and I couldn't take her home for fear Braga would follow us there." Micah shrugged. "So I brought her here. Do you mind?"

"Not at all. Does she know what you are?"

"Not yet."

Saintcrow grunted softly. "That should be an interesting discussion."

"Yeah." Definitely not one Micah was looking forward to having.

"Why don't you stay at Blair House?" Saintcrow suggested. "It's the safest lair next to my own."

"Thanks."

"I'll put the wards up on the bridge."

"You want to keep Braga *in* if she comes here?"

"No, you idiot. I'll reverse the wards to keep her out."

"What about her bodyguard? Will they work on him, too?"

"They'll keep everybody out, except for you, me, and Kadie. Everybody, and everything."

Micah nodded, then frowned. "You're not afraid of her, are you? Braga, I mean?"

"No. I can handle her. It's Mahlon that worries me. Like I told you, I don't know what he is, but she's invincible when he's with her. A lot of hunters have tried to take her out. They're all dead." He lifted one shoulder in a negligent shrug. "It's not me I'm worried about. It's Kadie. I sired her, and that makes her more powerful than most. But she's no match for Leticia. And neither are you."

"Yeah, thanks for reminding me."

Saintcrow flashed a wry grin. "Bring your friend up to my place tomorrow night. I'm sure Kadie would like to meet her."

Micah glanced at the woman in his arms. Somehow, he doubted Holly would be interested in meeting Kadie.

Holly woke with a start to find Micah watching her, his expression pensive. "What happened?" She glanced around the room, eyes narrowed and filled with confusion. "Where are we? How did we get here?"

"I needed to get out of California in a hurry," he said, choosing his words carefully. "And I brought you with me."

She sat up, her gaze quickly taking in her surroundings. They were in a large, sparsely furnished, rectangular room. A fireplace took up most of one wall. A tall bookcase dominated the opposite one. A coffee table separated the sofa on which she sat from the one across from it. "Brought me where?"

"Morgan Creek."

"But, that's impossible. You said it was in Wyoming." She cradled her head in her hands. "I feel so strange."

"Look at me, Holly."

She looked at him warily, fear replacing the confusion in the depths of her eyes. "I want to go home."

"Yeah. About that, I'm afraid it's not an option at the moment."

"Are you kidnapping me? If it's money you're after, you're out of luck. My folks aren't millionaires by any means."

"It's late. Why don't you get some rest and we'll talk tomorrow?"

"No! We'll talk now."

"You're tired," he said, his voice low, hypnotic. "So tired you can't keep your eyes open."

"Tired," she murmured.

"That's right. Just relax. You're going to go to sleep now, and you won't wake up until the sun sets tomorrow."

Her head lolled back on the sofa, her eyelids fluttering down as her body went limp.

Lifting her into his arms, Micah carried her down the hall and into one of the larger bedrooms. He lowered her onto the mattress and undressed her down to her lacey black bra and panties. Desire knifed through him. Tucking her under the covers, he wondered if she had expected him to seduce her, or if she just liked pretty underwear.

He studied her for several moments before leaving the bedroom.

He had never been inside Blair House before. It had once been the lair of the Morgan Creek vampires.

Now, he wandered from room to room. A number of vampires— seven men and one woman—had lived here for decades. Their scent lingered in the drapes and the carpets, in the very air. Kiel had been killed by Saintcrow for attacking Kadie. Micah wondered where the rest had gone—Nolan, Trent, Felix, Quinn, Wes, Darrick. Though he hadn't known any of them well, he couldn't help wondering how they were faring out in the human world on their own. They had been prisoners as much as the humans they preyed on in Morgan Creek, but they had been safe from hunters.

He paused outside one of the doors. Though he had never been here before, he knew the room had belonged to Morgan Creek's lone female vampire. Lilith. Even after five years, her scent remained strong. She had died in this room, destroyed by a hunter, after Saintcrow sent the humans and vampires away.

Leaving the house, Micah strolled through the town. Once the vampires left, Shirley and her friends had turned Morgan Creek into a popular rest area for tourists and travelers. The homes in the residential area, once inhabited by mortals whose sole purpose had been to supply the vampires with blood, had been rented out to tourists in the summer. The restaurant had been redecorated. Some of the old buildings, like the movie theater, had been spruced up.

A new pump had been installed at the gas station, although the old hand pump remained, for sentimental reasons. It had been a favorite picture spot for those visiting the area. Some of the older buildings had been demolished. With Shirley's passing, Micah had locked up the town. As far as he knew, no one had stayed here until Saintcrow and Kadie returned.

He paused when he passed the restaurant. Seeing it always reminded him of Shirley.

When she had first gotten sick, Micah had insisted she go see a doctor. Sure, she had been pushing fifty, but hell, these days fifty was still young. In spite of numerous tests, the doctor hadn't been able to diagnose her illness.

Micah had his own ideas about the cause of her rapid decline. He blamed it on the years she had spent nourishing the vampires of Morgan Creek. To his way of thinking, the deaths of her friends could also be blamed on the vampires. It just wasn't natural for humans to be trapped in one place like rats in a cage, or to give blood so often. Of course, they hadn't really "given" their life's blood. It had been taken from them, by force, if necessary.

But that was old news.

A thought took him to the cemetery located not far from Saintcrow's lair.

The two women who had most influenced his life, save for his sweet mother, were buried here. He stood at Lilith's grave, remembering the night she had turned him. If he lived to be a hundred, he would never forget the horror of waking as a new vampire, abandoned by his sire, with no idea how to survive in a world that was no longer his.

Had Saintcrow not taken pity on him and taught him how to survive, had Shirley not given him the love and support he so desperately needed, Micah feared he would have turned into nothing more than a killing machine, some mindless monster without a hint of humanity.

Moving to Shirley's grave, he knelt to run his hands over the earth that covered her. Murmuring, "Rest well, sweetheart," he headed back to Blair House to check on Holly.

After tomorrow night, Holly's life, her view of the world around her, would never be the same again.

Leticia Braga cursed long and loud as the vampire she was hunting vanished. One minute he had been in a booth with some mortal female; the next he was gone, taking the woman with him.

She was not surprised by the fact that he had disappeared so quickly, or the fact that he'd recognized her as one of the Undead. Both were abilities known to all vampires. What surprised her was that he knew she was hunting him.

How had he known that? And who was he, anyway? What was his connection to Saintcrow? Had Saintcrow turned him?

She shook her head. Whoever the vampire was, he had been recently turned and not by a master vampire.

Saintcrow. Just the thought of him filled her with unspeakable anger. She had spent centuries alone, estranged from her twin brother ever since the night she had turned him against his will. Seeking companionship, she had wandered the world, becoming more and more bitter with every passing year, losing more and more of her humanity.

And then she'd met Gavin. His love had given her hope for the future; his acceptance of what she was, his willingness to accept the Dark Gift, had taken the sting from the past. She had felt reborn, alive again. She had never been a beauty, but Gavin made her feel feminine, soft. Desirable.

Most astonishing of all, his love had somehow filled the emptiness inside her. Suddenly, she didn't need to feed as often. Hunting no longer thrilled her. Now, it was Gavin who satisfied her craving for blood, for acceptance, for love. Her sire had abandoned her. Her parents were long dead. Her brother would not speak to her. But none of that mattered now. Gavin had become her whole world.

And then, all too soon, he was gone, destroyed by Ryan Saintcrow. Gavin's death had stripped away the last of her humanity, snuffed out any and all hope for the future, leaving her with nothing but hatred that burned away every other thought, every other emotion, save one: her need to destroy Saintcrow.

And do it she would, if she had to chase him across the world and through all eternity.

Chapter Eight

Holly woke abruptly, the lingering images of her dreams still fresh in her mind.

Strange dreams, she thought, until she sat up and realized she was in a strange bed in a strange room, and that it was dark outside.

She glanced at her watch, then bolted upright. Good Lord, had she been drugged? She had been asleep for almost twelve hours!

Swinging her legs over the edge of the bed, she realized she wasn't wearing anything but her bra and panties. Who had undressed her?

"Good evening."

Holly pulled the covers up to her chin at the sound of his voice. "So, it wasn't a dream." He looked well-rested, she noted, and as roguishly handsome as always. She clutched the blankets tighter, as if they could protect her. "Did you undress me?"

"Yes, but I didn't look."

She lifted one brow in blatant disbelief.

"Well, not much. I went back to your house late last

night and packed you a few things." He jerked his chin toward a familiar dark blue suitcase near the door.

"That was very thoughtful," she said politely, "but I'd like to go home now."

He shook his head. "Not just yet."

Holly stared at him, a trickle of unease skittering down her spine. "Micah, I want to go home. Now." She tried to sound adamant, but there was no mistaking the apprehension in her voice. She heard it, and so did he.

"It isn't safe." He held up a hand when she started to speak. "Just listen for a minute. Someone's after me. They know I've been with you, which means your life might be in danger."

"I don't believe you." She darted a glance at the open door, wondering what the chances were of getting past him, but even if she could, she could hardly go running into the night in her underwear. Who knew what lurked out there? "Why would some stranger want to hurt me?"

"Because they think by hurting you, they would be hurting me."

"But . . . but that's ridiculous. We hardly know each other."

"She doesn't know that."

"She?" Visions of a jealously insane wife flitted through her mind. "Good Lord, you *are* married!"

"It's nothing like that, believe me." He dismissed the notion with a wave of his hand. "She's actually after Saint-crow. I guess she's hoping I'll lead her to him."

"Is he the man I saw last night before I . . . before I fainted?" She shook her head. "I've never fainted before."

"Well, you had good reason. Why don't you get dressed? There's some food in the kitchen. You must be hungry."

Now that he'd mentioned it, Holly realized she was

starving. She would get dressed and grab something to eat, and then she was leaving, one way or another.

With a wry smile, he left the room, closing the door behind him.

Holly sat there for several moments, trying to gather her thoughts. Last night, she had been in California. Tonight she was in Wyoming. Someone was looking for Micah and because of that, her own life might be in danger. . . .

Wyoming. How had they gotten to Wyoming? It was a blur, making her wonder again if he had drugged her. She had no memory of leaving the club, no memory of how they had gotten here, or of what had happened in between.

Tamping down her growing sense of anxiety, she got out of bed and rummaged through her suitcase. She dressed quickly in a pair of jeans and a sweater. She found her hairbrush, which she put to good use. Her handbag was on the chair. Reaching inside, she withdrew her cell phone, frowned when there were no bars. *Maybe outside*, she thought, tucking the phone into her pocket as she left the bedroom.

The house was large and cold, and for no reason she could pinpoint, the place gave her the creeps. There was no sense of anyone living there, no knickknacks, no pictures on the walls. She peeked into the rooms she passed on her way downstairs. The bedroom she had slept in was just one of many. All were furnished with a bed and a dresser and nothing more.

In the kitchen, she found a large ice chest on the floor filled with soft drinks and a couple of apples. A bucket of take-out chicken waited on the counter, along with a plate and a fork. There were no appliances to be seen, no table or chairs. Curious, she looked inside the cupboards. They were all empty. Did Micah live here? Maybe he had just moved in and his new appliances hadn't yet arrived.

Feeling as though she were trapped inside some bizarre universe, she filled the plate with fried chicken, mashed potatoes, and coleslaw, grabbed a Coke from the ice chest, and went into the living room to eat.

Micah sat on one of the sofas, waiting for her.

Holly sat on the opposite couch, the plate balanced on her lap. "Aren't you having any?"

His gaze moved to the hollow of her throat. "I've already eaten."

Holly nodded. She ate quickly, conscious of him watching her, but too hungry to care. When she finished, she put the plate aside, took a deep breath, and said, "I think you owe me an explanation."

"I thought I gave you one earlier."

"How did we get here?"

Micah stretched his legs out in front of him and folded his arms over his chest, watching her like a cat at a mouse hole all the while.

The stillness of the house, combined with his unblinking gaze, unnerved her. She was far from home, alone in a strange place with a man she scarcely knew. He could be some kind of lunatic, a serial killer, a sexual predator. She told herself she was letting her imagination get the best of her.

"A lunatic? Really?" he remarked, his voice tinged with amusement.

Her eyes widened with the realization that he had read her mind.

"I'm not going to hurt you, Holly."

"I'd like to believe that!"

"Believe it." He took a deep breath and let it out in a heavy sigh. "There's something else I need you to believe."

"What's that, I'm afraid to ask?"

"You remember the other night, when you asked me if I believed in vampires?"

"Yes, why?" She plucked at the hem of her sweater, trying to ignore the cold knot of fear growing in her belly.

"You asked why anyone would want to be one."

"Didn't we already have this discussion?"

He heard the tremor in her voice, saw the tension in the stiffness of her shoulders. She was afraid, but had nothing concrete to focus her fear on. That was about to change.

"Vampires are real, Holly."

She stared at him. "If you're making a joke, it isn't funny."

"Am I laughing?"

"So you're telling me you believe in vampires?"

"Actually, I'm telling you that I *am* a vampire."

"I've had enough of this," she said, rising. "Take me home. I don't know who you think you are, or where we are, but I insist you take me home. Now!"

Micah shook his head. "I can't do that."

"Why not? You brought me here."

"I told you, it isn't safe for you to go home right now."

She scrubbed her hands up and down her arms, as if she had a chill. "I have a feeling it isn't safe for me here, either."

"You're not in any danger from me, or from anyone here. Believe that if you believe nothing else."

But Holly wasn't listening. Turning on her heel, she ran for the front door and out into the night, her only thought to get away from him. She didn't believe in vampires, but she believed in maniacs. She ran as if her life depended on it, which she was very much afraid it did.

She ran down the hill as fast as her legs would carry her, ran until the spooky old house was far behind her and she was gasping for breath. Afraid to stop, she pressed her hand to her side and kept going.

After what seemed like forever, she saw dark shapes ahead. Shapes that turned into houses. She hurried toward the closest one. The windows were dark, but she pounded on the front door. "Hello? Is anyone home? Hello? Please, somebody, I need help!"

Relief flooded through her when an inside light came on.

Relief that quickly turned to defeat when Micah opened the door.

He stared at her, one brow arched. "Where do you think you're going?"

"Away from you!"

"There's nowhere for you to go, sunshine. Saintcrow and his wife would like to meet you."

Holly shook her head vigorously. "Well, I don't want to meet them." For all she knew, his *friends* were as crazy as he was. With a bravado she was far from feeling, she folded her arms across her chest. "If you're a vampire, prove it."

"I brought you here from L.A. What other proof do you need?"

"You could have drugged me and brought me here while I was unconscious." That certainly made more sense than anything else.

"You don't believe that," he muttered. "Okay, how's this?" he asked, and he dissolved into a dark, silvery mist, floating just above her head.

Holly uttered a word that would have scandalized her father and made her mother blush.

Laughing, Micah materialized in front of her. "Convinced?"

"Let me see your fangs."

"Only if I can bite you." He grinned inwardly. Little did she know, he had already done that.

"No!" She backed away from him, her eyes wide and scared, her heart pounding a wild tattoo.

Damn. He could hear the blood flowing through her veins, smell it just beneath the surface of her skin. "It won't hurt," he said, his voice thick. "In fact, you'll like it."

Cupping her hands around either side of her throat, she shook her head.

"Maybe some other time." Micah pried one hand from her neck and interlocked his fingers with hers. "Come on, we need to go. Saintcrow and Kadie are waiting."

Before she could protest, Holly found herself standing in front of a large fireplace in a room that looked like the interior of an old-world castle. A tapestry, its colors faded by time, adorned one of the walls. An ornate bookcase took up space on another. A suit of armor stood in one corner, a pair of crossed swords hung over the fireplace. The armor and swords looked out of place in the same room as the Jonathan Adler sofa, love seat, and armchair arranged in front of the hearth. The sofa was flanked by a pair of exquisitely carved end tables.

The furnishings received only a cursory glance. It was the couple on the sofa that held Holly's attention. The man was incredibly handsome, with inky-black hair and deep black eyes. A thin white scar ran from the outer corner of his left eye, down his cheek, to where it disappeared under his shirt collar. Power radiated from him like heat from a forest fire.

She glanced from Saintcrow to Micah and knew they were the same. Both vampires. Their combined power filled the room and raised the hairs along her arms. She remembered meeting Micah for the first time and thinking he was like no other man she had ever met. Now she knew why.

The woman had lovely dark, wavy brown hair and golden-brown eyes. She possessed the same aura of preternatural power as the men.

Vampire.

Rising, the woman hugged Micah, then smiled at Holly. "I'm Kadie," she said. "Welcome to our home."

Holly nodded, unable to speak past the lump of fear clogging her throat. She was leery of the woman, but the man terrified her. He was a killer. A predator. She knew it as surely as she knew she was prey.

Micah squeezed Holly's hand. "No need to be afraid of Saintcrow. He won't bite you."

"Unless you ask me to," Saintcrow remarked, flashing a hint of fang.

"Rylan!" Kadie glared at her husband. "Behave yourself."

Grinning, he reached up and squeezed her hand. "Yes, dear."

With a shake of her head, Kadie resumed her place on the sofa. "Please don't be afraid of us, Holly. We mean you no harm. Sit down, won't you?"

Holly looked up at Micah, a silent plea in her eyes. She was wary of him, but far more afraid of Saintcrow.

Micah grinned. So, he was the lesser of two evils. "I think I'll take Holly back to Blair House," he said. "This is a lot for her to process."

"Of course, she must have a lot of questions," Kadie said with an understanding smile. "Holly, you can trust Micah. He's a good man. He won't hurt you." She sent a warning glance at Saintcrow. "And neither will we."

"Maybe we'll see the two of you tomorrow night," Micah said.

"Just a minute." In a move too quick for human eyes to

follow, Saintcrow stood in front of Holly. Her cell phone appeared in his hand as if by magic.

"What are you doing?" she exclaimed. "Give me that!"

"I'll just hang on to it while you're here."

Indignant, Holly stared at Micah. He shrugged, then wrapped his arm around her waist.

Moments later, they were back in the living room at Blair House.

Releasing his hold on Holly, Micah went to stand near the fireplace, putting some distance between them. "Are you okay?"

"I don't think I'll ever be okay again." She curled up in a corner of the sofa, her legs tucked beneath her, arms tightly folded across her chest. "I can't believe the nerve of that . . . that vampire! What gives him the right to take my phone?"

"It's his town, Holly. He makes the rules. Maybe he was afraid you'd call for help."

"Humph! I already tried. No bars. Was that his doing?"

Micah shrugged. "Perhaps." He wasn't surprised by her confession. Had he been in her shoes, he would have called for help as soon as an opportunity presented itself. Back when Saintcrow and the vampires had lived here, Saintcrow hadn't allowed any of the vamps or humans to have phones or computers or anything that would put them in touch with the outside world. In those days, when vampires who had grown tired of dodging the hunters came seeking refuge in Morgan Creek, they had become prisoners, in their own way, as much as the humans they fed on.

"So, do you have questions?" he asked.

"Thousands," Holly muttered irritably.

"Ask away."

"Is it true—all the things the books and movies say?

You drink . . . blood? And don't age? And you can't go out in the sun? Or have children?"

He nodded. "And a wooden stake in my heart will kill me, in case you were wondering."

"And you can read my mind." It wasn't a question.

"Yeah."

"Do you sleep in a . . . ?" She couldn't say the word. It was just too gross to even think about.

"No, I don't sleep in a coffin. Just a bed."

Her relief was almost palpable.

Suddenly filled with restless energy, Micah paced the floor in front of the hearth.

Holly watched him a moment. How had she dated him, kissed him, and never realized what he was? It seemed obvious now. The way he moved, as if he weren't tethered to the earth the way she was, the ever-present hunger lurking in his eyes. She had foolishly thought it was desire; she knew now it was a yearning for blood. Her blood.

Suddenly uncomfortable at the silence between them, she blurted, "Kadie and Saintcrow seem . . . happy."

"No reason why they shouldn't be. They're very much in love."

Vampires in love? That was a whole new concept. What kind of life did they have? What was the point of living forever if you couldn't have a family? How did they fill their nights when they had no purpose in life other than to feed? "Have you ever been in love?"

Micah snorted. "You just learned vampires are real and you're asking about my love life?"

"Have you? Been in love?"

"Just once," he said quietly. He paused in front of the hearth, one hand braced against the mantel. "Her name was Shirley." The memory of losing her knifed through him again, as fresh as if it had just happened. "She passed away a year ago."

"Did you . . . ?"

Micah didn't have to read her mind to know what she was asking. "Yes, I drank from her. And no, I didn't kill her." He spoke sharply, aggravated that she would even think such a thing. "What about you?" he asked, turning the tables on her. "Have you ever been in love?"

"Not really." Her gaze slid away from his. She had been falling in love with him, Holly thought. Thank goodness she had learned the truth before it was too late. Still, he seemed nice enough. For a vampire. But she didn't trust him. And she still wanted to go home.

Vampire . . . She gave herself a mental shake. In spite of all he had told her, all she had seen with her own eyes, it just didn't seem possible such creatures actually existed.

"Creatures? Really?"

She blushed from the soles of her feet to the top of her head. She had to remember he could read her thoughts. "How long are you going to keep me here?"

"As long as necessary."

"Are you going to . . ." She lifted one hand to her throat. "Bite me?"

"I already did, sunshine. I already did."

And with that bit of disturbing news, he vanished from her sight.

Micah stood in the shadows outside the house. His annoyance at Holly for thinking he had killed Shirley, combined with his resentment at Shirley for not letting him bring her across, filled him with impotent anger. And that anger, like so many strong emotions, sparked his hunger. He envied Saintcrow. The man was a rock, able to control his hunger and his emotions, to come and go as he pleased day or night, to spend eternity with the woman he loved. Dammit, it wasn't fair!

A thought took him to the nearest town. He prowled the night, searching for prey, but it was Holly who dominated his thoughts. The fact that he was drawn to her only made matters worse. He didn't want to care for her. He had vowed if he fell in love again it would be with a vampire, someone who would understand him, someone to share the next couple of hundred years with, but he was afraid it was too late for that. Like it or not, he couldn't get Holly Parrish out of his mind. He wanted her, for a lifetime or an eternity, it didn't matter.

He wanted her.

And he would have her.

One way or another.

He had bitten her. The thought made Holly sick to her stomach, and she thrust it aside. She tried to push all thoughts of Micah from her mind, as well, but it was impossible. Why, of all the men in the world, did Micah have to be a vampire? Sure, she hardly knew him, but she had been attracted to him from the night they'd met. She had been so certain that he was different from other men. Well, she had been dead right about that, she thought dryly. She just hadn't known how different!

Tomorrow, when he was sleeping in his coffin—*no, his bed*, she amended—she was leaving this place. There had to be a road nearby. Sooner or later, roads led to freeways, and freeways led to towns. She would hitchhike if she had to. Maybe she would get lucky and a nice, fatherly cop would pick her up and make sure she got safely home.

She wondered where Micah had gone, then decided she

didn't want to know. There were times when ignorance was bliss, and she was certain this was one of those times.

Moving to the window, she stared into the darkness. What was it like, to drink blood to survive? She couldn't even begin to imagine it. It was one thing to lick your own blood from a paper cut, another entirely to drink it—drink it!—from a stranger. How much had he taken? A tablespoon? A cup? A pint? She shuddered. More?

She lifted a hand to her neck. When had he bitten her? And why couldn't she remember? It seemed impossible that she could forget something so horrendous.

She added that to the list of things she didn't want to think about, afraid she might go a little crazy if she let herself dwell on it.

What was it like for Micah from day to day—or rather, night to night? Did he miss the warmth of the sun on his face? Vampires were supposed to live for hundreds, maybe thousands, of years. What did they do for excitement when they had seen everything, done everything? Did they ever get tired of existing on a warm, liquid diet?

She frowned. Micah had eaten lobster and rice when they went out to dinner together. How was that possible?

Had he wanted to be a vampire? Had it happened the way it did in movies? Vamp drinks from human. Human drinks from vamp, and *voila!* A new vampire is created.

She pressed a hand to her forehead. Just thinking about it gave her a headache.

Stretching out on the sofa, she tried to force all thoughts of vampires from her mind, but, of course, that was impossible. Every time she closed her eyes, she envisioned Micah bending over some poor, unfortunate soul, or worse, sinking his fangs into her own throat.

She tossed and turned for hours until, at last, she tumbled into a restless sleep.

* * *

The sun shining through the front window roused Holly. Remembering her decision to leave here while Micah slept, Holly bolted upright. Rising, she straightened her clothes as best she could, grabbed an apple from the ice chest in the kitchen, and ran out of the house.

Walking briskly, she left the house on the hill behind. Last night, it had seemed as if the other houses were miles away, but as she neared the residences now, she realized they were much closer than she'd thought.

Micah had told her Morgan Creek was a ghost town. It certainly felt that way, even though the homes she passed looked well-tended.

More buildings loomed ahead. Drawing closer, she saw a grocery store, a library, a restaurant. All closed up tight.

Farther down the street, she noticed a movie theater and a gas station. What had happened to the people who lived here? Had Micah and Saintcrow killed them all and taken over the town? Maybe there really were ghosts here. That would explain the sudden chill that swept over her as she hurried down the deserted street.

Her steps quickened when she saw the bridge up ahead and the road beyond. With any luck at all, she would find a ride into the nearest town and be home by tomorrow.

Chapter Nine

Grumbling under his breath, Saintcrow rolled out of bed, pulled on a pair of jeans, a hooded jacket, and sunglasses, and left the house. A thought took him into the town proper. Eyes narrowed against the light and heat of the sun, he spotted Micah's woman running toward the far end of the bridge, frantically waving her arms in hopes of flagging down a passing car.

He didn't waste time trying to reason with her—simply wrapped his arms around her and willed the two of them into Blair House.

As soon as he released her, she ran for the front door, a cry of dismay erupting from her throat when the door refused to open. Like a doe trapped by a mountain lion, she whirled around to stare at him, her heart pounding like a trip hammer, her eyes wide with fright.

"Where the hell did you think you were going?" Saintcrow removed his sunglasses and slipped them into his jacket pocket.

"Home."

"Didn't Ravenwood tell you that was a bad idea?"

She nodded. She was visibly trembling now, her face pale.

Saintcrow blew out a breath, annoyed by her fear. Not that he could blame her. He was a very old vampire. Even humans who didn't recognize him for what he was sensed his preternatural power and strength. "Relax," he said quietly. "I'm not going to hurt you."

"Then let me go."

"Lady, you can't be that dumb. I know Micah told you about Braga. She's a dangerous, vengeful creature who wouldn't think twice about draining you dry and tossing your corpse into a ditch. If you go back home and she gets your scent, you're as good as dead."

She glared at him, arms akimbo. "What if I don't believe you?"

"Why would I lie?"

Holly couldn't think of a logical reason, but that didn't mean he was telling the truth. "How can you be awake? It's daytime."

"I've been a vampire a very long time. I can be awake during the day as long as I don't spend too much time in the sun. Now, if you'll excuse me, I'm going back to bed. We'll talk later."

And with those ominous parting words, he vanished from her sight.

Holly stared at the place where he had been standing. How had he done that? And how had he known she was at the bridge?

She looked at the door. Curious, she tried to open it again. The handle turned, but the door remained closed. She tried the windows and the back door with the same results.

With her mind still reeling from her conversation with Saintcrow, she returned to the living room and sank down on the sofa. She hadn't believed Micah when he told her that her life was in danger if she went home, but in spite of her words to the contrary, when Saintcrow said her life was in danger, she believed every word.

How strange was that?

Micah rose with the setting of the sun. He would have preferred to take his rest upstairs, in one of the bedrooms, but he didn't feel comfortable doing so with Holly in the house, so he slept in the basement with the heavy iron door bolted from the inside. Not that he was afraid she would try to destroy him—although that was always a possibility. It was more that he didn't want her to see him when he was trapped in the dark sleep, helpless, vulnerable. He had never seen a vampire at rest, had no idea what he, himself, looked like.

He still found it unsettling, sinking into that deathlike oblivion. No dreams, no tossing and turning. He grunted softly. No trouble falling asleep. Once the sun went down and he closed his eyes, it was, indeed, like death. If he lived long enough, he would be able to be active during the day, but that was decades maybe centuries—down the road.

He dressed quickly, ran a comb through his hair. As soon as he opened the basement door, he knew Saintcrow had been in the house.

What he didn't know was why.

Racing up the stairs, he found Holly in the kitchen, drying her hands on a dish towel. His gaze moved over her, lingering on the curve of her neck. "Are you all right?"

She nodded. "Why wouldn't I be? There's no one else here."

Micah frowned. "What's wrong?"

"Nothing."

"What did Saintcrow want?"

"How do you know he was here?"

"I can smell him. What happened?"

Holly leaned back against the counter and folded her arms over her chest. "I left."

"Left?" Micah raised one brow. "What do you mean, you left? Where did you go?"

"I was going home. I would have made it, too, if Saintcrow hadn't grabbed me and brought me back here."

"Why would you do that? I told you it wasn't safe for you to leave."

"Why?" she asked, her voice rising as anger and frustration replaced her fear. "Why? Maybe I don't want to be here! Maybe I don't like being held prisoner by vampires! Maybe I'm scared out of my mind because some psycho vampire who doesn't even know me wants to kill me!"

"All good reasons," Micah allowed with a grin. "Although, if you ask me, that last one seems like reason enough to stay."

"It's not funny, damn you!"

"You're right—it's not funny. It's serious as hell."

"What is this place? What kind of town has businesses and houses but no people?"

"A very strange town." Micah jerked his head toward the living room. "Let's go sit down and I'll tell you what I know."

Holly hesitated a moment, then went into the front room and sat on one of the sofas, her hands tightly folded in her lap.

Micah took a place on the other couch. "Years ago, and I don't know how many years exactly, this town was inhabited by a coven of vampires. Saintcrow was their leader. He put some sort of supernatural whammy on the bridge that also extended to the mountains that surround the town, so that anyone who wandered into Morgan Creek was unable to leave. The vampires provided the people with food and shelter, books and movies . . ." He paused, wondering how to explain the rest without making Saint-crow and the others sound like monsters, only to realize it was impossible.

"What happened to the people?"

"Not what you're thinking, exactly, but . . . the vampires preyed on the men and women who lived here. The vamps weren't allowed to hurt anyone. Or kill them," he added quickly. Although that had happed from time to time. "But they did drink from them."

Holly's eyes widened in horror. "They kept people here to feed on? Like cattle? That's disgusting! It's . . . it's . . ." She shook her head. "How could you do that? What about children?"

"Hey, I wasn't even here then. This was all set in motion long before I met Saintcrow. And as far as I know, they never kept any children here."

"As far as you know." She shook her head. "He's a monster."

"I don't know about that."

She stared at him, aghast. "You think what he did was right? Is that what you intend to do with me? Keep me here like your own private stock?"

"Of course not!"

"So, where are all those people now?"

"Kadie convinced Saintcrow to let all of them go."

"For someone who says he wasn't here, you seem to know an awful lot about what went on."

Micah nodded. "Three of the women who lived here decided to stay when the others left. I fell in love with one of them. I told you about her."

Holly nodded. "I just don't understand what any of that has to do with the woman who's after you."

"There's no connection that I know of. It was just bad

timing that Braga and I crossed paths. I don't know how she put it together that Saintcrow and I know each other. All I know is Saintcrow told me she's dangerous, and so is the man she travels with."

"So," Holly murmured, "if I'd never met you, my life wouldn't be in danger, and I wouldn't be here now."

"That about sums it up."

"Talk about bad luck."

"I'm sorry you feel that way."

"How else would you expect me to feel?"

"I'm trying to help you, sunshine, whether you believe it or not. If you want to leave, leave."

Holly chewed on her thumbnail. If everything he had said was true, going home would be foolhardy, perhaps fatal. "How did Saintcrow know I was at the bridge? I left in the morning, when your kind is supposed to be dead to the world—you should pardon the pun."

Micah shook his head. "He has incredible power. I don't know how he does it, but he knows everything that goes on in this town. It's like he's got some kind of physical connection to the place."

She nodded, her expression thoughtful.

Micah sat back, hands resting on his thighs, watching her, reading her thoughts. Some of her fear had evaporated, replaced by what she considered morbid curiosity about the history of Morgan Creek and the vampires who had lived here, preying on those who'd had the misfortune to stumble into the town. Kept like rats in a trap, was the way she viewed it.

She wasn't far wrong, he thought. Still, from the vampire point of view, he could understand why Saintcrow had done it. Fifty years ago, vampire hunters had stalked their kind relentlessly. It must have seemed like a stroke of genius, taking over a ghost town, warding it so no one who entered could leave, thereby assuring that the town's location and inhabitants were kept secret from the rest of the world.

From a human standpoint, it was despicable. But if Micah had learned one thing in his short time as a vampire, it was that humans and vampires didn't live by the same codes of conduct.

Holly blew out a sigh. "I don't know what to do." Closing her eyes, she massaged her temples.

Micah watched her a moment; then, moving behind the sofa, he began to rub her back and shoulders. She started at his touch, then relaxed, her head falling forward, a sigh of pleasure escaping her lips.

"This is all so unreal," she muttered. "No one will ever believe it."

No one would ever know, Micah thought as he kneaded the tension from her neck. If she decided to leave, he would wipe all memory of himself, Saintcrow, Kadie, and Morgan Creek from Holly's mind. It was a handy talent, one he had used often on those he preyed upon.

All things considered, he couldn't help thinking that would probably be the best course of action for all concerned. Except . . . he wasn't ready to see the last of Holly Parrish. And wiping her memory wouldn't keep her safe. Ignorance might be bliss, but it wouldn't protect her from Braga.

"So, what do we do now?" she asked.

"I guess that depends on you."

Holly didn't pretend she didn't know what he was talking about. Even now, knowing what he was, she couldn't deny the attraction that hummed between them like the sizzle in the air before a storm. She had tried to ignore it, told herself it wasn't real, but to no avail. It intrigued her, tempted her, even as it frightened her.

She folded her arms over her chest. "What if I still want to go home?"

"If you're determined to leave in spite of everything, then I'll take you back." Saintcrow might have been able to justify keeping people against their will, but Micah couldn't do it. He wasn't Holly's keeper or her jailer. She was a big girl, old enough to make her own decisions, no matter how stupid they were.

She leaned forward, her hands on her knees. "Do you mean it?"

He nodded. He didn't tell her he would erase her memory before he released her.

Decisions, decisions, Holly thought, settling back on the sofa. Now that Micah had agreed to take her home if that was what she wanted, she hesitated. Did she really want to go home and take a chance on facing a vindictive vampire? Or stay in Morgan Creek with an attractive one until the danger was past?

In the end, there was really only one decision that made any sense. "As much as I hate to admit it, I guess staying here *is* the smart thing to do. But you promise you'll take me home when that other vampire is no longer a threat?"

He nodded again.

"All right," she murmured. "I'll stay. Oh, wait! I can't. I have a job! My boss expects me to be at work tomorrow. I have an appointment with a new client at ten, and I'm supposed to interview a new secretary for one of the partners, and . . ." Her voice trailed off.

"Can't you take some time off?" Micah asked.

"My vacation starts next week."

"All right, here's what we'll do. I'll take you home late tonight. You go to work in the morning. Tell your boss something's come up and you need to take your vacation a little early. Don't go out for lunch. Work overtime if you have to, but don't leave the building until I get there. You should be safe as long as you're surrounded by people. When the sun goes down, I'll bring you back here."

"Can the Braga woman go out during the day?"

"I don't think so. But her bodyguard, Mahlon, can, and I don't want to mess with him. Even Saintcrow's afraid of him."

If that was true, Mahlon must be scary indeed. "Are you sure all this is necessary?"

"It's *your* life."

When he put it like that, there was nothing else to say.

As promised, Micah took Holly home that night. He sat on the sofa, watching an old Steve McQueen movie, while she went into her room. He heard the water come on, detected the scents of soap and shampoo as she showered and washed her hair. Soon after, he heard the sound of a blow-dryer. Fifteen minutes later, she stepped into the living room clad in flowered PJs and a light blue robe.

After a moment's hesitation, she joined him on the sofa. He noted she left as much room as possible between them.

"You remember what I told you about staying inside tomorrow?" he asked.

She nodded. "Are you going back to Morgan Creek tonight?"

"No."

"You don't intend to stay here, do you?"

"Uh-huh."

"Tonight *and* tomorrow?"

"Is that a problem?"

"Where will you spend the day?"

"In your closet probably."

"My closet?"

"It's dark and quiet."

"Oh." She had never let a man stay the night, Holly mused, grinning inwardly, and the first time she did, it was a vampire who intended to sleep in the midst of her jeans and dresses. On one hand, she was less than thrilled with the idea. On the other, she would at least have someone to protect her on the off chance that Braga came sniffing around tonight. "Well, I think I'll go to bed. Do you need anything?"

His gaze moved to the curve of her throat. The heat of his eyes was a palpable thing, almost like a physical caress.

Holly lifted a hand to her neck, suddenly remembering that he claimed to have bitten her. "When?" she asked. "When did you bite me?"

"While we were dancing at Gabriella's."

"I don't believe you. I'm sure I'd remember something like that."

"Not if I didn't want you to."

She stared at him. Not only had he bitten her, but he had also compelled her to forget it. How many times had he done such a despicable thing?

"Just once."

Holly grimaced. It was yet another grim reminder that he could read her thoughts.

"Why should I believe you? You could have done it a hundred times and I wouldn't know."

"True enough, but I didn't." Reaching into his pocket, he pulled out her cell phone and tossed it to her. "Saint-crow thought you might need this."

"How thoughtful of him."

"Why don't you get some sleep, sunshine? It's late."

Nodding, she went into her bedroom and locked the door, although that seemed pointless, since he could easily turn into mist and slip through the cracks.

She brushed her teeth, tossed her robe on the foot of the bed, crawled under the covers, and all the while, she imagined Micah bending over her, his fangs piercing her flesh, drinking her blood. . . . Such thoughts were not conducive to a good night's rest.

When she finally drifted off, it was to dream of Leticia Braga chasing her through a dark, shadowy world. Micah ran at the other vampire's side, his eyes as red as the fires of hell, his fangs dripping blood.

Her blood.

Chapter Ten

Several years before she passed away, Holly's grandmother had decided she needed a walk-in closet with built-in shoe racks and sweater cubbies. And mirrored doors because they were all the rage. The rest of the family had considered the remodel an extravagance, but not Holly. She had bragged to all her friends about how hip her granny was. Not only did Grandma Parrish drive a Dodge Challenger, but she had mirrored doors in her bedroom.

One of the last things Holly had promised her grandmother was that she would be worthy to wear white on her wedding day. In college and beyond, Holly had come close to breaking that promise several times, but her vow to wait had kept her from crossing the line. So far. She had a terrible feeling that if anyone could make her break that vow, it would be Micah, whether she was willing or not.

In the morning, Holly stood in front of the closet doors, checking to make sure nothing was showing that shouldn't be. And all the while, her hand itched to slide one of the doors open and steal a peek at Micah while he was at rest. Would it wake him up? Was it possible to wake a sleeping vampire? Did he look gross while trapped in that deathlike sleep?

Shaking the impulse aside, she stepped into her shoes, grabbed her handbag, and hurried out to her car. Sliding behind the wheel, she quickly locked the door and pulled out of the driveway. She told herself there was nothing to worry about. Braga was a vampire. She had to sleep when the sun was up. But her bodyguard . . . what was his name? Oh, yes, Mahlon. He was human. And Saintcrow was afraid of him. Having met Saintcrow, she found it hard to imagine that he was afraid of anything, human or otherwise.

All the way to work, she kept glancing in the rearview mirror, a quiver of unease slithering down her spine every time she saw a car with a man behind the wheel following close behind her.

She didn't relax until she was safely inside her office with the door closed. By then, she was a nervous wreck.

Holly breathed a sigh of relief when five o'clock rolled around. She had just backed up her work when Micah materialized beside her desk.

"You about ready?" he asked, glancing around her office. It was small and square. A window overlooked the street, a framed painting of a running horse adorned one wall, a whiteboard hung beside the door.

Holly pressed a hand to heart. "Don't do that!"

"Do what?"

"Just zap into my office."

"Sorry."

Scowling, she quickly shut down her computer and gathered her things.

"Did you talk to the boss about taking your vacation early?"

"Yes. He wasn't happy about it, but he said it would be all right."

"Good. Let's go."

All Holly's senses came alive as they rode the elevator down to the parking garage. As she walked toward the car, her gaze darted left and right. Was there someone lurking in the shadows?

She quickly unlocked her car, and Micah slid into the passenger seat. His presence, so close, made her pulse race. The car seemed smaller with him in it. With her hands clenched on the wheel, she drove out of the garage and headed for the freeway.

He chuckled softly when she glanced in the rearview mirror for the tenth time in as many minutes. "Relax. There's no one following us."

"How can you be so sure?"

"I'd be able to sense her if she was nearby."

"What about that bodyguard of hers? Can you sense him, too?"

"Yeah."

A handy talent, she thought as she pulled off the freeway.

At home, Holly changed into jeans and a T-shirt. A peanut butter and jelly sandwich, washed down by a glass of milk, served as dinner. She cleaned out her refrigerator, disposing of everything that would spoil, then asked her neighbor's teenage son, Josh, to water the yard until she returned, and to collect her mail—most of which was junk these days, since she paid her bills online.

And all the while, she was keenly aware of the attractive vampire idly thumbing through a magazine in her living room.

Doubts assailed her as she packed a bag with enough

changes of clothes to last three weeks. Another small case held her toiletries. Was she doing the right thing? She was going off to a ghost town with a man she scarcely knew, putting her life—and her future—in the hands of a vampire and his two friends—who were also vampires.

Muttering, "I must be insane," she closed her suitcase, slung her handbag over her shoulder, and picked up the smaller of the two bags.

"I'm sorry about all this," Micah said from the doorway. "I didn't mean to put your life in danger."

"I know. It's not your fault." She glanced around the room. "I guess I'm ready."

"You can trust me, Holly. I won't let anything happen to you."

Looking up, she met his gaze. In some ways, she was more afraid of him than she was of Saintcrow and Braga combined. They could harm her physically, but caring for Micah could bruise her soul.

Micah grabbed the other suitcase, then wrapped his arm around her waist.

Moments later, they were back in Blair House.

Feeling nervous and ill at ease, Holly looked at him. Why had she agreed to this? What was she going to do in this place for three weeks? The town was deserted. There was nothing to do here. He slept during the day.

He set her suitcase on the floor beside the sofa; then, as if he knew his nearness made her uncomfortable, he put some space between them. "I need to go out for a while. You'll be safe here."

She dropped her purse and the small bag on the sofa. "Where are you going?"

"Just where you think," he said, his gaze meeting hers. "I need to feed."

He said it so casually, she thought. As if it were no big

deal to go out and prey on some poor, unsuspecting man or woman.

"I know you think it's awful, but it's necessary."

Holly sank down on the couch. "Do you like being a vampire?"

"Like it?" Micah frowned as he thought it over. He had never stopped to think about it. It was a fact of life, something that, once done, couldn't be undone. "What difference does it make?" he asked bitterly. "There's no going back."

"But would you, if you could?"

Would he? Sure, there were things he missed, like playing football with his brothers on Saturday mornings, digging into his mother's homemade lasagna and apple pie, teasing Sofia and Rosa about their dates while driving them to early church services on Sunday. But there were things about being a vampire he would also miss, like his preternatural strength and speed, his enhanced senses, his immunity to disease, never growing old and feeble.

And things he wouldn't miss, like the hunger that clawed at his vitals even now, urging him to sink his fangs into Holly's throat and savor the warm, rich nectar that flowed through her veins.

"I'll be back in a while." And with those few words, he was gone.

Holly shook her head, wondering if she would ever get used to watching him vanish in the blink of an eye. Wondering what she was going to do in this dreary place for the next three weeks, and what she would do if Braga was still a threat when those three weeks were up. She couldn't stay locked in this place forever. She had a job she loved, friends, family.

She closed her eyes, her mind reeling with questions for which she had no answers.

In the morning, Holly woke with a start. For a moment, she couldn't remember where she was, and then it all came rushing back to her.

She was in Morgan Creek, alone with three vampires.

In the cold light of day, being trapped in a ghost town with Micah and his friends suddenly seemed like the worst decision she had ever made.

Grabbing her handbag, she fled the house. If she was careful to always be home before dark, if she armed herself with a sharp wooden stake and a bottle of holy water and a big silver cross, surely she'd be safe from the monsters.

She was out of breath by the time she reached the bridge. She glanced over her shoulder, but there was no sign of Saintcrow.

Gathering her courage, she started across the wooden expanse, repeatedly glancing over her shoulder, constantly wondering if she was doing the right thing.

Only another few steps until she reached the road.

She heard a car in the distance. If she hurried, maybe she could flag down the driver and hitch a ride.

Almost there!

Relief flooded through her when she reached the end of the bridge. And then a strange thing happened. She couldn't go any farther. She couldn't see anything blocking her way, couldn't feel any kind of barrier, but try as she might, she couldn't get past the edge of the bridge to the roadway beyond.

She let out a wail of frustration as the car drove past.

"Going somewhere?"

Feeling like a child caught playing hooky, she whirled around to face Rylan Saintcrow.

He shook his head, his expression rueful. "Micah told me you had agreed to stay here for a while. What changed your mind?"

She clutched her handbag to her chest, as if it would protect her. "What do you think?"

"I find it hard to believe that any rational person would rather face a vampire she's never met than stay with the ones who are trying to protect her. Or do you have a death wish?"

"Rational?" She swallowed a burst of hysterical laughter. "I think I'm losing my mind."

"Try pretending you're here because you want to be," he suggested. "This is a nice place. The mountains are pretty this time of year. Pretend you've come here to relax. Take a look around, pick one of the houses you like, and I'll give it to you. Once it's yours, we won't be able to enter unless you invite us, which means you won't have to see any of us if that will make you feel safer. I'll open the movie theater and the other stores and stock your house with food and whatever else you want."

"Why can't I cross the bridge?"

"A little vampire magic. You and Kadie can't go out. No one else comes in."

"So, you've decided to spend the rest of your existence in prison?"

"Hardly. But for now, this is the safest place for you. And for Kadie." He glanced at the sky as he pulled the hood of his jacket forward. "Think about what I said."

"I don't have much choice, do I?"

"Not really." He jerked his chin at her handbag. "I'll be needing that phone back."

She was tempted to refuse, but what was the point? She

couldn't outrun him. Couldn't hope to fight him off. She glared at him as she reached into her bag, withdrew the phone and tossed it at him.

He caught it easily, sketched a bow, and vanished from her sight.

She stared at the place where he had been standing, thinking how cool it would be to be able to just disappear like that.

Since she couldn't leave and she didn't have anything else to do, Holly decided to take Saintcrow up on his offer. Walking the few blocks to the residential section, she noted that the houses were set on large lots, well back from the street. Most of them had wide front porches and old-fashioned picture windows.

She spent the rest of the morning going from one house to another. Although the floor plans were basically the same—one large bedroom, living room, kitchen, bathroom, service porch—the furnishings, paint, and wallpaper were all different, no doubt reflecting the tastes of the former occupants, she thought with a shudder. Men and women had lived in these houses, helpless prey to the vampires who had ruled the town. How had they endured such a horrible life? She couldn't imagine such a thing. And even though the houses were lovely, a prison was a prison no matter how richly furnished.

In the end, she decided on a house painted pale green with white shutters, partly because she liked the color and partly because it was closest to the town and farthest from the house on the hill. The previous owner had had a preference for French blue, and the color was predominant in all the rooms, from the flowered sofa and chairs in the living room to the quilt and matching drapes in the bedroom. The appliances in the kitchen were stainless steel. She found a set of flowered china and glassware in the cupboards, silverware in the drawers, pots and pans in the lower cupboards. The bathroom had a nice whirlpool tub, as well as a shower. In the living room, a pair of built-in bookshelves filled with books and DVDs bracketed a widescreen TV. As prisons went, it was better than most.

She was here, she thought glumly, and here she would stay for the better part of a month. Might as well try to make the best of it.

Returning to Blair House, she gathered her belongings and made the long walk back to the cozy little house that was to be hers.

It didn't take long to put her things away. Her stomach was growling by the time she finished. Being one of the many women addicted to chocolate, she always kept a candy bar in her handbag for emergencies.

With a Midnight Dark Milky Way in hand, she went into the living room and perused the bookshelves. The previous prisoner had had a penchant for mystery novels and sci-fi and fantasy movies. *The Lord of the Rings* trilogy, *X-Men, Pirates of the Caribbean, The Mummy, Ghostbusters, The Avengers, Men in Black, Mission Impossible.*

All of her favorites, Holly noted, pulling the first *Pirates* movie from the shelf. What could be better than dark chocolate and Johnny Depp? she mused as she turned on the TV, slipped the DVD into the player, then settled back on the sofa.

Micah woke with the setting of the sun. He sensed immediately that Holly wasn't in the house. He wasn't worried; he knew she couldn't leave town. But it was dark outside. Where would she go?

Rising, he pulled on a pair of jeans, tugged on his boots, and went outside. Opening his preternatural senses, he honed in on the scent of her blood. It led him to one of the houses in town.

Shirley's house.

He stared at the front door, remembering the first night he had met her as though it were yesterday.

He had been wandering through the residential area, looking for a secure place to spend the daylight hours, when he heard someone crying. . . .

Curious, he walked around to the rear of the house. He found the woman lying in a heap at the bottom of a set of stairs that led into the kitchen. There was blood matted in her hair. One ankle was swollen.

She let out a shriek when she saw him.

"Hey, calm down. I'm not going to hurt you."

She stared at him, her eyes wide with panic, her heart beating wildly as she tried to scrabble away from him.

He knelt beside her. "Take it easy."

"Go away!"

"You need help, lady. That's a nasty bump on your head. What happened?"

"I . . . I slipped on the steps. I think I might have passed out." She cringed when he reached for her. "What are you going to do?"

"I'm going to take you inside and bandage your head and your ankle."

"No! You can't come inside!"

Micah snorted. "Lady, if I was going to kill you, I could just do it here."

She blinked at him, as if that had never occurred to her.

He settled her in his arms. "So, are you going to invite me in or not?"

* * *

He had been surprised by how quickly they had become friends. And, eventually, lovers.

Dammit, he'd left Holly at Blair House. What was she doing here, of all places? He reached for the doorknob, determined to find out, only to frown when the door refused to open. For a moment, he considered breaking it down; instead, he dissolved into mist, intending to slip inside, only to discover that he couldn't.

Materializing, he rang the bell.

"Who is it?"

"Who the hell do you think?" He heard a click as Holly unlocked the door.

Hands fisted on her hips, she glared at him. "Do you intend for me to starve to death? There's nothing to eat in this place."

Micah blinked at her, amused by her temper. "What would you like?"

"I don't care! I'm starving. I haven't eaten since last night!"

"Tell me what you want and I'll get it for you."

"Anything! If you're going to keep me imprisoned, the least you can do is feed me." Saintcrow had promised to stock the cupboards. Apparently, he had forgotten.

"As you wish," Micah retorted, his own anger rising.

Before she could say anything else, he was gone.

"People come and go so quickly here," she muttered. "I feel like Dorothy in the Land of Oz."

A short time later, there was a sharp rap on the door. When Holly opened it, she found Micah on the porch, his arms laden with grocery bags.

"Are you going to invite me in?" He frowned, wondering

why he couldn't enter the house. He thought about it a minute, then decided it must be Saintcrow's doing.

"No."

A muscle worked in Micah's jaw, but he didn't say a word. He placed the bags on the porch, turned, and walked away.

Holly stared after him. What was she doing? Did she want to spend the next three weeks stuck in this house with no one to talk to? Micah was the only friend she had in this place. Well, he wasn't exactly a friend, she thought. Still . . . she started to call him back, but it was too late. He was already gone.

She had pulled the bags into the foyer and was about to close the door when a silver Mercedes pulled up in front of the house. She frowned when Saintcrow stepped out of the car.

"Evening, Holly."

"How did you know I was here?"

He lifted one brow.

Oh, right, she thought. More vampire hocus-pocus.

Moving to the rear of the car, he opened the trunk, removed several large boxes, and stacked them in front of the door. "I'd bring them in for you, but I'm pretty sure you'd rather I didn't."

"What is all this?"

"I promised to feed you, didn't I? I think you'll find everything you need in there. If not, just let me know. I'm not up-to-date on today's food choices, so Kadie made me a list. A rather long list," he added ruefully.

"Thank you."

Saintcrow glanced past her. "I thought Micah would be here."

"He was. He brought me some groceries, too."

Saintcrow nodded. "Cut the kid some slack, why don't

you? He's only doing what's best for you. It's easy to see that he cares about you. And just as obvious that you care for him."

"Don't be ridiculous. He's a vampire."

"He's still a man." Saintcrow gestured at the boxes. "You'd better get those inside before the ice cream melts. If you get lonely, I know Kadie would love some female company." With a wave of his hand, he slid behind the wheel of the Mercedes and pulled away from the curb.

Holly stared after him. He seemed so friendly, so normal, except for that aura of power that clung to him.

With a sigh, she pulled the boxes into the house, locked the door, and then carried the groceries into the kitchen. Saintcrow had, indeed, bought everything she would need, and more. Added to what Micah had brought, she had everything she could possibly want. She grinned as she found several bags of candy, including one of miniature Midnight Dark Milky Ways.

Murmuring, "Bless you, Kadie," Holly unwrapped one and popped it into her mouth.

Kadie Saintcrow might be a vampire, but it was obvious she hadn't forgotten what it was like to be human and female. Every woman knew that, whatever the problem, chocolate was the answer.

Holly opened the front door, her gaze sweeping the darkness. Overhead, thick gray clouds played hide-and-seek with a bright yellow moon. A faint breeze stirred the leaves on the trees. Shivering, she closed and locked the door, trying not to think about the fact that she was the only game in town. It reminded her of those old horror movies—helpless female stranded in a town of vampires.

All that was missing was Christopher Lee and some creepy background music.

Earlier that evening, she had washed all the dishes and silverware in the kitchen, just to have something to do. She had changed the sheets on the king-size bed, scrubbed the sinks and the bathtub, dusted the furniture, vacuumed the rugs with an old Hoover she found in one of the hall closets. Then she had spent a long, lonely night watching one movie after another.

One day down, only twenty to go, she thought glumly. Going to the front window, she drew back the curtains but there was nothing to see other than her own reflection.

Where was Micah? Was he as bored as she? Or was he out preying on some poor unsuspecting soul? How did vampires spend their nights when they weren't hunting the helpless?

If she called his name, would he hear her? Could he read her mind when they weren't together?

"Micah?" she whispered. "Can you hear me?"

Micah slouched in the back row of the movie theater, his feet propped on the back of the seat in front of him. On the screen, Steve McQueen chased a fugitive across an airport runway. It was one of Micah's favorite movies.

He jerked upright when he heard Holly call his name. From the subdued tone of her voice, he knew she wasn't hurt or in trouble.

Curiosity and a burning desire to see her again took Micah to her door. Instead of knocking, he spoke to her mind. *I hear you. If you want to talk, I'm on the porch.*

The door opened a moment later, and Holly stood there, looking more than a little surprised to see him.

He leaned his shoulder against the jamb. "You called?"

"You really heard me. That's so . . . so . . . fantastic."

"Yeah, well, I wouldn't be here if you hadn't called," he said, his voice flat. "Last time I was here, you made it pretty clear you wanted to be left alone."

"Can you blame me? All this supernatural stuff isn't easy to process, you know. When you've spent your whole life believing vampires are myths, it takes some time to get used to the idea that they're real."

He snorted. "Tell me about it."

"Then you know what I mean. And if vampires are real, what about werewolves and zombies and . . ." She waved her hand in the air. "Who knows what else?"

"Well, I've never met any werewolves. I'm not sure what Mahlon is, but I'm pretty sure he's not a zombie."

Holly folded her arms over her breasts.

"Was there something you wanted?" Micah asked.

"Just some company."

He nodded. "I know you don't want me inside, so why don't you come out here and sit on the swing?"

She hesitated only a moment before crossing the threshold. The swing creaked when she sat down.

Micah leaned against the porch rail across from her.

"Tell me about your life," Holly said. "What do you do for fun?"

"Fun?" He shrugged. "The same things as most people, I guess. I like movies. Rock concerts. A good murder mystery. Going to the beach. Of course, a suntan is out of the question."

Holly laughed, and some of the tension drained out of her. "What did you do before . . . you know?"

"I was pursuing a career as an actor. A well-known director saw me in a low-budget film and offered me a part in a big-budget movie shooting in Cody, Wyoming. It was supposed to be my big break. I wasn't the star, but

I was in several pivotal scenes with the main character. The director had high hopes for me, said I had the right 'look' for his next project.

"And then one night I met Lilith in a bar. We had a few drinks and a few laughs. Later she took me to what I thought was her house." He shook his head. "I was more than a little drunk, and she was very persuasive. One thing led to another. . . . Hell, I don't even remember most of it. When I woke the next night, I was a vampire and she was gone. Being a new vampire pretty much put an end to my career in showbiz."

"That must have been terrible for you." Holly couldn't begin to imagine how he must have felt, how frightening it must have been, to realize that in one night his whole life had been turned upside down.

"Terrible doesn't begin to describe it. I think I went a little crazy in the beginning. The hunger will do that to you if you don't keep it in check. Later, Saintcrow told me that when a vampire turns someone, they're supposed to hang around awhile, at least long enough to explain what's happened, you know? Long enough to teach their fledgling how to survive."

"What did Saintcrow teach you, exactly? I mean, once you became a vampire, didn't you just instinctively know what to do?"

"Not quite. The only thing I knew that first night was a searing, insatiable thirst unlike anything I'd ever experienced. I would have done anything to put an end to it. Saintcrow taught me how to hunt. How to satisfy my hunger without killing. He showed me how to make feeding pleasant for those I preyed on." Micah regretted his choice of words when Holly grimaced with revulsion. "Sorry."

"How do you do that? Make it pleasant?"

"I'd be happy to show you," he said with a wicked grin.

"No way!"

"It's a little like making love. You can do it slow and easy and give your partner pleasure, or you can just take what you want with no thought for anyone but yourself."

His voice, low and sexy, moved over her like invisible fingers. The sensation was so real, she would have sworn he was caressing her. But that was impossible.

Feeling her cheeks grow warm, she said, "Go on."

"Slow and easy is always best." Micah grinned at her. "He also taught me the importance of finding a safe place to spend the day. How to detect hunters. How to use all the preternatural powers that were now mine."

"Have you ever turned anyone?"

"No. I don't want the responsibility."

"I guess I can understand that." She regarded him a moment, then said, "I asked you once before if you liked being a vampire. You never answered me."

Micah shrugged. "It has its perks. I like the strength and the speed. Never being sick. Not having to worry about getting old and helpless." He'd been eight or nine when his maternal grandfather had gotten sick. The old man had hung on for over a year, growing weaker with every passing day. The thought of lingering like that, slowly wasting away, had given Micah nightmares for months.

"But?"

"I miss the sun. Food." He paused. "My family."

"They don't know what happened to you?"

"It's not an easy thing to talk about. What do I say? Hi, Mom and Dad. What's new with you? Oh, by the way, I'm a vampire now."

"Maybe you should just tell them. I'm sure they'd understand."

"You mean the way you did?"

"I'm not your mother, but if I was, it wouldn't make any difference in my feelings. It's not like you're some kind of out-of-control monster."

"Believe me, I think about it all the time," he admitted. "I don't go home as often as I'd like, because it's hard to hide what I am. Hard to make excuses for why I can't stay for dinner, why I can't play a round of golf with my dad, or play catch with my nephews, stuff like that. It's easier to stay away. As far as they know, I'm still pursuing my acting career." He blew out a sigh. "In a few years, I won't be able to go home at all."

"Why not?"

"Sooner or later, they're bound to notice I'm not getting any older."

"Oh, right. I hadn't thought about that. But that's all the more reason to tell them the truth."

"You could be right. But I've got a big family. A secret like this is hard to keep. All it takes is one of my nieces or nephews letting it slip to one of their friends, or a teacher, that their uncle is a vampire."

"I doubt if anyone would believe it."

"At the moment, it's not a risk I'm willing to take."

Holly looked pensive a moment, then asked, "What about the blood?"

"What about it?"

"How can you . . . ?" She shuddered.

"I can't survive without it," he said flatly. "It's as simple as that. I've tried, believe me, but not feeding . . . it's not worth the pain." He shifted from one foot to the other. "Why did you pick this house?"

"What?"

"This house. Why did you choose this one?"

"I liked the colors inside, the furniture. It probably

sounds silly, but it just felt right. Why? Is there something wrong with it?"

He shook his head, wondering if he should he tell her this had been Shirley's place.

"Micah?"

"You remember the woman I told you about? Shirley?"

"Yes. Oh, no! This is her house, isn't it?"

"Yeah."

"I'll look for another one tomorrow."

"No, it's okay. You're all settled in. Besides, it suits you."

Holly shook her head, then sighed. "Sometimes you seem so normal," she murmured, then clapped her hand over her mouth. "I didn't mean that the way it sounded."

He raised his eyebrows. "Normal, huh?"

"I just meant that if I didn't know what you are . . ." She waved her hand in a vague gesture of dismissal. "Just forget what I said."

"Don't worry about it, sunshine. Do you need anything?"

"No." She shivered as a gust of wind blew down out of the mountains.

"You're cold," he said. "You should go inside."

"I guess the cold doesn't bother you."

"No. Hot or cold, it's all the same to me." Pushing away from the railing, he shoved his hands into his pants pockets. "Call me if there's anything you need."

She nodded, then bit down on her lip as he started down the stairs. "Micah, wait."

Pausing, he glanced over his shoulder. "What is it?"

"I don't want to be alone." She didn't want to admit that Morgan Creek made her uneasy. She had never been afraid of the dark, but this town spooked her. It was so quiet, and kind of eerie tonight, with the moon peeking through the clouds, as if it were spying on her.

"There's nothing to be afraid of," he said, reading her thoughts. "No one here will hurt you." No one alive, anyway, he thought, recalling that Saintcrow had told him Kadie believed there were ghosts in the graveyard. He'd never seen one, but it wouldn't surprise him if one showed up. Lots of people had died here, not all of them peacefully.

"Please stay."

"I can't spend the day here," he said. "But I'll stay until the sun comes up."

"Thank you." Hoping she wasn't making a huge mistake, Holly hurried into the house; then, remembering he couldn't follow unless invited, she said, "Micah, please come in."

She felt the oddest sensation as he stepped over the threshold. It was a feeling she couldn't explain, an odd vibration in the air that whispered over her skin and raised goose bumps on her arms.

When she shivered this time, it had nothing to do with the cold.

Chapter Eleven

Holly slept late. When she woke, she lay there for a while, thinking about last night's conversation with Micah. What would it be like, to be turned into a vampire against your will and left with no one to guide you, no one to tell you what to expect? She couldn't imagine the horror a newly-turned vampire must feel as she slowly realized that the life she knew—the future she had planned—was gone, with no hope of ever getting it back.

What would have happened to Micah if Saintcrow hadn't come along to teach him what he needed to know? It must have been scary as hell, at least in the beginning, not knowing exactly what he had become or what to do. How awful, not to be able to tell his family the truth, to have to tell one lie after another to keep those he loved the most from learning what he had become.

Like he'd said, sooner or later, there would come a time when he wouldn't be able to go home at all, because his family would grow old and he would always look the way he did now.

When she was eighty—should she live so long—he

would still look the way he did today—handsome, virile. Young.

Shaking off her dismal thoughts, she went into the kitchen for a cup of coffee.

Three weeks wasn't a terribly long time, but it suddenly seemed like an eternity.

Micah knocked on her door shortly after the sun went down. After a day spent alone with her own thoughts, Holly was delighted to see him.

"You busy?" he asked.

She arched one brow. "Busy dying slowly of boredom."

"Yeah, I figured that, so I came to spring you for a few hours."

"What do you mean?"

"It's my mother's birthday. If we leave now, we'll get there right on time."

"What about Braga?"

"She doesn't know where my folks live, or where we are. We should be safe enough for an hour or two."

"What about Saintcrow?"

"I already told him we were going. He's going to meet us at the bridge to lower the wards. Otherwise, you wouldn't be able to leave."

It took less than a heartbeat to make up her mind. "Just let me change my clothes."

"Are you sure you want to do this?" Saintcrow glanced at Micah and Holly, who stood side by side near the end of the bridge.

"We won't be gone long," Micah assured him. "An hour or two, three at the most."

"Be careful."

"Always." Micah put his arm around Holly's waist. "You ready?"

Holly nodded. She had only a fuzzy memory of the journey from her house to Morgan Creek. As before, she felt a sudden dizziness, a sense of moving swiftly through a long, dark tunnel. When the world righted itself, they were standing in front of a florist shop. Micah bought two dozen long-stemmed red roses. He held the flowers in one hand, wrapped his arm around her waist, and the next thing she knew, they were standing on the sidewalk in front of a large, two-story house located between a ranch-style house that was for sale and a vacant lot.

"Home sweet home," Micah murmured, and Holly didn't miss the wistful note in his voice. Light blazed from every window. Music and laughter spilled through the open front door.

"Dammit," he muttered, "they haven't eaten yet."

"What are you going to do?"

He shook his head ruefully. "Mass hypnosis," he muttered. "Come on."

Mass hypnosis? On his own family? Was he kidding?

Taking her by the hand, Micah led her up the stairs to the veranda. "If anyone asks how we got here, we flew. By plane," he clarified. "And we have to leave by ten to catch a flight back because I've got an early call in the morning. Got it?"

"Got it."

There was chaos the minute Micah stepped into the foyer. Everyone—men, women, and children—ran to greet him, all talking at once as they smothered him with hugs, kisses, and questions.

Afraid of being trampled in the rush, Holly stayed out of the way.

"Mikey!" A tiny woman with short, thick black hair hurried in from the kitchen, her face wreathed in smiles, her sparkling brown eyes shining with tears. "You came!"

The crowd in front of Micah parted like the Red Sea.

Micah passed the bouquet to Holly, then swept the woman into his arms. "I couldn't miss your birthday, Ma."

She hugged him fiercely. "Can you stay?"

"Just for a few hours. I have to be on the set early in the morning."

"You're here now," she said, wiping her eyes with the hem of her apron. "That's all that matters. Come, we were just about to eat." She paused when she saw Holly standing off in a corner. "Who's this lovely lady?"

"Ma, this is Holly Parrish. Holly, my mother, Lena."

"I'm pleased to meet you, Mrs. Ravenwood," Holly said. "Happy birthday."

Lena shook her finger at her son. "You didn't tell me you had a girl!"

Murmurs and speculation ran through the crowd. A couple of men punched Micah on the arm. Others winked at him.

Ignoring them, Micah said, "She's just a friend, Ma. Here," he said, taking the flowers from Holly. "Happy birthday."

Lena beamed at her son as she accepted the bouquet. "Come, you two. Dinner is ready. Let's eat."

Holly was amazed by the size of the Ravenwoods' kitchen and the adjoining dining room. Both were huge, but judging from the size of the crowd in the house, they needed the space to accommodate their nine children, and their assorted spouses and kids. In the dining room, two long trestle tables, covered with white damask cloths, were set with gleaming silverware and candles. Two large, round tables had been set up in the kitchen for the kids.

Lena found a beautiful crystal vase for the flowers.

When everyone was seated, Micah introduced Holly to his family, but she forgot most of their names as soon as she heard them. All except for his youngest sister, Sofia. Dressed in ubiquitous black, her dark eyes lined in kohl, she looked like a crow in a field of wildflowers, albeit a beautiful one.

Following Holly's gaze, Micah said, "She's into the whole vampire-goth scene. My folks are hoping she'll outgrow it."

Holly nodded, thinking she had never seen a more beautiful family in her life. They could have all been movie stars, from Micah's father, Luciano, to his youngest niece, Maiya.

Holly had expected to be bombarded with questions about herself and her relationship with Micah, and while there were numerous inquiries, none were too personal.

Holly answered their questions, marveling at the amount of food it took to feed such a large crowd. There were three kinds of pasta, two kinds of sauce, loaves of homemade bread, salads, and several kinds of wine. She had never been surrounded by such a large, exuberant family, or felt such an abundance of love. No wonder Micah was homesick.

After dinner, the children and grandchildren sang happy birthday to Lena, and then they all trooped into the living room to watch her open her presents.

Of course, there was cake—the biggest birthday cake Holly had ever seen—along with four kinds of ice cream, including spumoni. Micah's favorite, Lena told Holly with a wistful smile.

Later, after Micah's married siblings and their kids had said their good-byes and his two single sisters had gone off with their dates, Holly and Micah relaxed in the living room with his parents.

"So, Holly, how long have you and Micah known each other?" Lena asked.

"We just met a few days ago," Holly replied.

Lena glanced from Holly to Micah and back again. "You're the first girl he's ever brought home to meet us," she remarked, smiling. "Can I hope . . . ?"

"Ma, you're embarrassing her," Micah said.

"Pshaw, no reason to be embarrassed. It's past time you settled down. You can't blame a mother for wanting to see all of her children happily married."

"Ma . . ."

Holly grinned, amused by Micah's discomfort. It was obvious this was a topic that had been discussed before—and often.

"Will we be seeing you on the big screen soon?" his father asked.

"I'm afraid not," Micah replied. "They scrapped the film I was working on. I'm not sure why. So, it's back to square one."

"You'll make it," his mother said, a note of pride in her voice.

When Lena went into the kitchen to make a fresh pot of coffee, Micah's father slipped him a hundred-dollar bill.

Micah shook his head. "Dad, I don't need this."

Luciano snorted. "Right. Don't tell your mama."

Looking somewhat sheepish, Micah slipped the bill into his pocket.

It was a few minutes before ten when Micah stood. "I've got to go, Ma. Happy birthday."

"Your being here was the best gift of all."

Taking her in his arms, he hugged her tight. "I love you, too."

"Don't stay away so long next time," his father said, giving him an affectionate slap on the shoulder. "You know how your mama misses you."

"And bring Holly with you when you come back," Lena said, squeezing Holly's hand.

"You have a wonderful family," Holly remarked as they walked away from the house.

"Yeah."

"How did you do it?" she asked. "Make them all believe you were eating when you only drank the wine?"

"I don't know how to explain it. It's just one of the many perks of being Undead."

Holly didn't miss the faint note of bitterness in his voice. She had expected him to magically transport them back to Morgan Creek. Instead, hands shoved deep in his pockets, he strolled down the street.

"Where are we going?" she asked, looking around.

He shrugged. "Nowhere. I just feel like taking a walk. You mind?"

"Is it safe?"

"Don't worry about Braga. I'll pick up her scent long before she appears. Besides, the odds of her being here are pretty slim."

Holly nodded, hoping he was right. "I've never been to Arizona before."

"It's a nice place, if you don't mind the heat."

"Probably not a lot of vampires here," she said, thinking about the long, hot sunny days.

"None that I know of, although I'm sure there are probably a few."

"Alaska seems like the place to go," Holly said. "Aren't

they supposed to have a lot of long nights there during the winter?"

"So they say."

They walked in silence for a short time. It was a nice, upscale neighborhood. The yards were well-tended, the houses in good repair. Dogs barked at them as they passed by; a few growled deep in their throats.

"It's because of me," Micah said as yet another dog growled. "Animals have a keen sense of smell. They know I'm different."

"All animals?"

"I don't know about all of them. But dogs and cats don't like me."

Holly pondered that as they crossed the street. No pets for vampires. It was kind of sad, actually.

Her breath caught in her throat when Micah took her hand in his. She felt him tense a little, perhaps waiting to see if she would pull away. When she didn't, he stopped walking and drew her slowly into his arms.

She gazed up at him, caught in the web of his stare, her heart beating wildly. *Vampire.*

"Holly . . ." Her scent surrounded him, seeping into his pores, filling his senses, spiking his desire. And his thirst. He glanced at the pulse throbbing in the hollow of her throat. "You're driving me crazy."

"Micah . . ." She shook her head as his arms tightened around her. Imprisoning her like iron bars. "Please."

"Please what?" he asked, his voice husky with need.

His power enveloped her, raw, primal. Exhilarating. Frightening. "Don't hurt me."

"Never. Just a taste, Holly."

"And if I refuse? Will you take it anyway?"

He took a deep breath. "No."

Torn by indecision, she worried her lower lip. What would it feel like, to let him bite her, to know he was drinking her blood? What if he didn't stop? Maybe she was crazy, but morbid curiosity trumped her good sense. "Promise you'll only take a little?"

"I promise."

With a sigh, she closed her eyes. "Do it."

She tensed when his tongue laved her neck, just below her ear.

He murmured, "Relax, sweetheart," and then she felt the scrape of his fangs at her throat. She had expected it to hurt, maybe like getting a flu shot. She closed her eyes, the tension draining out of her, as a delicious warmth spread through her, followed by a wave of sensual pleasure.

It was over all too quickly.

Holly opened her eyes to find him smiling down at her. "Didn't I say you'd like it?"

She blinked at him, pursed her lips to keep from asking him to bite her again.

Micah cocked his head to the side. "Are you all right?"

She nodded. Lord have mercy! If people knew how amazing being bitten could be, they would be lining up in droves for the privilege.

"In droves?" Micah laughed softly. "Seriously?"

Holly glared at him. "Stop reading my mind! It isn't polite."

He laughed harder, then wrapped her in his arms again.

The next thing she knew, they were standing on the roadway that fronted the bridge. Saintcrow materialized almost immediately to lower the wards.

"Looks like the two of you had a good time," Saintcrow remarked. "Any sign of Braga?"

"No."

Frowning, Saintcrow regarded Holly for a moment, then shot a glance at Micah, one brow arched.

Holly had the strangest feeling the two vampires were communicating, and then Saintcrow was gone. "How do you do that?" she asked. "How can you just vanish into thin air?"

"We don't really vanish," Micah explained, taking her hand. "We just move faster than the human eye can follow."

"Is that how you got us to your parents' house so quickly?"

"Not exactly."

"How, exactly?"

"It's more a matter of thinking where I want to be and . . ." He shrugged. "I guess it's kind of like teleportation, vampire-style."

She pondered that on the walk back to Shirley's house.

Inside, Micah drew her into his arms. She didn't have to be psychic to know he was thinking about something even more intimate than taking her blood. She could feel his arousal, see the desire that burned like a flame in his dark eyes.

For a moment, it seemed as if someone had stolen all the air in the room. Holly couldn't breathe, couldn't think, as her mind filled with images of the two of them locked together in a sensual embrace.

And then the images were gone.

And so was he.

Holly blew out a sigh. Would she ever get used to the way Micah just disappeared? There one minute, gone the next. She should have been appalled at the erotic images that had flashed through her mind. But she wasn't. Instead, she had almost wished for him to make them come true. And how ridiculous was that? They had no future together. What girl in her right mind would fall in love with a vampire?

And yet, he didn't act like a vampire, at least not like the ones she'd seen in movies. Well, except for drinking her blood, she amended, lifting one hand to her neck. Micah was kind and sweet, he loved his family . . .

She wrapped her arms around her waist, wishing they were his arms. He wanted her. There was no denying it, just as there was no denying that she wanted him just as badly.

What would life be like, married to a vampire? Married! Why was she even thinking such a thing? She wasn't in love with Micah.

Was she?

It was ludicrous even to be thinking about love or marriage when all they had shared were a few kisses— all right, utterly fantastic kisses that had made her toes curl and her insides melt like butter on a hot day.

She thought of Saintcrow's wife. Kadie had fallen in love with a vampire—a vampire who had kept her prisoner and fed off of her! Holly shuddered. And now Kadie was a vampire. Did she have any regrets? Had it been Kadie's decision? Or had Saintcrow turned her against her will? Maybe he had tricked her into it, made her believe she loved him the way Micah had made his family believe he'd eaten dinner. After all, if vampires could read minds and manipulate them, how was a girl to know if what she felt was real, or merely an idea implanted by a supernatural creature?

Feeling a headache coming on, Holly massaged her temples. How was she going to endure three weeks of this?

She needed to talk to someone. And her only option was Kadie Saintcrow.

Holly glanced at her watch. It was late, she thought, but probably not too late to pay a call on a vampire.

Chapter Twelve

"Holly!" Kadie exclaimed as she opened the door. "Is something wrong?"

"No. I . . ." Now that she was face-to-face with Kadie Saintcrow, Holly decided she had made a terrible mistake. What insanity had made her think asking a vampire for advice was a good idea?

"Please, come in," Kadie invited. "I've been hoping you'd come to see me."

Gathering her courage, Holly stepped inside. She shivered when the door closed behind her.

"What is it?" Kadie asked. "You look troubled."

"Can we talk? Just the two of us?"

"Of course. Rylan's gone out to check the perimeter."

"Is Braga nearby?"

"I don't think so." Kadie gestured for Holly to have a seat, then perched on the sofa beside her. "What did you want to talk about?" she asked, smiling. "As if I didn't know."

"Can *you* read my mind, too?"

"No. To be able to do that, I'd have to . . . never mind."

"Have to what?"

"Drink from you." Without giving Holly a chance to respond, Kadie said, "Now tell me, what's bothering you?"

"I thought you said you knew."

"I don't have to read your mind to see that you're bothered by your feelings for Micah."

"Am I that transparent?"

Kadie leaned back on the sofa. "Vampires are notoriously attractive to mortals."

"What do you mean?"

"For starters, they have a kind of innate allure that's very hard to resist."

"So what I'm feeling for Micah isn't real—is that what you're saying?"

"Not at all. The attraction wanes if it isn't genuine."

Holly clasped her hands in her lap. "Maybe this is none of my business, but . . . did you *want* to be a vampire?"

"No. And yes. It's a long story."

"I'd like to hear it."

"I'll just give you the highlights. I was badly wounded, with no hope of surviving. Rylan gave me the choice of dying or becoming a vampire and staying with him." She smiled faintly at the memory. "Becoming a vampire was really the only choice."

"Have you ever regretted it?"

"No. How could I, when it means living forever with the man I love?"

Holly chewed on the corner of her lower lip for a moment before asking, "If it hadn't been a matter of life or death, would you still have made the same decision?"

"I honestly don't know. Probably not at that moment. And yet, sooner or later, I know I'd have asked him to turn me because it was really the only way for the two of us to stay together."

"Is he as fierce as he seems?"

Kadie laughed softly. "He can be. He's a master vampire, after all. He's incredibly strong and powerful. And, yes, arrogant. And at times condescending. But he's never been anything but kind to me."

"But he kept you here against your will. He *fed* on you. How could you fall in love with him?"

"Because I'm incredibly handsome and irresistible."

Holly's cheeks flamed at the sound of Saintcrow's voice.

"Am I interrupting a gossip session?" he asked, rounding the sofa.

"No." Kadie smiled up at her husband. "I was just answering some of Holly's questions."

"Not giving away any of our secrets, I hope."

"Rylan!" Kadie shook her head. "We don't have any secrets, Holly."

Taking a place beside Kadie, Saintcrow draped his arm around her shoulders. "Speak for yourself, wife."

Holly stared at the two of them. Saintcrow frightened her in ways she didn't understand. She could feel his power moving over her. It was much stronger than Micah's. She assumed it was because Saintcrow was so much older. A master vampire. Would Micah one day have that kind of power?

Feeling suddenly like a goldfish in the company of sharks, she stood. "I should be going."

Rising, Kadie walked Holly to the door. "I hope you'll come again," she said. "And please don't be afraid of Rylan. He's really a pussycat."

"Somehow I doubt that," Holly said dryly. "Good night."

* * *

When Holly reached the end of the road, Micah stepped out of the shadows. "I came to walk you home."

"Thank you." The closeness that had been between them earlier that evening seemed to have vanished like morning dew. He walked at her side, careful not to touch her.

It was a long walk. And a little scary. Holly glanced at the dark clouds drifting across the sky. It was easy to imagine monsters lurking behind every shadow. Even the mountains seemed sinister, somehow, like jagged teeth waiting to tear her to shreds. Or vampire fangs . . .

"How did you know where I was?" she asked, unable to endure the silence between them a moment longer.

"Where else would you be? Did Kadie answer all your questions?"

She looked up at him. "Are you reading my mind again?"

"No."

"Then how . . . ?"

He tapped his ear with his forefinger. "Vampire hearing. Very acute."

Holly bit down on her lower lip, trying to remember everything she had said. Everything Kadie had said. She supposed Micah hadn't heard anything he didn't already know, including the fact that she was attracted to him. "Earlier tonight, why did you leave so abruptly?"

"Because I want you."

His words, spoken softly and intimately, sent a sudden warmth pulsing through her.

"And I know you want me."

She thought of denying it, but what was the point when he could read her mind?

Micah kicked a rock out of their path. "The thing is,

my desire to make love to you is hard to separate from my thirst, and vice versa. I'm afraid of what might happen if I succumb to either one."

Holly didn't know what to say to that, but it gave a whole new meaning to the expression "dying for love." He could easily kill her without meaning to. Accident or not, she would be just as dead.

"You remember that you had to invite me into the house before I could cross the threshold?"

"Yes."

"If I'm ever there and you want me gone, all you have to do is rescind the invitation."

"And you'll leave?" she asked incredulously. "Just like that?"

"Just like that." He fell silent again.

During the rest of the walk home, Holly was lost in thought, her mind replaying everything Kadie and Micah had told her.

"We're here."

Holly looked up, surprised to find they were at the foot of the porch stairs. "Thank you for this evening," she said as he followed her up the steps. "I enjoyed meeting your family."

"Can I kiss you good-night?"

"Is that a good idea?"

"Probably not," he admitted.

But when he reached for her, she didn't pull away. Holly went up on her tiptoes as his arms circled her waist, drawing her body against his. She closed her eyes as his mouth covered hers and a warm, sweet heat spread through her. When his tongue slid across her lower lip and delved inside, she felt it in the deepest part of her being. Suddenly weak and wanting, she clung to him, breathing in his scent, reveling in the strength of his arms around her.

Drowning in a sea of sensual pleasure, she let out a cry of protest when he released her.

"Get in the house, Holly." His voice, razor sharp, left no room for argument.

She blinked at him, alarmed by the faint red glow in his eyes.

"In the house. Now!" Reaching past her, he opened the door and shoved her inside. "Revoke my invitation."

"Micah Ravenwood, you're no longer welcome here!" Heart pounding, she slammed the door, then leaned back against it. "I rescind your invitation." She peeked out the window, but there was no sign of him.

Had she only imagined that hellish red glow?

Holly wandered through Morgan Creek, bored out of her mind. Last night, every time she'd closed her eyes, she had seen Micah's eyes. Red and glowing. She had expected to have nightmares after that; instead, her dreams had been filled with erotic images of the two of them making love in a variety of bizarre locations—in a bathtub filled with blood, on the floor of a castle dungeon, in the middle of a graveyard. She had never had such outlandish dreams in her whole life. Until she met Micah.

Shaking the nightmares away, Holly turned her thoughts to more mundane concerns. She was accustomed to working every day, used to making decisions and solving problems, meeting people, keeping busy. Her options in Morgan Creek were severely limited—stay in the house and read or watch TV, go to the movie theater, or take long walks.

She was tired of reading, tired of movies, tired of walking when there was no place to go. If only she had a phone or a computer, she could at least get in touch with her folks or one of her friends at the office, or lose herself in some mindless online game.

Damn Rylan Saintcrow for taking her phone. Did he really think she would call for help and put her family or friends or the police at his mercy? The man was a vampire and a killer.

She glanced at the lowering sky. The weather suited her mood perfectly. Cold and gray.

"Feeling sorry for yourself?"

She jumped a foot at the sound of Saintcrow's voice coming from behind her.

"A vampire and a killer?" he asked, amusement evident in his tone. "Is that how you see me?"

Summoning her courage, she turned to face him. "Isn't that what you are?"

"Indeed. But very few mortals—or vampires, for that matter—have the nerve to call me a killer to my face."

"I didn't say it to your face," she muttered. "I didn't even know you were here." Head cocked to one side, she frowned at him. "How can you read my mind?" She lifted a hand to her neck. "Did you . . . ?"

"I'm a master vampire."

"I thought you had to drink my blood to read my thoughts."

"How do you know I haven't?"

She went cold all over as she imagined him bending over her while she slept, or hypnotizing her and then wiping the memory from her mind. "Have you?"

He shrugged. And then he grinned. That one simple smile made him seem almost human.

"Put your mind at ease, Holly. I've never bitten you."

"Then how can you read my mind?"

He tapped a finger to the side of his head. "Master vampire."

"Oh. I'm surprised to see you out and about."

He shrugged. "Kadie is at rest, and I sensed you needed some company. Do you play cards?"

"What?"

"Do you play cards? We can while away an hour or two playing poker, gin rummy, or canasta. Blackjack? Whatever you like."

Holly stared at him. Was he serious?

"Well?"

"I'd like that. I think."

"There are cards in the tavern."

In a move quicker than her eye could follow, he wrapped his arm around her waist, and the next thing she knew, they were in a large room dominated by a bar that ran the length of the back wall. A number of booths lined one side of the room; a dozen small, round tables occupied the other side.

"Make yourself at home," he invited.

Holly chose a table near the front window, watching as Saintcrow went behind the bar.

"Would you like something to drink?" he asked. "We've got wine and soft drinks."

"A soda, please. Coke, if you've got it."

He quickly filled a tumbler with ice and soda, then poured himself a glass of wine. Reaching under the counter, he pulled out several decks of cards, which he spread on the counter. "What'll it be?"

"Gin rummy?"

Nodding, he picked up a deck and shoved it into the pocket of his jeans.

Holly watched him walk toward her, thinking he moved like a sleek black panther stalking its prey. Once again, she felt his preternatural power roll over her, making the hair on her arms tingle. "What does being a master vampire mean, exactly?"

He set the glasses on the table, then took the chair across from hers. "Basically, it means I'm very old and very powerful."

"And yet you're afraid of the Braga woman."

"No. She doesn't bother me. It's her companion. Mahlon." He sipped his wine. "No one is quite sure what he is. At night, he's no threat to our kind. But during the day . . ." Saintcrow shook his head. "He worries me."

"Because you're vulnerable?"

"Because Kadie is vulnerable. Micah must have told you that thresholds have power. They can repel my kind. Whatever else Mahlon is, he's still human and, as such, thresholds have no power over him. Braga has used that to her advantage against her enemies many times."

"If he comes here, will he be able to cross the bridge?"

"I don't think so, but I'm not certain. And that worries me most of all." He pulled the cards from his pocket. "Shall I deal?"

At her nod, he opened the deck, shuffled, and dealt the cards.

Holly looked at her hand, and then at Saintcrow. "I'm never going to win, am I? I mean, you probably already know what cards I'm holding."

He held up his hand, as if he were taking an oath. "I promise not to read your mind while we play. You have my word."

"I'm surprised you have soda in here," she remarked, lifting her glass. "I thought you could only drink blood. And wine."

"I bought it just for you."

"That was very thoughtful. Thank you." He constantly surprised her, she thought.

He shrugged. "Kadie used to like it."

To Holly's surprise, Rylan Saintcrow proved to be remarkably good company. They played several hands, and then, unable to restrain her curiosity, she asked the inevitable question. "How long have you been a vampire?"

He studied her face for several moments, then laid his cards aside. "A very long time. It happened during the Crusades. A lot of men died on the way to the Holy Land. They were the lucky ones. Many of us died from lack of food and water, or from the heat. We all learned firsthand what hell was like as we marched across the desert in full armor.

"In the beginning, we thought it was exciting, riding off to war for God and glory, but our enthusiasm quickly waned, replaced by the stink of fear and death.

"I was wounded in battle. It was a mortal wound. I dragged myself off the field to die. A woman found me there. A beautiful woman with long blond hair and the face of a saint. She gave me a drink of water, sang me a song."

He paused, a faraway look in his eyes. "She spoke to me in a quiet voice. I don't recall much of what she said. I was close to death when she asked me if I wanted to die. A foolish question at such a time," he said with a wry grin. "I was too far gone to answer.

"What happened next is only a hazy memory. 'The lust for life burns strong and bright within you,' she said. 'It would be a shame to let that flame be snuffed out so quickly.' I can still feel the sting of her teeth at my throat, but it didn't really hurt. I was drifting away in a sea of red when she slapped me. It jerked me back from the brink of eternity. Lifting my head, she held her bleeding wrist to my mouth and told me to drink." He grunted softly. "When I woke the next night, I was a vampire, although I didn't realize it at the time. All I knew was that I was ravenous.

"I heard voices in the distance. Three men were gathered around a small fire. I called out and they invited me to join them. I must have looked pretty awful, my clothes all torn and stained with blood. When they drew their weapons . . ." He shrugged. "I did what vampires do."

"What does any of that have to do with Braga?"

"Nothing. Her quarrel with me happened centuries later."

"And the vampire who turned you?"

"I never saw her again."

So, Holly thought, like Micah, Saintcrow had been turned and left to fend for himself. Was that why he had taken Micah under his wing, because he'd known what Micah had been going through?

Saintcrow glanced out the window.

Holly followed his gaze. The clouds were gone; the sun was a bright blaze of light in the clear blue sky.

Saintcrow rose with a rueful grin. "Alas, I fear I must take my leave."

The words were barely out of his mouth before he was gone.

Holly took a deep breath and blew it out in a long, slow sigh. How quickly her life had changed from the mundane to the bizarre!

Picking up the deck, she shuffled the cards, then dealt a hand of solitaire, only to sit there, staring at the ace of spades.

Saintcrow had been alive during the Crusades.

Micah was a vampire. Would he live as long as Saintcrow?

But Micah's lifespan wasn't the question she contemplated on the walk back to Shirley's house. Rather, it was Micah himself and her deepening feelings for him that troubled her. Against her better judgment, she was falling in love with him. And how dangerous was that? If she let herself love him, she might one day find herself having to make the same kind of life-and-death decision Kadie had made.

Holly paused at the bottom of the porch steps. If she had to make such a choice, what would it be? Leave the man she loved? Stay with him and grow old while he remained forever young? Or give him her heart and soul and become a vampire?

It was a question for which she had no answer.

A decision she hoped was never placed before her.

Chapter Thirteen

Leticia Braga paced the floor of the abandoned warehouse she was currently using as a lair. "We've searched the town from one end to the other," she muttered. "There's no trace of the vampire or the girl he was with. Where could they have gone?"

From his place in the corner, Mahlon shrugged. "The trail is cold."

"You have a gift for stating the obvious!" she snapped. "Now, how are we going to find him?"

"The girl's house."

"What about it?"

"Maybe I can find something useful inside."

"Well, don't just stand there!"

"Yes, mistress."

Leticia shook her head as she watched him shamble out the door. He was as strong as an ox. And as dumb as a stump. But he was unfailingly loyal, due in no small part to the fact that she had once saved him from a mob bent on burning him at the stake. She wasn't sure what he was—part fairy or demon, part troll or ogre—but it didn't matter. They were both stronger when they were together.

Restless, she changed into a long black dress, then transported herself to a small tavern located on a side street in North Hollywood, a place inhabited by vampires and their human companions.

It was early and the crowd was sparse. She had been visiting vampire hangouts across the country for decades. She was well aware that the odds of running into anyone acquainted with Rylan Saintcrow were slim at best. Nevertheless, sooner or later, she was certain her luck would change. Fate would not be so cruel as to deny her the satisfaction of destroying the man who had killed Gavin.

She was on her way out of the club several hours later when she passed two vampires standing near the door. Neither posed a threat, and she spared them hardly a glance until she overheard one of them mention Saintcrow's name. She paused just outside the door, her attention focused on their conversation. They mentioned Saintcrow again, and then a new name, one she had not heard before. Micah Ravenwood.

Keeping the pair in sight, she returned to her table to wait for Mahlon.

He arrived twenty minutes later.

"Did you find anything in the woman's house?" Braga asked, never taking her gaze from the vampires near the door.

"The vampire we saw has been in her house. There was no sign of either of them. Her refrigerator was empty."

"You looked in there?"

"I was hungry, mistress."

Leticia gestured at the pair near the entrance. "We may have another lead. One of them mentioned . . . Come," she said, rising. "They're leaving."

She followed the two men out of the club. Mahlon trailed after her.

The vampires strolled down the street, whispering to each other, until they reached an alley and darted into it.

Leticia grinned. Fools, she mused, if they expected to take her unawares, or elude her so easily.

A thought carried her to the far end of the alley, while Mahlon followed the vampires, neatly trapping their prey between the two of them.

Before her quarry could dissolve into mist and disappear, Leticia pinned the nearest one against the side of the building. "Don't move," she warned. "I can tear your throat out before you summon your power."

Mahlon slammed the second man against the opposite wall, then dropped a silver chain around his neck, negating his ability to dissolve into mist.

Leticia glanced from one unknown vampire to the other. "Who are you?"

"Who are you?"

She stared at the man in her grasp, surprised by his impudence. Eyes burning red, she hissed, "I won't ask you again."

Whatever else he was, the vampire had the good sense to answer. "Trent Lambert."

"And your friend?"

"Quinn. What the hell do you want?"

"Just some information."

Lambert regarded her warily. "What kind of information?"

"In the bar, you mentioned the name Saintcrow. Would that be Rylan Saintcrow?"

"Maybe. Who wants to know?"

"Leticia Braga. I'm an old friend of his."

"Is that right? Funny, he never mentioned you."

"I'm hoping to renew our acquaintance. I'd take it kindly if you'd tell me where to find him."

Lambert shrugged. "I don't know. I haven't seen him in years."

Leticia summoned her power and let it wash over him.

Lambert reeled under the onslaught, his fingers clawing at her hands in an effort to free himself.

She tightened her hold on his throat. "Are you sure you don't know where he is?"

"I haven't seen him in five years," Trent gasped. "I swear it. Not since I left Morgan Creek."

"Morgan Creek?" Her eyes narrowed. "Where might that be?"

"It's a ghost town in Wyoming."

Smiling, she withdrew her power. Lambert breathed a sigh of relief, followed by a hoarse cry of pain and horror as she slowly ripped out his throat, then tossed the body aside.

Galvanized into action, Quinn kneed his captor in the groin.

Grunting in agony, Mahlon loosened his hold on the chain.

Teeth clenched against the searing pain, Quinn yanked the chain from around his neck, dissolved into mist, and fled the alley.

Mahlon looked up at Braga, his face fish-belly white, his hands cradling his genitals. "Sorry, mistress."

Leticia shrugged. "No matter. I have the information we need. Let's go."

Chapter Fourteen

"You've been with Saintcrow."

Holly looked up from the magazine she had been reading, puzzled by the underlying note of disapproval in Micah's voice.

"We played cards earlier today," she said, shrugging. "He's not so bad, after all. He told me part of his life's story. It's almost inconceivable that anyone—even a vampire—could live so long."

"Yeah."

"Are you mad at me?"

A muscle twitched in his jaw. "Why should I be mad?"

Holly closed the magazine and tossed it on the coffee table. "You tell me."

"Hell, I don't know. Maybe I'm jealous of his power. Jealous because he can be with you during the day and I can't. Because he made peace with what he is centuries ago, and I'm still trying."

"I'm sorry we can't be together during the day, too, but there's nothing I can do about it," she snapped. "Instead of being angry, you might try being glad that I had some company!" She glared at him, almost sorry she had let him in.

"You're right. I'm sorry." He dropped onto the sofa beside her. "I know this isn't easy for you."

"My grandmother always said what can't be changed must be endured. I guess it's good advice, though right now it's a little hard to follow."

"Yeah." His gaze met hers, slid to the hollow of her throat, then returned to her face. "Holly?"

Her heartbeat quickened at his unspoken question. It was madness to let him drink from her again, but for all that, it was a pleasant kind of insanity.

When he reached for her, she went willingly into his arms. She had expected him to bite her. Instead, his mouth covered hers in a hot, searing kiss that drove everything else from her mind. His tongue dueled with hers, evoking new sensations deep within her. His hand moved up and down her back, slid around to cup her breast. Desire shot through her and she leaned into his touch, willing, eager, to give him anything—everything—he wanted and more, as long as he kept holding her, kissing her.

"Sweet," he whispered, his breath mingling with hers. "So damn sweet."

He kissed her again, gently this time, the kind of kiss a man bestowed on the woman he loved. She moaned softly, bereft when he took his mouth from hers. He brushed a lock of her hair aside, and then she felt the heat of his tongue against her skin, the prick of his fangs at her throat.

But there was no pain. Only pleasure washed through her, as warm and liquid as sun-kissed honey.

She whimpered in protest when he lifted his head. "Don't stop."

"Don't tempt me, sunshine."

She blinked up at him. "Why do you call me that?"

"Because you're the only light in my life, Holly. Because

your smile brightens my nights like the sun I'll probably never see again."

She stared at him. Never in all her life had a man's words touched her so deeply.

"Stay with me," he murmured.

"What?"

"I can't lose you now. I need you in my life, sunshine. Say you'll stay."

"Micah . . ."

"I know what you're thinking. We just met a few weeks ago. We're still strangers in many ways." He shook his head. "I know you have a life waiting for you when you leave here. Friends. Family. I won't keep you away from them. Just let me be part of your nights."

His arms tightened around her, and then he was kissing her again, slow, deep kisses that turned her blood to fire. She clung to him, wanting to be closer, closer, as desire unfurled within her. There was a touch of desperation in his kisses, a hunger, a need that went beyond the physical, wending its way into the very depths of her heart and soul.

She knew she should refuse. Agreeing to share her life with a vampire she scarcely knew was madness. But when she gazed into his eyes, when she saw the naked yearning reflected there, she could no more deny him than she could stop breathing.

"Holly?"

"I don't know how we'll make it work when we leave here," she murmured. "But I'm willing to try."

He didn't say anything, merely held her close, his face buried against her neck.

It was an odd feeling, she thought, comforting a man who was virtually immortal, a being who could easily break her in half. Yet, at this moment, he seemed as vulnerable as she.

Had she made a mistake? She searched her heart and soul for some sense of doubt or apprehension, but all she felt was an abiding sense of peace.

Standing outside in the shadows, Saintcrow grunted softly as he listened to the discussion between Micah and Holly. He hadn't meant to eavesdrop on what had turned into a very intimate conversation. He had come to ask Micah if he wanted to accompany him while he checked the outskirts of Morgan Creek, and then maybe go into the nearby town in search of prey.

Saintcrow rubbed a hand across his jaw, somewhat surprised that Holly had agreed to stay with Micah. Did she realize what she was getting into? Micah had tasted her blood. She was bound to him now. No matter where she went, Micah would always be able to find her, read her thoughts, bend her will to his, if he so desired.

It was a heady thing, being a vampire, he mused. The power. The strength. The vitality. The ability to move from one place to another with blinding speed, to dissolve into mist, to transform from human to animal. The overwhelming need for blood that plagued every fledgling for the first decade or so. The boredom that came after hundreds of years of existence. Not every vampire could handle the drastic changes. Some, unable to control the power, lost all trace of their humanity and turned into killing machines—true monsters that left nothing but death and destruction in their wake. Such behavior quickly caught the attention of mortals, thereby putting the survival of every vampire at risk. Such rogue vampires rarely lasted long. Sooner or later, an older vampire destroyed them. He had taken down more than one in his time.

Micah had been on the edge of becoming just such a creature when Saintcrow found him.

Rylan grinned inwardly as he turned away from the house and headed for the bridge. Whether a man was mortal or vampire, there was nothing like the love of a good woman to keep him on the right track. Kadie had certainly been an influence for good in his own life. He didn't know what he would do without her, remembered all too clearly how close he had come to losing her.

Theirs was a unique love story, he thought wryly. Kadie had wandered into Morgan Creek like so many others, but unlike the rest, Saintcrow had wanted her the moment he'd laid eyes on her. Little had he known that she would turn his world upside down.

It had been Kadie who had convinced him to free the mortals the vampires fed on. Kadie who had made him realize how cruel he had been. He had broken up families, deprived children of their parents. Until Kadie, he had salved his conscience with the fact that he was a vampire, a predator. And mortals were prey. Wanting to please her, he had freed them all—mortals and vampires alike.

The biggest surprise had been learning that Kadie's father was a hunter. That little surprise had almost cost Saintcrow his life. Had it not been for the timely arrival of Kadie and Micah, he might have died at her father's hands. Instead, Kadie had been mortally wounded. She had never wanted to be a vampire, but when given a choice between life as a vampire with him, or death, she had chosen to stay with him.

To his relief, she had never been sorry. And neither had he.

It would be interesting, he mused, to see what path Holly followed when she had to make the same choice, as she surely would, sooner or later.

Chapter Fifteen

In the morning, Holly lingered in the shower, wondering if she had imagined the note of longing in Micah's voice last night, the yearning in his eyes. It seemed inconceivable that a vampire, possessed of incomparable strength and immense power, could be so vulnerable, so needy. He had said nothing of loving her, but then, they had only known each other for a few weeks.

Lust came instantly, she thought. Love took longer. Still, it was hard to believe that he could need her so desperately in such a short time.

Frowning, Holly rinsed the soap from her hair. What if it had all been an act? What if Micah had said all those things in hopes of keeping her close? Preying on her sympathy to ensure a ready blood supply.

She shook her head. That hardly seemed likely. He had never taken more than a few sips. Of course, that could change and she would be helpless to stop it.

She blew out a sigh, then turned off the water. Stepping out of the stall, she grabbed a towel and wrapped it around her hair, used another to dry herself before pulling on her robe.

The day yawned before her.

She hadn't given it much thought last night, but if she stayed with Micah—and that was a big if in spite of what she'd said—she would never see him during the day. There would be no shared Easter or Christmas mornings together, no breakfasts in bed, no days tanning at the beach or wandering through the zoo, no picnics in the park.

No children.

Carrying a cup of coffee into the living room, she found herself thinking about the woman who had once lived in this house. What had it been like for her? Holly couldn't help thinking she would have gone quietly insane if she had been in that woman's place. How awful, to know you couldn't leave, that you would never see any of your friends or family again.

To know you had become nothing more than a source of food for a bunch of bloodthirsty monsters.

Micah had loved the woman. Shirley. Holly heard the underlying pain in his voice whenever he spoke of her. It was strange to think that vampires were capable of such a tender emotion. Yet the evidence was here, before her eyes. There was no denying that Saintcrow and Kadie were very much in love. You could hear it in Saintcrow's voice whenever he spoke Kadie's name. See it in Kadie's expression whenever she looked at him.

Curling up on the sofa, Holly sipped her coffee. What kind of lovers did vampires make, anyway? If Micah's kisses were any indication, he was probably fantastic in bed. And with a vampire's stamina, undoubtedly tireless.

She hit her forehead with the heel of her hand. Why was she even thinking about such things? He wasn't really human anymore. Shoot, technically, he wasn't even alive. And yet there was no denying the fact that she came vibrantly alive in his arms.

Brow furrowed in thought, she put her cup aside. What if Micah was lying to her? What if he intended for her to take Shirley's place? What if he had no intention of ever letting her go home?

A chill ran down her spine as another troublesome possibility wormed its way into her mind. Micah could read her thoughts. She knew he was capable of making people believe whatever he wanted them to. Hadn't she seen the proof of that with her own eyes at his mother's house? He had manipulated his whole family into believing he had eaten dinner with them.

How hard would it be to make her believe she wanted to stay with him forever?

A gasp escaped Holly's lips when Micah materialized in the living room that evening. "You've got to stop that!" she exclaimed.

"Sorry."

"You don't sound sorry," she said irritably. "Why can't you enter a room like normal people?"

"Normal people?" He lifted a brow. "I guess because I'm not normal."

"You know what I mean."

"What are you so grumpy about? Did you wake up on the wrong side of the bed this morning?"

"Maybe I'm grumpy because I didn't wake up in *my* bed. Did you ever think of that?"

"Hey, I'm sorry, all right?"

"No, I'm sorry," she said. "I know you're trying to keep me safe, and I appreciate it, I really do."

"But?"

"I miss my house. I miss working. I miss my freedom."

He nodded. "I hear ya."

"If I ask you something, will you answer me honestly?"

"I always have."

"Can you force me to do things I don't want to?"

"What do you mean?"

"Micah Ravenwood, you know darn well what I mean! Did you compel Shirley to fall in love with you?"

"Hell, no! Why would I do that?"

"So she wouldn't object when you fed on her."

Micah raked a hand through his hair. "Is that what you think? Dammit, Holly, I'd never do anything like that. Maybe you find it hard to believe that a woman could love me, but she did. And I loved her. And it was real, whether you believe it or not. Dammit!"

Holly huffed a sigh when he vanished from her sight. Why hadn't she kept her big mouth shut? Now he was gone and she was going to have to spend the rest of the evening alone, which was the last thing she wanted. She hadn't meant to hurt his feelings. She had just wanted some reassurance that he wouldn't compel her to do something she would find repulsive, like letting him feed on her. A little nibble once in a while was one thing, but quenching his thirst for the rest of her time in Morgan Creek was quite another.

How was she going to endure this for the next two and a half weeks?

How had Shirley and all the other unfortunate souls endured it year after year with no end in sight?

Of course, Shirley had had Micah for company, Holly mused. And whether she wanted to admit it or not, being loved by a hot young vampire couldn't have been all that bad.

Going into the bedroom, she changed into a pair of jeans and a T-shirt, her gaze lingering on the bed with its pretty quilt. Micah had made love to Shirley in that bed.

Holly blew out a sigh of exasperation. No matter how many times she warned herself that making love to Micah would be foolish, it was something she yearned to experience for herself.

Going to the window, she stared into the darkness.

He wanted her.

She wanted him.

It was just a matter of time.

Chapter Sixteen

The blankets fell away as Kadie sat up, nervously chewing on her thumbnail as she listened to Saintcrow's conversation with Quinn. Quinn! She remembered him all too well from the days she had been a prisoner in Morgan Creek. He had accosted her soon after her arrival, but never again. Saintcrow had seen to that.

By the time Rylan ended the call, she was perched on the edge of the bed.

"You heard?" he asked.

She nodded. "You don't think she'll come here, do you?"

"It wouldn't surprise me." Tossing his cell phone on a padded rocker, he began to pace the floor. Lambert was dead. Braga knew about Morgan Creek.

"Even if she finds this place, she won't be able to cross the bridge, will she?" Kadie asked anxiously.

"She shouldn't be able to."

"And Mahlon?"

Saintcrow shook his head. "Neither one of them should be able to set foot on it, but I can't guarantee that."

"You're scaring me," Kadie said. And then grimaced. She was a vampire. She shouldn't be afraid of anything.

But Saintcrow was worried, and that was enough to scare the pants off her.

"Nothing for you to be afraid of."

"You wouldn't lie to me, would you?"

He flashed her a wry grin. "Only if I had to."

"Rylan!"

Sitting beside her, he drew her into his arms. "I won't let anyone or anything hurt you, sweetheart. Do you believe me?"

"Of course."

"That's my girl. I need to find Micah and let him know what's going on. I won't be gone long."

Saintcrow found Micah in the cemetery, sitting beside Shirley's grave.

"Thinking of joining her?" Saintcrow asked, hunkering down across from him.

"Not exactly. What brings you out here?"

"I just had a phone call from Quinn."

Micah frowned. "Quinn?"

"One of the old Morgan Creek vamps."

"Oh, yeah, I remember him. He killed one of the women, didn't he?"

"Leslie. But that's not why he called," Saintcrow said dryly. "It seems Braga knows about this place."

"He told her?"

"No. She forced it out of Lambert. And after he told her everything she wanted to know, she ripped out his throat."

Micah scrubbed a hand over his jaw before asking, "What else did Lambert tell her?"

"I don't know. Quinn wasn't very coherent."

"Where is he now?"

"Looking for a place to hide if he's smart."

"Are we still safe here?"

"That's the sixty-four-thousand-dollar question, isn't it? To tell you the truth, I really don't know."

"So, what do we do now?" Micah asked. "Wait around to see if the wards on the bridge are strong enough to keep her and the hulk out?"

"You got any better ideas?"

"No, dammit. But I've got a bad feeling about this."

"That makes two of us. What are you doing out here anyway?" Saintcrow asked.

Micah shrugged. "Just thinking. Wondering what my life would have been like if Shirley had let me bring her across."

"What are you really worrying about?"

Micah looked up, his gaze meeting Saintcrow's. "Holly, of course. I swore I'd never fall in love again, and if I did, it would be with another vampire. And now . . . shit, I'm making the same mistake again."

Saintcrow snorted. "I've lived a long time, and if there's one thing I've learned, it's that you can't pick and choose who you'll love."

"What would you have done if Kadie had said no? Would you have brought her across anyway?"

"Without a doubt. She probably would have hated me for it, but I'd rather live with her hatred than live without her."

"That's what I thought." Micah plucked a blade of grass from the edge of the grave. "Power's a dangerous thing, isn't it?"

"It always has been. What's wrong between you and Holly?"

"She thinks I compelled Shirley to fall in love with me so I'd have a constant source of blood."

"I'm beginning to see your problem."

"I don't know how to convince her otherwise. She knows I can read her mind. Now she thinks I'm going to force her to do things against her will. How the hell can I convince her that I won't?"

"You could let her drink your blood."

Micah snorted. "Yeah, right. Like that'll happen."

"She'll like it."

"How can you be so sure?"

"I've never known a mortal who didn't. On the plus side, she'll be able to read your thoughts if you want her to. And if you don't, you can block her without her knowing it."

"I've never heard of humans drinking from vampires."

"It's pretty common with the goth crowd. Sometimes couples drink from each other. They only take a little and they don't bite each other. Usually, they use an X-Acto knife or a small surgical blade to make a small incision. They only drink a drop or two."

"That's . . . I don't know. Sick, I guess," Micah muttered, and then laughed. He was a fine one to judge, considering he consumed a lot more than a drop or two.

"It'll give Holly a high like nothing else," Saintcrow remarked. "Some mortals get so addicted to our blood, they can't live without it. But that's rare."

Micah shook his head. "I'm not sure it's a good idea."

"Well, it's up to you. Right now, we need to decide whether to stay here and stand our ground, or cut and run."

"You're the master vampire. What do *you* think we should do?"

"Stay here, at least for now."

"And if Braga and her hit man show up?"

"Let's worry about that when and if it happens."

"How old is Braga, anyway?"

"Three or four hundred, I guess."

Old enough to be powerful, Micah thought, *but relatively speaking, still young for a vampire.* "You said you'd tell me what caused the rift between you."

"So I did." Saintcrow gazed off into the distance. "I ran across Braga in Spain about three hundred years ago. I was hunting, and so was she. Turned out we were after the same prey. We had a good laugh over it. Then, being the gentleman that I am, I quit the field and went looking elsewhere.

"We ran into each other another time or two after that, and then I didn't see her again until about two hundred years ago. As fate would have it, I was hunting in London when I chanced upon another vampire. He was newly turned, a little uncertain, and belligerent as hell. At the time, I'd staked out a small portion of the East End as my hunting ground and very politely told him to get the hell out of my territory. He refused, and then he challenged me. I was younger then, full of piss and vinegar. I told him to bring it on. We fought." Saintcrow shrugged. "I killed him. Braga found me while I was disposing of the body. I tried to tell her what happened, but she wouldn't listen. Not that I blame her. She loved the guy. We fought. I won, but I couldn't bring myself to kill her. Big mistake."

Rising, Saintcrow slapped Micah on the shoulder. "Go home. Your woman is missing you."

"I doubt that," Micah muttered.

But the thought that it might be true took him to Shirley's. . . . He sighed in exasperation. He had to stop thinking of it as Shirley's house.

It was Holly's place now.

Micah found Holly on the sofa, one leg curled beneath her, a bowl of buttered popcorn in her lap, a soda on the table beside her. He didn't miss the sudden uptick in her heartbeat when he entered the house—through the front door—or the sense of relief that followed it. Unless he was very much mistaken, she was happy to see him.

"I'm sorry I got angry before," he said, dropping onto the chair across from the sofa. "I can't blame you for being worried, or afraid. Or curious. This is all new to you. You have no reason to trust me or believe anything I say."

"I'm sorry, too."

"I was talking to Saintcrow a few minutes ago. He said drinking my blood would allow you to read my thoughts. . . ." He nodded as a look of revulsion crossed her face. "I was pretty sure you wouldn't like the idea. He just suggested it because he thought it might put your mind at ease if you knew what I was thinking."

"Wouldn't that make me a vampire?"

"No. I'd have to drain you to the point of death and then give you my blood to bring you across."

Judging from the look of horror in Holly's eyes, he figured she was visualizing the transformation. And not happy with what she saw.

"Could we talk about something else?" she asked.

"Yeah." He hesitated a moment before saying, "I'm afraid I've got some bad news."

"I'm not sure I want to hear it."

"It's up to you."

Holly set the bowl on the end table, sipped her drink, then folded her hands in her lap. "All right. Tell me."

"Braga ran into a vampire who used to live here. He told her about this place."

All the color drained from Holly's face. "So now we're not safe here, either?"

"I don't know. Neither does Saintcrow. We've decided to wait and see."

Holly licked lips gone suddenly dry. She wasn't safe at

home. She might not be safe here. "What if Braga does show up? What if Saintcrow's magic doesn't work on her, or on Mahlon?"

"There's no reason to panic, Holly. I won't let anything happen to you."

"I'd like to believe that," she said, her voice rising. "And I would except for one thing—even Saintcrow's afraid of Mahlon. And Saintcrow is a lot older and stronger than you are."

He couldn't argue with that, Micah thought. Compared to Saintcrow, he was little more than a fledgling. But if Saintcrow gave him some of his blood . . .

It was something to think about.

Holly's anxiety grew with every passing day. She woke each morning wondering if Mahlon would come knocking on her door, spent every night worrying if the wards around the town would hold, or if Leticia Braga and her burly assassin would find a way across the bridge.

Her appetite suffered. When she looked in the mirror, there were dark shadows under her eyes.

"You look like hell," Micah remarked when he came calling that night. "You've got to stop worrying."

"How can I?" But fretting about Braga wasn't the only thing preying on Holly's mind. The more time she spent with Micah, the more she wanted to be in his arms. She told herself it was crazy to want a man—a vampire!— the way she wanted him, but she couldn't help it. When she wasn't lying awake worrying if she would live to see another sunrise, she tossed and turned anyway, thinking about Micah, wishing he was in bed beside her, his arms holding her close, his lips moving in her hair.

"I know you're afraid, sunshine, but if Braga or Mahlon breach the wards, Saintcrow will know as soon as it happens. He'll get us out of here before they can do any damage."

"What can he do if Mahlon comes during the day?"

"You've got to trust Saintcrow. He hasn't survived this long by being weak or careless. If anything happens, he'll get you and Kadie out first." Micah's gaze moved over her face. "You need to eat something, Holly. Tell me what you're in the mood for, and I'll get it for you."

"I don't know."

"Well, set the table. I'll be back in a few minutes."

With a shake of her head, Holly went into the kitchen and set the table. Maybe Micah was right. There was no sense worrying about something over which she had no control. Every time she had tried to leave town, Saintcrow had known about it. There was no reason to think he wouldn't know the minute someone tried to enter.

It hardly startled her at all when Micah suddenly appeared in the kitchen, his arms laden with carry-out bags from the Olive Garden, Red Lobster, and Steak and Stein. He also had two bottles of wine, one red, one white.

"Since you didn't know what you wanted," he said, placing the sacks and the bottles on the table, "I brought you pasta, steak, and lobster."

"I can't eat all that," Holly protested.

"Eat what you want tonight," he said with a shrug. "Save the rest for tomorrow."

Sitting at the table, she opened the Red Lobster sack and withdrew a plastic container. "It's too bad you can't join me," she remarked as she opened the carry-out box.

"Yeah." He leaned back against the counter, arms folded over his chest. "I used to love lobster and rice. And pasta.

And steak." Going to the cupboard, he found two goblets. After setting them on the table, he opened both bottles of wine. He filled one glass with red, the other with white, which he handed to Holly. "Bon appetit."

"Does it bother you," she asked, "watching me eat?" At first, dining in front of him had made her self-conscious, but she'd eventually gotten over it.

"No." He grinned inwardly, thinking it would certainly bother her if *she* watched *him*.

Later, after Holly had finished dinner and put everything away, she joined Micah, who was in the living room watching a movie. After a moment's hesitation, she sat beside him on the sofa, careful to leave a fair amount of space between them.

He slid her an amused glance. "Maybe you could build a fence."

Heat flooded Holly's cheeks. If he only knew that was the furthest thing from her mind. Her cheeks grew hotter under his knowing gaze. Of course he knew what she was thinking! He was reading her mind again. Why did she keep forgetting about that?

His gaze burned into hers. "I want you, too, sunshine. In more ways than you can imagine."

"I can imagine quite a lot," she said, her voice suddenly thick.

Micah chuckled softly as he took her hand in his, his thumb making lazy circles on her palm. "Just say the word, and I can make you forget all about Braga and Mahlon and everything else that's bothering you."

"Right now, the only thing that's bothering me is *you*," she muttered.

"But in a good way," he said with a wink. "You want me. Admit it."

She glared at him, but didn't deny it. Nor did she resist

when he drew her into his arms. How could it feel so right to be there when it was so wrong on so many levels? Saintcrow and Kadie might be deliriously happy together, but Holly didn't want to be a vampire, didn't want to give up the life she knew for a life of endless night and a warm, liquid diet.

"Holly, I think I'm falling in love with you."

Speechless, her heart pounding, she stared up at him.

"I'm just as surprised as you are," he admitted ruefully. "I tried to fight it, but . . ." Cupping her face in his palms, he kissed her lightly, his tongue sweeping over her lower lip, dipping inside to caress hers.

Gasping with pleasure, she melted against him, her arms twining around his neck. All thought of right or wrong fled her mind as he kissed her again, one hand stroking her back, her hair, as his other hand drew her closer. Lost in his touch, enflamed by his kisses, she couldn't think, could scarcely breathe. There was only Micah.

His scent surrounded her.

His kisses intoxicated her.

She shivered with anticipation when his tongue stroked the sensitive skin beneath her ear.

He was going to bite her.

She turned her head to the side to give him access to her throat, moaned softly at the touch of his fangs. Why had she waited so long for this? She writhed in his arms as pleasure flowed through every fiber of her being. She wanted to be closer, closer. Wanted to crawl inside of him so she could feel what he felt.

She wanted to taste him. . . .

She jerked back, alarmed by the thought.

Micah lifted his head, his expression wary. He knew what she was thinking. Knew the very idea repulsed her even as curiosity gnawed at her.

"Did you plant that idea in my mind?" she asked.

"No, darlin'."

She regarded him through eyes narrowed with suspicion. "Even if I wanted to do such a gross thing, *I* don't have fangs."

"You don't need them. For all our strength, vampires are remarkably vulnerable."

Holly licked her lips, then shook her head. "Forget it. I've changed my mind."

"You're lying. You're just afraid you might like it."

"Maybe I am," she retorted. "Can you blame me?"

He shrugged. "It's your decision."

Holly's gaze settled on Micah's throat, her curiosity growing with every passing moment.

"Don't be embarrassed." He held out his left arm, palm up, tapped his wrist with his forefinger. "Start here."

"Why?"

He shrugged. "Blood's closer to the surface. You don't have to bite so hard or so deep."

"Then why don't you bite me there?"

"Because nibbling on your neck is far more intimate."

She flushed at his answer.

Laughing softly, Micah drew her gently into his arms and kissed her again. "Come on, sunshine. Take a walk on the wild side."

She hesitated a moment, then ran her tongue over the inside of his wrist. She smiled when he groaned low in his throat. Was it pleasurable for him, being bitten? She nipped him lightly, felt his body grow taut.

Truly curious now, she bit him again, hard enough to draw blood. She had expected to feel revulsion; instead, a wave of sensual heat exploded deep within her and spread outward, like ripples on a pond.

Micah's arm tightened around her, threatening to crush a few ribs. Unable to breathe, she tried to wriggle free.

He released her immediately. His dark eyes were cloudy with desire when he looked at her. A knowing smile that clearly said, *I told you so*, played over his lips.

Holly blinked when she heard his voice in her mind, as clearly as if he were speaking aloud.

We're truly bonded now, sunshine. No matter where you go, I'll always be able to find you, just as you will always be able to find me.

There was a sense of comfort in his unspoken words.

But not enough, she realized, to overpower the worrisome thought taking root in the back of her mind. What if she didn't want him to find her? What if, once the danger was past, she never wanted to see him again?

Chapter Seventeen

We're truly bonded now, sunshine. No matter where you go, I'll always be able to find you, just as you will always be able to find me.

Those words followed Holly to sleep that night and replayed in her mind upon waking in the morning. Again, she wondered if tasting him had been such a good idea. What if she didn't want him to find her? What if she didn't want to find him?

And what if she did? Did she just twitch her nose to make him appear? Or maybe, like the Bloody Mary legend, she could look in a mirror and call his name three times.

Sitting up, she swung her legs over the side of the bed and pulled on her robe. "All right, Mr. Ravenwood, if it's true, where are you?"

And suddenly, without knowing how, she knew where he was.

Barefooted, she followed the invisible link that led her out of Shirley's bedroom—it would never be *her* bedroom, Holly thought, or her home—and up the hill to Blair House.

She had expected the front door to be locked, but it opened at her touch. All the drapes in the house were drawn tight, but the blood bond led her unerringly through the dark rooms, down a set of narrow wooden steps she had never noticed before, to a heavy steel door.

Micah was behind it. She knew it as surely as she knew her own name.

With the sound of her heartbeat thundering in her ears, she put her hand on the latch and pushed. It opened on silent hinges. Chewing on her lower lip, Holly stepped inside. The floor beneath her bare feet was icy cold. A basement, she thought.

Or a crypt.

Moving cautiously, she followed the pull of the invisible link. She stopped when her knee hit something. Reaching down, her fingers brushed cool flesh. Micah?

She stood there a moment, the sound of her breath loud in the room's absolute silence. Then, suddenly spooked, she turned and hurried up the stairs.

She paused at the top, one hand pressed to her chest. She needed a light. A candle, she thought, recalling that she had seen one in a holder, along with a book of matches, when she had stayed here with Micah. It took only minutes to find them.

The basement was less spooky in the candlelight, although the shadows gave her a start.

Her hand shook as she held the light over his resting place. In the flickering glow of the candle, he looked . . . not exactly asleep, but not quite dead, either. His skin seemed paler than usual. Most disturbing of all was that he didn't seem to be breathing. When she laid her hand on his shoulder and shook him, he didn't respond.

Was he truly dead when the sun was up? Unable to feel anything? If she screamed, would he hear her?

Completely creeped out, Holly turned and ran out of the basement and out of Blair House as if pursued by demons.

* * *

With the return of awareness, Micah's nostrils filled with Holly's flowery scent. At first, he thought her scent was coming from his clothing, but then he realized it was too fresh. She had been there, in the basement, only hours ago.

Exclaiming, "What the hell!" he bolted upright. Muttering curses, he made his way upstairs. He showered, pulled on clean clothes, ran a hand through his hair, and all the while he imagined her standing beside the bed, staring down at the monster. Dammit! Why the hell had she come here? Had it satisfied some morbid curiosity to see him like that? Helpless and vulnerable and, hell, he didn't know how he looked at rest. Why hadn't he locked the damn door? Shit!

A thought took him to the front porch of her house. He was about to storm inside when he paused, overcome by a sudden, unexpected wave of embarrassment. She had seen him when he was, for all intents and purposes, dead to the world. And suddenly he couldn't face her.

Feeling like an ass, he willed himself out of Morgan Creek. He needed to feed and he needed a woman, in that order.

Since he wasn't overly picky, prey was easy to find. He stopped at the first tavern he saw, perused the lone females, and called one to him.

She smiled uncertainly as she sidled up beside him. Sensing her confusion, he spoke to her mind again, assuring her that she was in no danger.

"I'm Micah," he said.

"Julie."

"Can I buy you a drink?"

"Sure." Her gaze moved over him like he was a side of grade A beef. "I've never seen you in here before."

He shrugged. "It's a little early for me."

When she smiled this time, it was genuine. "Woman trouble, I'm guessing."

"It shows, huh?"

"Just a little."

"What are you drinking?"

"Whiskey sour."

He signaled the bartender and ordered a refill for her and a glass of red wine for himself. They made small talk while waiting for their drinks. She was divorced, living with her married sister while she looked for a job.

Later, he asked her to dance, and then, exerting his will on hers, he took her to the small hotel around the corner.

Leticia Braga prowled back and forth along the road that fronted Morgan Creek. Thick brambles and underbrush heavy with thorns bordered both sides of the bridge. She had tried to cross the structure several times to no avail. Even with his bull-like strength, Mahlon couldn't batter his way through Saintcrow's wards. She felt a sudden longing for her twin brother, Leandro. She had brought him across soon after she was turned. He had never forgiven her, refused to speak to her. There were times, like now, when she sorely needed him. He was smart, clever, resourceful. But no matter how many times she apologized or begged him to forgive her, he refused to respond.

Shaking off thoughts of Leandro, she dissolved into mist, thinking to float over the obstacle. But Saintcrow's wards formed a protective barrier over the bridge and the land and the whole damn perimeter.

Cursing a blue streak, she materialized beside Mahlon.

"Now what?" he asked, his burly arms folded across his massive chest.

Leticia whirled on him. "How the hell should I know? I've tried everything I can think of!"

He dragged a heavy hand across his jaw. "We could blow it up."

"What good would that do?"

"It might shatter whatever mojo he worked on the bridge and the town."

Leticia stared at him. She didn't think it would work, but what the hell. It was worth a try.

Every survival instinct Micah possessed went into over-drive as he neared Morgan Creek. Dissolving into mist, he drifted over the bridge and willed himself to Saintcrow's lair.

After resuming his own form, he knocked on the door.

Saintcrow opened immediately. "From the look on your face, I'm guessing you've been near the bridge."

"You know, then?"

Saintcrow nodded. "Come on in."

"What do you think she's up to?" Micah followed Saint-crow into the living room. Nodded at Kadie as he took a seat in the chair across from her.

Saintcrow dropped down on the sofa beside her, arms crossed over his chest. "I wish I knew."

"So, what do we do now?" Micah asked.

"Wait for her next move, I guess."

"I think it's time to get the hell out of Dodge."

Saintcrow glanced at his wife. "What say you?"

"I don't know. Where would we go?"

"I've got a few other lairs," Saintcrow remarked, "but none of them are as secure as this one. Well, there is one other, but it's out of the country."

"If it wasn't for me, you'd just confront her and be done with it, wouldn't you?" Kadie asked.

Saintcrow didn't say anything, but he didn't deny it.

Micah cleared his throat. "Can I ask you something?"

"Ask away."

"I've heard drinking from a master vampire can make a younger vampire more powerful. Is that true?"

Saintcrow nodded. "Are you feeling a sudden need to be stronger?"

"With Braga and her bodyguard sniffing around? You're damn right."

Saintcrow rolled up his shirtsleeve, then held out his arm, palm up. His eyes took on a faint red glow.

Micah's whole body tensed as Saintcrow's preternatural power rolled over him. It was a fearsome thing, that ancient power, heavy and dark. It was more than age that molded that power. It was centuries of experience, of lives taken and lives spared, of internal battles won and lost. One drink, Micah thought, and a small part of that incredible power would be his. If he had the courage to take it.

Saintcrow cocked his head to the side. "Well?"

Micah blew out a breath as he knelt in front of the master vampire and grasped his arm. He looked up at Saintcrow a moment, then sank his fangs into his wrist.

The sheer power of Saintcrow's ancient blood exploded through every nerve and fiber of his being, more potent, more satisfying, than anything he had ever known. It burned through his veins like hellfire, making him feel reborn.

One taste, and he wanted more. Wanted it all.

"Enough."

Saintcrow's voice penetrated Micah's mind, but he ignored it. Just a little more.

"Enough!"

Power slammed into Micah like a sledgehammer, driving

him backward, into the wall. Slightly dazed, he stared at Saintcrow.

The vampire flashed his fangs. "Hard to let go, isn't it?"

Micah nodded.

"One taste, and you think if you could just drink it all, you'd never thirst again."

Micah licked a bit of blood from his lips, felt it sizzle like liquid fire on his tongue.

"It's not true, that feeling," Saintcrow said. "You're a vampire. No matter how long you survive, you'll always need to feed. Maybe not as often as you grow older. But the hunger is always there." He paused, one brow raised. "Are you listening to me?"

Nodding, Micah stood. "That was amazing. I feel like I could conquer the world with one hand tied behind my back."

Flashing a wry grin, Saintcrow said, "For now, let's concentrate on conquering Braga."

Braga's unmistakable scent still lingered in the air when Saintcrow went to check the bridge later that night. Mahlon's scent was there, too, though less evident.

Saintcrow frowned into the darkness. It was obvious his wards had held. But he had expected that. He was older and stronger than she, but they were both tenacious, both unforgiving when one of their own had been hurt or threatened. She would never give up, any more than he would.

Perhaps he should just hunt her down and take her out. And yet, he couldn't blame her for wanting revenge. Had Braga or Mahlon hurt Kadie, he would have hunted the culprits to the ends of the earth, and when he caught them, they would have begged for mercy, pleaded for death long before it came.

For centuries, he had ignored Braga's threat, but that had been before Kadie came into his life. As long as Leticia Braga lived, Kadie's life would forever be in danger.

Mahlon was another problem. Was he Braga's minion by choice, or compulsion? If the former, he might seek revenge for Braga's death. If the latter, Mahlon would likely be glad to be free of her.

Saintcrow glanced over his shoulder, his desire stirring as he heard Kadie's footsteps hurrying toward him. It amazed him that his feelings for her continued to grow stronger, deeper. "What are you doing out here, love?"

"I missed you. Is something wrong?" She wrinkled her nose against a cloying smell. "Is that her?"

He nodded. "She was here shortly after dark, but she's gone now." Taking Kadie's hand in his, he started walking back toward their lair.

"What are we going to do, Rylan? She's never going to give up."

"I haven't yet decided."

"Do you think Micah and Holly will stay together?"

"They will if Micah has anything to say about it. I'm not sure Holly wants to tie her life to a vampire's." He slid a glance in Kadie's direction. "You're not sorry, are you?"

She glared at him. "Rylan Saintcrow, how can you even ask that?"

Pausing, he pulled her into his arms and kissed her soundly. "Just checking."

"Where are we going?" she asked when they passed the turnoff to the house.

"Nowhere in particular. It's a beautiful night and I've

got a beautiful woman by my side. I'm just not ready to go back inside yet."

"If we leave here, where will we go?"

"I've got an old castle in Sibiu. I haven't been there in a century or two. The place isn't in my name, so it's unlikely Braga would think to look for us there."

"A castle sounds great, but where the heck is Sibiu?"

"Transylvania."

"I should have known," Kadie said, laughing. "A vampire castle in Transylvania. What a novel idea."

"It's not much of a place," he warned as they continued on. "Might not even be habitable after all this time."

"Well, it's nice to know we've got somewhere to go." Her steps slowed as they neared the cemetery. Some of the friends she had made in Morgan Creek were buried there. Mona had died of natural causes; Leslie had been killed by one of the resident vampires, most likely Quinn. And Shirley was there, along with Rosemary and Donna.

Saintcrow squeezed her hand. "Are you all right?"

"I was just remembering another time when I came here."

He grunted softly.

On impulse, Kadie opened the rickety wooden gate and entered the cemetery. It hadn't changed since the last time she'd been here—row after row of weathered wooden crosses. No headstones. No flowers. Most had no names or dates to identify the dead or the year of their passing. Shirley's grave, marked by a tall marble cross, stood out from the others.

Feeling suddenly melancholy, she made her way to the graves of her friends. She hadn't been present when they were buried, so she'd had no way of knowing who lay in which grave. It had bothered her that nothing marked their final resting places so she had fashioned crosses and placed them at random on the graves.

She frowned when she looked at the crosses. Someone had switched them.

"You had them backwards," Saintcrow remarked. Coming up behind her, he wrapped his arms around her waist.

She leaned back against him. "There was no way for me to know." At the time, she had told herself it didn't matter if the right name was over the right grave. Mona and Leslie had been past caring. She had etched their names on the crosses so they wouldn't be forgotten. "Do you feel that?" Twisting out of Rylan's arms, she glanced around.

"Feel what?"

"That sudden chill," she said, shivering. "It's the same feeling I had once before, like someone—or something—was trying to warn me of danger."

"Well, Braga's been sniffing around," he remarked. "That's danger enough for one day." Taking her by the hand, he said, "Come on. Let's go home."

Hand in hand, they strolled toward the gray stone house.

They had just reached the foot of the hill when an explosion shook the ground. Flames leaped toward the sky, momentarily turning the night to day.

"The bridge," Saintcrow muttered darkly. "May her black soul rot in hell, she's blown up the damn bridge."

Chapter Eighteen

Holly jumped to her feet. "What was that?" She glanced nervously around the living room. "An earthquake?"

Micah shook his head. "I don't think so." Moving to the window, he parted the curtains. Bright orange flames lit the sky. Sparks, ash, and bits of debris drifted through the air.

Moving up behind him, Holly peered out the window. "Is the town on fire?"

"No. The fire's coming from the direction of the bridge. Saintcrow's here."

Before she had time to ask how he knew, there was a knock at the door.

"You want me to answer that?" Micah asked.

"I'll do it," Holly said. "After all, *I'm* the one who has to invite him in."

It was a grim-faced vampire who stood on the other side of the door. He lifted one brow in silent inquiry as he waited for her to decide whether or not to admit him.

"Oh, just come in," she said, again feeling that peculiar vibration as Saintcrow stepped over the threshold.

"Evening, Holly," he said.

She nodded, then followed him into the living room.

Micah still stood near the window. "Was it Braga?"

"I don't know if she lit the fire," Saintcrow said, hands clenched at his sides, "but she's the one responsible."

"Why would she do that?" Holly asked.

"I can't say for sure, but if I had to guess, I'd say she's testing the wards."

Micah left the window to perch on the arm of the sofa. "Why didn't they hold?"

"It wasn't just the bridge that was warded," Saintcrow explained. "I set wards around the whole town to repel intruders. I never expected anyone to set off a bomb or whatever the hell they used. I should have planned for that, too. Lack of foresight on my part, I guess."

Holly sat on the sofa near Micah. "Where's Kadie?"

"She's packing."

Holly's eyes widened. "Where is she going?"

"Nowhere without me," Saintcrow said dryly. "I told her to be ready in case we need to make a quick getaway."

Holly stared at him.

"You might do the same," Saintcrow suggested. "Feel free to rescind my invitation when I leave." He glanced at Micah. "I'm going down to check the damage if you want to come along."

"Yeah, I think I will." Micah looked at Holly. "I won't be long."

She nodded. *A quick getaway*, she mused as the two men left the house. *A quick getaway to where?*

"So," Micah remarked as he surveyed the scorched pile of wood that had once spanned the deep ravine. "What now?"

"I've decided you were right. It's time to get the hell out of Dodge."

"You're thinking about that place you mentioned, the one out of the country."

"Yeah. I'm not worried about Braga or Mahlon coming after us here. The wards should repel them, but a man armed with a rocket launcher could do a hell of a lot of damage."

"You don't really think she could get her hands on that kind of firepower, do you?"

"I don't doubt it for a minute."

"Shit."

"Go tell Holly to throw some things in a suitcase. We're leaving tomorrow night."

"Leaving? Where are we going?"

"Saintcrow's got a place in Transylvania."

"Transylvania! I can't go gallivanting off to the vampire capital of the world. For one thing, I don't have a passport. For another, I have to go back to work soon. I—"

Micah shut Holly up the only way he knew how. He kissed her, long and slow and deep.

Holly felt herself drowning, going down for the third time, when Micah lifted his head. She stared up at him, breathless, her whole body yearning for him, ready to give him anything he desired. "Where did you say we were going?"

In the morning, Holly showered and ate breakfast. What kind of magic had Micah worked on her last night to convince her to go off to Transylvania with three vampires?

She smiled inwardly as she ran her fingertips over her lips. What kind, indeed? All he'd had to do was kiss her and she was ready to agree to anything.

What was she going to do about her job? Even though Mr. Gladstone had been kind enough to let her take her vacation early, it seemed unlikely that he would give her more time off. He might, she thought, if he knew her life was in danger. Unfortunately, even if she had her phone—which she didn't—she couldn't very well tell him the truth. Even if she could tell him about Saintcrow and Micah and Braga, he wasn't likely to believe her. Sometimes she couldn't believe it herself.

Her anxiety grew with every passing hour. Was she doing the right thing? What would she do in Transylvania? How long did Saintcrow intend to stay? Questions, questions, and no answers.

She thought the day would never pass.

Holly was in the bedroom making sure she hadn't forgotten anything when Saintcrow and Kadie arrived. She heard their voices as they greeted Micah, who had appeared with the setting sun. Try as she might, she couldn't discern their words. Were they talking about her? Did they think of her as excess baggage? Were they worrying about what to do with a helpless mortal?

She looked up when Micah entered the room.

"Are you ready, sunshine?"

Her throat dry, she nodded.

"Hey, don't ever think of yourself as excess baggage, sweetheart. I love having you around. You must know that." He drew her into his arms. "I'm sorry I got you into this. I know you'd rather be anywhere else, but I'm glad you're here." He stroked her cheek with his fingertips. "I love you, Holly. I'll keep you safe, and when the danger's passed, I promise to take you home."

Holly blinked up at him. *He loves me*. Three little words

and they changed everything. In that instant, she felt certain that the only place where she would ever feel at home was in his arms. For the first time, she was glad that he could read her mind. Smiling up at him, she thought, *Kiss me.*

For a moment, he gazed deep into her eyes. Then, murmuring, "My pleasure," he bent his head to hers. His kiss, when it came, was achingly tender.

When he kissed her a second time, she knew her life had changed irrevocably.

"Traversing an ocean takes a little longer than going to Arizona," Saintcrow said. "It might make you sick to your stomach, but that's normal."

Holly nodded.

"Since it's such a long journey, you'll be going with me."

"What?" Stricken, Holly looked anxiously at Micah. *Please, I don't want to go with him.*

"I know," Micah said, "but it's for the best. Saintcrow is more powerful, more experienced. Kadie and I can make it on our own. But I'm not sure I'm strong enough to get us both there."

Holly shook her head. "But . . ."

"I understand your misgivings," Saintcrow said. "But you need to trust me. I know what I'm doing."

Micah reached for Holly's hand and gave it a squeeze. "If you can't trust him, sunshine, trust me. I'll be close by."

In the end, she had no choice. She gasped as Saintcrow lifted her effortlessly into his arms. At his command, she closed her eyes and held on tight.

If traveling between cities was like moving through a long, dark tunnel, traveling across the ocean was like flying through time and space at warp speed.

She had no idea how it was done, didn't want to know, didn't ever want to do it again. When this was all over, she was taking a plane home!

It took almost half an hour before her stomach stopped roiling and her head stopped spinning. And even then, she felt disoriented. When she finally had the strength to lift her head and look around, all she could do was stare—at age-old tapestries on high stone walls, at a fireplace big enough to hold a pair of elephants, at rugs and furniture that would have been at home in an antique shop. Flickering candles in huge standing candelabras, placed at intervals around the enormous hall, filled the room with light.

"Welcome to my humble home," Saintcrow said. "I apologize for the dust and the lack of amenities."

Humble? Holly stared at him. "It's a castle. A real castle."

"Only a small one." He waved a hand in the direction of the hearth, and a fire sprang to life.

More vampire magic, Holly mused. She curled her legs beneath her on the high-backed sofa. It was covered in silk damask—probably worth a small fortune back in the States, she thought absently. "Where are Micah and Kadie?"

"Making the bedrooms habitable. I trust you want one of your own."

"Of course." She regretted the words as soon as they were spoken. Did she really want to sleep alone in a room in this drafty old castle? She didn't know if there were ghosts in Morgan Creek, but she wouldn't be surprised if there were a few roaming the castle's dark halls and corridors.

"It's been awhile since anyone's lived here," Saintcrow remarked.

Holly nodded. She could have guessed that by the

cobwebs dangling from the high ceilings and the dust in the corners. "Did you buy this place?"

"No. It was given to me by a paramour a few centuries ago."

A paramour? Holly didn't think she had ever heard anyone use that word. It was an old-fashioned term for an illicit romance. She couldn't help wondering if Kadie had ever asked about the women in her husband's past. Silly question, she thought. What woman wouldn't?

What was she going to do in this place while Micah and his friends rested?

"You might want to alter your hours to coincide with ours," Saintcrow suggested.

Why hadn't she thought of that? Of course, she was already doing it to some degree. She had been staying awake until well after midnight and getting up later in the morning.

"You might want to start now," Saintcrow said. "Due to the time change, it's a little after four in the morning. I'll stock the kitchen before I take my rest. Stay inside tomorrow. The castle is warded against intruders so no one will bother you."

Holly nodded, her mind whirling. Braga had blown up a bridge. What was to stop her from blowing up a castle?

"Micah's waiting for you upstairs, first door on the left."

Taking a deep breath, she climbed the narrow set of stone steps to the second floor.

Micah was waiting for her there. The room was large and square, with a big, four-poster bed adorned with crushed velvet hangings. A pair of rosewood tables flanked the bed. A matching wardrobe took up most of one wall. Oriental rugs, their colors faded by time, covered the floor. She spied her suitcases at the foot of the bed. A fire crackled in the hearth, taking the chill from the room.

"I think you'll be comfortable here," Micah remarked.

She nodded.

"If you need anything tomorrow, call Saintcrow. He'll hear you." He kissed her forehead. "Sweet dreams, sunshine."

"You're not going to leave me!" She hated the note of panic in her voice, but who could blame her for being a little uneasy? After all, she was in the land of Count Dracula, the most infamous vampire of them all.

"Not if you don't want me to."

"Stay with me until I fall asleep."

"All right." He turned his back while she changed into her nightgown and slid under the covers. Removing his boots and shirt, he slid in beside her, his arm slipping around her shoulders.

And knew immediately that agreeing to sleep next to her had been a horrible mistake. Did she really expect him to lie beside her and just go to sleep as if there weren't a beautiful, desirable woman beside him? Sure, she was wearing a nightgown, but he could feel the heat of her body through the thin fabric, hear every breath, smell the scent of her hair and skin. The blood whispering through her veins.

Holly rested her head on his shoulder and closed her eyes. She was in an ancient castle in Romania with three vampires. But right now, all she could think of was the one lying beside her. His skin felt cool beneath her cheek. She felt the tension in the arm around her, the length of his leg alongside hers.

Maybe this hadn't been such a good idea, after all.

She shivered as his hand stroked her hair, followed by the touch of his lips. She sucked in a breath as he rolled onto his side. His arm slipped around her waist, drawing her body close to his. Even in the dark, she could see the desire in his eyes. He wanted her. Of that there was no doubt.

And she wanted him. There was no doubt of that, either.

She waited, breathless, her heart pounding in her ears.

And still he watched her. Was he reading her thoughts? Did he know how confused she was?

"Micah . . ."

He gazed deep into her eyes, eyes filled with longing and confusion.

He kissed her once, roughly, then threw the covers aside and left the room.

Holly stared after him, torn by a sense of loss, yet relieved that the decision had been taken out of her hands.

Holly spent the day exploring the castle in an effort to keep her thoughts off of what had nearly happened the night before.

The second floor contained only bedrooms and storage closets and a small room that she eventually figured out was the medieval equivalent of a toilet. The rooms were all furnished much the same as the one where she had spent the night. There was no sign of Micah, or Kadie and Saintcrow. No doubt they had a secret lair somewhere on the premises.

The downstairs housed the main room, a dining hall, and a primitive kitchen. There were no appliances, of course.

She found bread, sandwich makings, fruit, and sodas in an ice chest.

Holly had just finished eating dinner when Saintcrow

appeared. "We're going out," he said. "You're welcome to come with us, or you can stay here."

Holly bit down on the inside corner of her lip. "Going out" usually meant the vampires needed to feed. She didn't really want to go along while they hunted some poor mortals. On the other hand, she really didn't want to stay in this spooky old castle alone, either.

Nodding, she said, "I'd like to go."

"I thought you would," he said, smirking. "I'll tell Micah to bring you a jacket."

Holly had expected the vampires to teleport to wherever they were going, so she was relieved—and surprised—when Micah ushered her into the backseat of a late-model Cadillac convertible.

She leaned toward him, whispering, "Where did the car come from? Saintcrow said no one's been here in a while."

"I believe in being prepared," Saintcrow said, meeting her gaze in the rearview mirror. "I ordered the car a couple of nights ago."

"I didn't mean to pry," she muttered. Vampires had exceptional hearing. She had to remember that.

"Where are we going?" Kadie asked as Saintcrow put the car in gear.

"There's a village a few miles from here. There's a festival going on. Lots of strangers in town."

Holly folded her arms over her chest, trying to keep her mind blank, but it was impossible. No doubt "lots of strangers"—when translated into vampire-speak—meant "lots of prey" who wouldn't be missed by the locals.

"You catch on fast," Micah drawled. "But we don't intend to kill anyone."

Holly looked out the window, wishing she could just

disappear. It was disconcerting, having Micah read her mind. Vampire alliances must be awkward, she thought, glancing from Kadie to Saintcrow. How did their marriage even survive, when they could read each other's every thought? Every couple had arguments. People—and probably vampires—had unkind thoughts about their partners from time to time. Thoughts that were usually fleeting and didn't mean anything, but were nevertheless best kept private.

"Kadie can block her thoughts," Micah said, "just as Saintcrow can block his."

"You can learn to do it, too," Saintcrow remarked. "It just takes concentration and lots of practice."

"Is that how you do it?" Holly asked.

"No. It's just part of being a vampire."

Holly sat back. The more she learned about vampires, the more fascinated she became. True, there were drawbacks—needing blood to survive being the main one. But there were perks, too, like never growing old and the ability to just think yourself wherever you wanted to go. She glanced at the vampires in the car and grinned inwardly. Apparently a liquid diet wasn't fattening, because they were all in great shape.

Really looking at them for the first time, she realized that their skin was different from hers, though she couldn't quite put her finger on the difference. Their hair was thicker, more lustrous. The results of a great shampoo, or just another perk?

She smiled when Micah slipped his arm around her shoulders and drew her closer. He loved her. She pondered the reality of that for several minutes, trying to decide how she felt about it. There was no denying that she was attracted to him, that she enjoyed his kisses, that she longed for more. But was that love, or just a bad case of lust for an incredibly handsome and sexy man?

"Incredibly handsome?" Micah murmured, grinning at her. "And sexy? Really?"

"Oh, shut up."

He pulled her closer, his gaze caressing her, blocking everything from her vision save for beautiful dark eyes filled with desire. Heedless of the couple in the front seat, he covered her mouth with his, his tongue teasing, tasting, slipping inside, sliding seductively against her own. She felt his kisses in the deepest, most intimate part of her being, turning her blood to fire and her mind to mush. She had but one thought, one wish.

He growled low in his throat as he lifted his head. His eyes still burned, but now they blazed with a different kind of hunger.

When he expelled a deep, panting breath, she saw his fangs for the first time.

Chapter Nineteen

Holly twisted out of Micah's embrace as reality came crashing down on her. What was she doing, making out with a vampire in the backseat of a car?

"Change your mind?" Micah asked dryly.

"I . . ." She lifted a hand to her throat.

His gaze followed the gesture. "What are you afraid of?" he asked, genuinely puzzled. "Even if I bit you, it wouldn't be the first time."

To her chagrin, Holly felt herself blushing, and how stupid was that? She hadn't done anything to be embarrassed about, and she wasn't about to apologize for being shocked by the sight of his fangs. Sure, she knew he had them. She had felt them at her throat. But knowing and seeing were two different things.

She glanced out the window when the car came to a stop.

"Kadie thinks you two need some time alone, so we're gonna walk from here." Saintcrow tossed the keys over the seat. After getting out of the car, he opened the passenger door. "We'll meet you back at the house in an hour or two." He offered Kadie his hand and they moved on down the street.

Bemused by their sudden departure, Holly stared after them.

Micah stroked her cheek with his knuckles. It sent a shaft of heat spiraling to the pit of her stomach.

"Alone at last," he murmured.

"I thought you were hungry."

"Oh, I am."

"Or do you say thirsty?" she wondered aloud.

"Both." He traced the outline of her lips with his forefinger, then let his fingertips slide slowly down her chin to rest in the hollow of her throat. "I'm hungry for your body." His words were direct but softly spoken. "I'm thirsty for your blood."

"Micah . . ."

"I'm here, darlin'."

There was no doubt about that. His presence filled the car and her senses. When he touched her, every nerve ending came to vibrant life, thrumming at his touch like the strings of a guitar when plucked by a master's hand.

He leaned slowly toward her. "Tell me what you want, sunshine," he whispered.

"Don't you know?"

He nodded. "I want to hear you say it."

"You," she murmured. "Just you."

She closed her eyes as he lowered his head to cover her mouth with his. As always, everything else fell away until there was only the two of them, their tongues tangling in an erotic dance of discovery. She clutched at his shirtfront as the world spun out of focus. What power did he have over her? One minute, she was appalled to be making out with him in the backseat, the next she was melting against him, yearning for more.

Wrapped in a cocoon of sensual pleasure, Holly didn't immediately realize Micah was no longer beside her. The staccato bark of gunshots brought her swiftly back to reality. She let out a gasp when her door flew open, shrieked when someone grabbed a handful of her hair and yanked her out of the backseat, scraping her arm against the door, before flinging her to the sidewalk.

Holly tried to scream for Micah, but all that emerged from her throat was a hoarse cry of dismay when she saw him sprawled facedown on the sidewalk. A dark stain leaked from beneath him and spread across the pavement. Was he dead? How was that even possible?

She glanced around, desperately searching for help, only to realize they were in a commercial district. All the buildings were dark, the parking lots empty, the streets devoid of traffic.

Terror gripped her when a second man rounded the front of the car and came to join the man towering over her. Holly swallowed hard as they dragged her into an alley a short distance from the car. She tried to scream for help, but fear clogged her throat. Icy sweat beaded her brow. Even if she hollered her head off, there was no one to hear her.

She was going to die.

But she wasn't going down without a fight. Adrenaline surging, she scratched and kicked for all she was worth, let out a cry of satisfaction when her nails drew blood. A well-placed kick sent one of her attackers to his knees.

And then, miraculously, Micah was there.

Holly choked back the bitter bile that rose in her throat as he broke the neck of the first man, turned away when he sank his fangs into the throat of the second.

"What the bloody hell!"

At the sound of Saintcrow's voice, Holly glanced over her shoulder to see the master vampire striding purposefully toward them.

"I leave the two of you alone for five minutes," he exclaimed, his face as dark as a thundercloud, "and all hell breaks loose."

"It's under control," Micah said, wiping his mouth with the back of his hand.

"I can see that. What happened?"

Micah shrugged. "Isn't it obvious?"

"What's obvious is that they took you by surprise."

"Yeah, well, I was distracted."

Saintcrow looked at Holly, who blushed from the soles of her feet to her hairline.

"Where's Kadie?" Micah asked.

"Waiting around the corner." Saintcrow sent a fleeting glance at the bodies sprawled at Micah's feet. "Since you've fed, we'll take Holly home with us. You can take care of the bodies and meet us there."

Holly huddled on the sofa in front of the hearth, arms tightly clasped around her middle. In spite of the roaring fire in the fireplace, she couldn't stop shaking. Until she'd met Micah, she had been a stranger to violence. Sure, she had seen death and destruction in living color on the nightly news, but never like this, up close and personal. Try as she might, she couldn't get the graphic images out of her mind, or forget the smell.

Nor could she help wondering what Micah was going to do with the bodies. Would he bury them? Or just dump them in the woods, where they would eventually be found and identified? Did their attackers have wives, children, friends who would miss them?

She shivered as the front door opened and Micah stepped inside, followed by a blast of cold air.

"Did you dispose of the bodies?" Saintcrow asked.

"No one will ever find 'em." Micah spoke to Saintcrow, but his attention was focused on Holly. "Are you all right?"

"I don't think I'll ever be all right again."

He closed the distance between them, then knelt in front of her. "I'm sorry you had to see that."

She nodded, her gaze riveted on the dried blood caked on his shirtfront. He had been shot at close range. Any other man would be dead. Only he wasn't a man.

"Holly, look at me."

"You saved my life."

"Yeah, well, you wouldn't have been in danger in the first place if you hadn't been with me."

Holly shook her head. "Let's not go there."

"I'm going to turn in," Saintcrow said, glancing from Micah to Holly and back again. "See you tomorrow."

When they were alone, Micah held out his arms, wondering if Holly would rebuff him or let him comfort her.

Without hesitation, she slid off the sofa and onto his lap, sighed as his arms wrapped around her. "I was so afraid," she whispered. "I thought you were dead."

"You put up a hell of a fight."

"Were they hunters?"

"No, just a couple of thugs looking for a good time. They won't be bothering anybody again."

With a shudder, she buried her face in his shoulder.

"Listen, sunshine, I can make you forget it happened if you want me to."

"No," she said, her voice muffled. "You've messed with my mind too often as it is."

He laughed softly. "Only for your own good."

Lifting her head, she met his gaze. "Maybe you could think of another way to help me forget."

"Yeah," Micah said, his arms tightening around her. "Maybe I can."

She sighed as he claimed her lips with his. As always, his kisses drove everything else from her mind.

Somehow, they were lying on the rug in front of the hearth, their bodies tightly pressed together. She welcomed his caresses even as her own hands explored the hard contours of his back and shoulders. She had seen death firsthand tonight. Being in Micah's arms was a reminder that life went on.

He whispered in her ear, his words as arousing as the touch of his hands.

Holly clung to him. She wanted him desperately and yet she held back, knowing that if she surrendered her body, she would also be surrendering her heart and her future. Once they made love, there would be no going back.

She froze when she felt the brush of his fangs at her throat.

Micah cursed under his breath, damning his need for her blood. After what she'd been through tonight, what was he thinking? Lifting his head, he murmured, "I'm sorry, Holly. Forgive me."

She nodded, her gaze sliding away from his. How could he be thirsty, she wondered, when he'd fed on that man less than an hour ago?

Sitting up, Micah ran a hand through his hair. "It isn't the same," he said quietly.

"What do you mean? Blood is blood."

"Think of him as meat and potatoes," Micah said with

a faint smile. "Needed for survival. But you . . ." His knuckles caressed her cheek. "You're like dessert, warm and sweet and extraordinary."

Holly grinned in spite of herself. No one but Micah could make something as disgusting as drinking her blood sound like something rare and wonderful.

During the next two weeks, Holly's life took on a fairy-tale quality. She slept like Sleeping Beauty during the day and went sightseeing with the vampires at night.

With Saintcrow as their guide, they toured the cities of Romania—cities with exotic names, like Alba and Sighisoara, Brasov and Bucharest. They shopped in quaint village stores, walked ancient streets, stood in awe of magnificent churches and citadels.

Of course, if you were touring Romania with vampires, a visit to Transylvania was a must. Located in the center of Romania and surrounded by the Carpathian Mountains, it was known worldwide as the home of the world's most famous vampire, Dracula himself. Many believed that the count, villain of so many books and movies, was loosely based on Vlad III, Prince of Wallachia, also known as Vlad the Impaler, a warlord renowned for his cruelty and bloodletting.

With one night slipping into another, it came as a shock to Holly to realize that her vacation was over. And so, she feared, was her job.

Chapter Twenty

Hands fisted on her hips, Leticia Braga stood on the edge of the road that fronted Morgan Creek. Scowling, she glanced at her companion. "The wards are still in place, but it doesn't matter. They've gone."

Mahlon nodded.

Eyes narrowed, she paced back and forth for several minutes before wheeling around to face her companion. "Lambert and his friend mentioned another vampire. Micah Ravenwood. I want you to find out everything you can about him. From what I overheard, it sounded like Ravenwood and Saintcrow are friends. Perhaps Ravenwood will lead us to our quarry."

"Yes, mistress."

As every vampire quickly learned, threatening mortal family members was the fastest way to bring an enemy— mortal or Undead—to his knees. Saintcrow was ancient. He had no surviving family members. She had little hope of separating him from Kadie. But Ravenwood was still a young vampire. There was a good chance he had family still living, people he cared for—parents, siblings. Perhaps a wife. Thanks to the Internet, finding information about

Ravenwood and his family shouldn't take Mahlon more than a day or two.

She stared across the ravine, but it wasn't the ruined bridge she saw, or the road beyond. It was the face of her beloved Gavin, his beautiful eyes filled with love, his mouth curved in a smile that had been hers and hers alone.

Grief pierced her heart and hardened her resolve. One way or another, she would find Rylan Saintcrow. She would not rest until he was dead by her hand.

Chapter Twenty-One

Micah read the text message on his phone a second time. And then a third. It was succinct and to the point.

> We have your family.
> If you ever want to see
> them again, bring me
> Saintcrow. Alive.
> You've got 48 hours.

"Dammit!"

"Micah, what's wrong?"

He raked his fingers through his hair, then swung around to face Holly. "Wrong? This is way beyond wrong."

"What is it? What's happened?"

"Braga has my parents and probably Rosa and Sofia. She's given me forty-eight hours to deliver Saintcrow or she's going to kill them all."

Holly stared at him, eyes wide. "What are you going to do?"

"I don't know." He sank down on the sofa beside her, then rose to pace the floor. "Even if I was of a mind to do as she asks, there's no way I could accomplish it. I'm no match for Saintcrow. Even if I could take him unaware, which is never gonna happen, I couldn't defeat him." Frowning, he glanced over his shoulder. "Shit! He's here."

Micah stalked toward the door and flung it open. "What do you want?" he asked gruffly.

Saintcrow lifted one brow. "Nice to see you, too."

"Sorry. What can we do for you?"

"I was taking a walk, and I got the feeling that you were pretty shaken up. I came by to see if I could help."

"You're the only one who can."

"So what's going on?" Saintcrow glanced from Micah to Holly and back again.

"This." Micah held up his phone so Saintcrow could read the screen.

A muscle twitched in Saintcrow's jaw.

"Do you think they're still alive?" Micah asked.

"She's got nothing to bargain with if she kills them."

"Nothing?" Micah raked a hand through his hair. "I've got eight brothers and sisters. Nieces. Nephews. Cousins."

Saintcrow studied Micah through narrowed eyes. "You're not going to try anything stupid, are you?"

"You mean like trying to take you out? Hell, no. Besides, she wants you alive."

"Undoubtedly," Saintcrow muttered dryly. "So, what do you want to do?"

"Give her what she wants and save my family. There's just one problem. You."

"There's no problem. We'll give her what she wants."

Micah stared at Saintcrow. "What? You're going to walk in and give yourself up, just like that?"

Saintcrow twitched one shoulder. "I've never gone after her before. I know why she hates me, and I don't blame her. Until now, the fight's always been between the two of us. I figured we'd meet sooner or later and settle it between us. But she's crossed the line now. She's made it clear that as long as she's alive, Kadie's in danger and so are you. And now, apparently, so is your family. It's time to end this once and for all. She's helpless during the day, but I'm not. Neither is Holly. . . ."

"Holly!" Micah exclaimed. "No way! She's got no part in this."

"Just listen to me. Our best chance of getting your family out of danger without anyone getting hurt is to make our move when Braga is at rest. Holly's the only one of us who can cross your family's threshold uninvited during the day. I'll cause a distraction of some kind to draw Mahlon outside. Once he's out of the picture, Holly goes inside, tells your old man to invite me in. I'll take Braga out. End of story."

"Do you really think it will be that easy?" Micah asked.

"Barring any unforeseen complications, yeah. Holly, you in?"

Holly nodded. She didn't like the idea of being anywhere near Braga or her bodyguard, but she had met Micah's family. She liked all of them. And she loved Micah. How could she refuse to help?

"I won't let anything happen to you," Saintcrow said. "I promise."

And, as she had once before, Holly believed him.

Saintcrow timed their exit from Romania so that they arrived in Arizona an hour before dawn. Twenty minutes later, Holly and her vampire companions were ensconced in the best suite in the best hotel in town.

Micah and Kadie went to seek their rest immediately on their arrival.

Holly was too wound up to even think about sleeping. Her head ached, her stomach was in knots. She stared at Saintcrow, who stood at the window looking outside.

"Do you really think we can do this?" she asked.

"There's a risk, but I think we can pull it off."

"Why are you so afraid of Mahlon?"

"I'm not afraid of him. There are rumors about him— that he's a Djinn, he's immortal, he's Braga's lover, he's a demon. I think they're all stories Braga started to make him seem more dangerous than he really is. He's taken her blood, so he's incredibly strong. But he's still just a man. The only thing that ever worried me was his ability to hunt vampires while they're resting."

"Are we going to Micah's house today?"

Saintcrow nodded. "Around three. Braga will be at rest. Mahlon won't be expecting any of us. I'll draw him outside. Once he's out of the way, I'll stake Braga." He flashed a wry grin. "I know what you're thinking. Movies always show a fountain of blood gushing from the wound when a vampire is staked, but that only happens with fledglings."

"But to kill her like that, when she's helpless . . ." Holly shook her head. "It's . . . it's murder."

"She's already dead, Holly."

"So are you," she retorted, then clapped her hand over her mouth.

"Yes," he said dryly. "I know."

"I'm sorry, I . . ."

"Forget it."

"Do you feel . . . alive?"

"Right now, I just feel the need to rest."

She nodded, embarrassed that she had asked such an inappropriate question.

There were three bedrooms in the suite—one for Kadie and Saintcrow, one for Micah, one for her.

But, today, she didn't want to sleep alone.

After changing into her nightgown, she tiptoed into Micah's room. The heavy drapes were drawn against the light of the rising sun. He didn't stir when she slipped under the covers.

Propped on one elbow, she let her gaze move over his face. Straight black brows, smooth olive-hued skin, a fine, straight nose. She ran her fingers lightly over his lips, remembering the heat of his kisses, the way her stomach curled with pleasure at his touch.

He loved her, or so he'd said.

"Did you mean it?" she whispered. "And if you do, then what?" She lifted a lock of his hair and let it fall through her fingers. "I want to love you," she confessed, "but I'm afraid. Not afraid that you'll hurt me, but afraid of what you are, of the changes it will make in my life. I know I said I'd stay with you, but I don't think I can."

She had to tell him, she thought as she snuggled against him and closed her eyes. She had to tell him it wasn't going to work between them.

But not until this was over.

Saintcrow rose shortly before two that afternoon. When he went looking for Holly to let her know it was almost time to go, he was surprised to find her asleep in Ravenwood's bed.

He regarded the two of them for several minutes. Micah loved Holly. There was no doubt about that. Saintcrow was reasonably certain that Holly loved the boy in return, or at least cared for him a great deal. Did she have what it took to join her life with that of a vampire? It took a special kind of woman—a strong woman—to make the sacrifices necessary.

Heaving a sigh, he left the room. At the moment, he had other, more pressing matters to take care of.

Downstairs, at the gift shop, he bought a hooded sweatshirt, a pair of gloves, and dark glasses.

When he returned to their suite, he slipped the sweatshirt over his head, put the gloves and glasses in his pocket, then went into Micah's room to wake Holly, but she was already awake and dressed.

"Ready?" he asked.

"I guess so."

With a nod, he wrapped his arm around her.

Moments later, they were in the backyard of the Raven-wood home.

Saintcrow stood in the shade of the patio. Motioning for Holly to remain quiet, he opened his senses. Counting Mahlon, there were six mortals in the house—five adults and an infant.

Saintcrow frowned. Braga's scent was also there, but it was faint. Too faint. He swore under his breath when he realized he had underestimated her.

"What's wrong?" Holly asked.

"She's not here."

"What do you mean? Where is she?"

"I don't know. Dammit. She's not resting inside."

"What do we do now?"

"You go around to the front of the house. I'll make some noise out here. Hopefully, Mahlon will come to investigate."

"And if he doesn't?"

"I don't know. Right now, we're playing this by ear. You stay out of sight until I call you." Reaching into his jacket,

Saintcrow withdrew a pistol with a two-inch barrel and thrust it into her hand. "Hang on to this, just in case." Delving into another pocket, he pulled out his cell phone and a couple of twenties, which he tucked into the pocket of her jeans. "If anything goes wrong, run like hell. When you're safely away, call a cab to take you to a hotel. When the sun goes down, contact Micah."

Holly glanced at the pistol in her hand. "How do you know I won't change my mind and make a run for it? Or call the police?"

"Because you're not the kind of woman to turn her back on someone in trouble. And calling the police might get Micah's family killed."

"I don't know how to use a gun."

"There's nothing to it. Just point the damn thing and pull the trigger."

Holly stared at him a moment. Then, muttering under her breath, she headed for the front yard.

When she was out of sight, Saintcrow moved to the side of the house and began pounding on the trash cans. When that didn't attract any attention, he went into the garage, opened the door to the family car, and leaned on the horn.

He grinned when he heard the back door open, followed by the heavy tread of Mahlon's footsteps. Leaving the garage, he stepped outside to wait.

Mahlon lumbered into sight, his ham-sized hands fisted at his sides. He stopped abruptly when he saw Saintcrow. "You." With a snort of disdain, he flexed his muscles, cracked his knuckles, then took a step forward, arms outstretched.

Saintcrow danced out of reach. The man was big. He was powerful. But he was slow.

Mahlon grunted as he changed direction, then lunged forward. He caught Saintcrow around the middle, lifted him overhead, and hurled him against the garage.

Saintcrow landed hard, then scrambled to his feet. Damn! The brute wasn't as slow as he'd thought.

Smiling, Mahlon wiggled his fingers, silently beckoning Saintcrow.

Saintcrow shook his head. He hadn't existed this long by making the same mistake twice. He backed away, as if he was afraid, waited for Mahlon to close the distance between them.

Closer. Closer.

Mahlon was smiling when he sprang forward.

Saintcrow waited until the last moment, spun out of reach, and buried his hand in Mahlon's chest.

Holly hid behind a hedge in front of the Ravenwood house, the gun heavy in her hand. After a moment's hesitation, she shoved it into the waistband of her jeans and pulled her shirt over it. She almost jumped out of her skin when a horn blared. What was going on back there?

Her hand gripped the pistol. Could she really fire it if Mahlon came charging around the side of the house? Would a gun this small even do any damage to a man of his bulk?

She sighed with relief when she heard Saintcrow holler, "Holly, get back here!"

Leery of what she might find, she made her way around to the back of the house.

Mahlon lay facedown in a widening pool of blood.

"Is he . . . ?"

Saintcrow nodded. "Oh, yeah. Holly? Holly!"

She dragged her gaze from the body, only then noticing the bloody object in Saintcrow's hand. Was it . . . ? Revulsion swept through her at the realization that it was Mahlon's heart.

"You're not going to faint on me, are you?" Saintcrow asked.

She shook her head. "No. What do we do now?"

"I need to get in the house. Go inside and tell Micah's father to invite me in."

"Right." Holly opened the patio door and stepped inside. The kitchen and dining room were empty.

Micah's parents were seated on the sofa in the living room, their hands lashed behind their backs, their feet tied at the ankles. One of his sisters—she couldn't remember which one—knelt on the floor in front of her husband, desperately trying to untie his hands, while her baby wailed for attention.

They all looked up, startled to see her. Micah's sister stood and picked up the baby.

"Holly!" Micah's father exclaimed. "What are you doing here? Get out, quick!"

"I'm fine." She tried to untie his hands, but the knots were too tight. "I need you to invite a friend of Micah's and mine inside."

"What are you talking about? You need to get out of here before that goon comes back."

"He won't." Holly moved to Micah's mother but, again, the knots were too tight. "Please, Mr. Ravenwood, I don't have time to explain. Just please invite my friend, Rylan Saintcrow, inside, and he'll free all of you."

"Why can't you invite him in?" Micah's mother asked, her voice shaky.

"We're wasting time," Holly said curtly. "Please, Mr. Ravenwood, just say the words!"

Micah's parents exchanged worried glances; then his father said, "Rylan Saintcrow, please come in."

An instant later, Saintcrow stood in the middle of the living room. Holly was relieved to see that he no longer held Mahlon's heart and that he had wiped the blood from his hands.

Moving quickly, he untied Micah's family. "All of you, get in the car and get out of here. Go to a hotel. Stay together. Mr. Ravenwood, if you've got a gun, take it with you. Micah will join you tonight and explain everything."

Mr. Ravenwood regarded Saintcrow for several taut seconds. Then he pulled a rifle from the hall closet, grabbed a box of shells from the shelf, and herded his family out the back door.

"The body!" Holly exclaimed.

"Don't worry. It's gone." Saintcrow jerked his chin toward the back door. "Maybe you should go with them?"

Holly bit down on the inside corner of her lip, then shook her head. "What do we do now?"

He regarded her a moment, as if weighing her resolve. And then he shrugged. "I'm gonna have a look around."

She trailed behind him as he moved through the house. "What are you looking for?"

"Just getting a good whiff of her scent."

"Then what?"

"I drank a little of Mahlon's blood before I killed him." Holly grimaced.

"It will lead me to her. Are you ready for this?"

"I guess so."

"You don't have to come along, although I might need your help if she's holed up in someone else's home."

Holly swallowed hard, then nodded. "Let's go."

Saintcrow put on gloves and dark glasses, pulled up the hood of his sweatshirt, and stepped outside. He stood on the porch a moment, head lifted, turning slowly from right to left. Was he scenting the air?

Grunting softly, he descended the stairs.

Holly trailed behind him. She had expected Saintcrow to zap them to wherever Braga was hiding out. Instead, they went on foot, following a track or a scent only he could detect. It took them to a part of town where older homes were being torn down to make way for new apartments.

Holly shivered when he came to a stop, not certain if the sudden chill had been caused by an attack of nerves or by the dark clouds gathering overhead. She glanced at Saintcrow.

His attention was focused on the last house still standing. It was a small, single-story dwelling. "She's inside," he muttered. "Come on."

Holly knew it was only her imagination, but it suddenly seemed as if the house had developed a dark aura.

She trailed behind Saintcrow. What was she doing here? She wasn't a vampire hunter. If anything happened to Saintcrow, she would be defenseless.

"I won't let anything happen to you."

This time, she wasn't sure she believed him.

He paused at a pile of rubble. Holly watched him sort through it until he found a short piece of jagged wood that had a sharp point at one end. Wordlessly, he handed it to Holly before approaching the front door.

It opened at his touch.

Holly stopped breathing as he put one foot over the threshold. Tossing her a grin, he stepped inside.

Her mouth dry, her knuckles white around the makeshift stake in her hand, she followed him inside.

"Stay behind me," he said. "And stay close."

She could hardly hear him over the rapid pounding of her heart.

They found the vampire in a small walk-in closet. She looked dead.

"You're still against this, aren't you?" Saintcrow said, a note of exasperation in his voice. "You're as bad as Kadie."

"I don't know how you can do it, just kill her while she sleeps."

"Would you rather I did it while she was awake?"

"Of course not! But . . ."

"I don't relish doing this," Saintcrow said quietly. "But she's never going to give up, and frankly, I'm tired of playing the game."

"Are you worried you can't beat her in a fair fight?"

He snorted his disdain. "If that's what you think, you're sorely mistaken. I'm doing her a kindness by destroying her while she's at rest. It'll be quick and painless. She won't feel a thing. But I'm a patient man, so I'll leave it up to you, Holly Parrish. I can take her heart while she sleeps, or . . ."

He shoved Holly against the wall as Leticia Braga lunged to her feet. Teeth bared, fingers like claws, she attacked Saintcrow, all the while screeching at the top of her voice that he had killed the love of her life.

Holly was too stunned to scream, too terrified to move.

Never, in all her life, had she seen anything as savage as the battle being waged before her eyes. Saintcrow was older, stronger, but Braga fought like a wild animal, biting, clawing, scratching, somehow dancing out of reach whenever it looked like Saintcrow was going to rip out her heart.

And always, Braga screamed her hatred at him.

Just when Holly thought the fight would go on forever, Saintcrow slammed Braga against the wall beside Holly, grabbed the stake from her hand, and drove it into the other vampire's heart.

The sudden silence was deafening.

The smell of blood filled the air.

As though freed from a spell, Holly fled the house as if pursued by the devil and his fallen angels.

Chapter Twenty-Two

Holly glanced over her shoulder, expecting to find Saintcrow in hot pursuit. But he wasn't there. Unless he had dissolved into mist and was, even now, hovering above her like some disembodied spirit.

She ran until she was out of breath, then stopped in front of a liquor store, her heart racing, her mind spinning. What to do, what to do?

What to do? What was she thinking? She had a phone and cash in her pocket. She was free!

With fingers that trembled, she located the number of a cab company.

Fifteen minutes later, she checked into a small hotel on the other side of town. In her room, she locked the door, then slumped onto the sofa and closed her eyes, only to snap them open when visions of Saintcrow holding Mahlon's heart, Saintcrow staking Braga, flashed through her mind.

She had a terrible feeling those images would haunt her for days—maybe months—to come.

She plucked Saintcrow's cell phone from her pocket, then paused as another image flashed through her mind.

Micah. True, she was anxious to put all this behind her, anxious to go home, but did she really want to leave Micah behind, as well?

She bit down on her lower lip, then shook her head. She'd had enough adventure to last a lifetime. She needed space, time to think. She needed to go home.

Using Saintcrow's phone, she called the airport and arranged for a flight to take her home first thing in the morning. The sooner she was in her own house, sleeping in her own bed, the better.

Micah woke with the setting of the sun. His first thought was for Holly. Was she safe? And what about his family? Had Saintcrow destroyed Braga and Mahlon?

He bolted upright when he realized Holly wasn't anywhere in the hotel. Muttering, "Where the hell is she?" he stormed into the suite's main room.

Kadie was curled up on the sofa, reading a book. Saintcrow stood at the window, gazing outside, hands shoved into his back pockets.

"Where's Holly?" Micah demanded.

"I don't know. She took off after I staked Braga."

"Why didn't you go after her?"

"Hey, I'm not her keeper."

Micah took a deep breath, almost afraid to ask. "My family?"

"I sent them to a hotel for the time being. You might want to call your folks and let them know it's safe to go back home."

Micah stared at Saintcrow's back. "Do they know about me?"

"I didn't ask."

"Did she feed on them?"

Saintcrow nodded.

Micah cursed softly. Did his family know the truth about him now? If they did, how could he ever face any of them again? He had lied to all of them for years. How could he make them understand? They would never look at him in the same way. Hell, he wouldn't be surprised if they never wanted to see him again.

"Kadie and I are going back to Morgan Creek," Saintcrow said, turning away from the window. "You're welcome to come along."

Micah nodded absently. "Thanks."

"If it makes you feel any better, there's a good chance your parents don't know."

"Whether they do or they don't, they're going to have a lot of questions about vampires after what happened here. And probably a few suspicions about me."

"Sucks to be you," Saintcrow said with a wry grin.

"Very funny."

Saintcrow laid a hand on Micah's shoulder. "They're your parents. They have to love you."

"And Holly loves you, too," Kadie said.

"Just give her a little time," Saintcrow advised. "She's been through a lot in the last few weeks."

"Yeah, time," Micah muttered bleakly. He had plenty of that.

"We'll be leaving for home later tonight," Saintcrow said. "If you need us, you know where to find us."

Micah nodded. After giving Kadie a hug, he left the hotel.

Outside, he took several deep breaths, then closed his eyes and concentrated on the blood link that bound him to Holly. She was in a room—probably in a hotel—asleep.

He blew out a sigh of relief. Holly was safe. His main concern now was facing his family.

* * *

On the other side of the world, Leandro Braga was ripped from the deathlike sleep of his kind. He bolted upright, gasping. Pain exploded through his chest, as if someone had driven a stake deep into his heart.

It was followed by an acute sense of loss as the blood link that had bound him to his sister, no matter the distance between them, vanished. It left him feeling oddly empty and adrift.

It could only mean one thing.

Leticia was dead.

He had hated her for centuries, refused to speak to her. As his sire, she could have compelled him to keep in touch with her, to return home, to do anything she wanted. But she had never done so, certain that, sooner or later, he would forgive her for turning him against his will.

Now it was too late. Forever too late.

He fell back onto his bed as the dark sleep curled around him yet again.

He couldn't mend the rift between them, he thought as he sank back into the darkness of oblivion, but he could avenge her death.

Micah stood in front of his parents' home. A deep breath carried the scent of Mahlon's blood, leading him to believe Braga's bodyguard had died on the premises. Before calling his parents he had gone through the house and then checked the backyard, but he'd found no evidence that blood had been shed there. Saintcrow had been thorough, indeed.

Micah had intended to be waiting for his folks when they arrived, but his courage had deserted him. After calling his folks to let them know the house was safe, he had disconnected the call before his father could ask any questions. And then he had fled the scene, unable to face them. He had spent the last half hour walking the streets, trying to figure out what to say, how to explain what had happened, who Braga was and why she had invaded their home. Steeling himself to face his family's disbelief, their revulsion, when they learned the truth about him.

Shit. Might as well get it over with.

For the first time since he had left home, he knocked on the front door, then stood there, jaw clenched, his whole body tense, as he waited for someone to answer the door.

Fear and uncertainty emanated from the house in waves.

After what seemed like hours, his father opened the door a crack. He looked like he'd aged ten years, but the rifle in his hands was rock steady.

One look at his father's face confirmed Micah's worst fears—his secret was no longer a secret. With a shake of his head, he muttered, "Unless that Winchester is loaded with silver bullets, it won't do you any good, Dad."

Color washed into his father's cheeks. "I didn't know it was you," he mumbled.

"Would you rather I left?"

"Are you alone?"

"Yeah."

Heaving a sigh, his father stepped away from the door.

Micah hesitated a moment before crossing the threshold. He had been so preoccupied wondering what his parents would think, he hadn't noticed that his whole family—minus his nieces and nephews—was gathered in the family room. Damn, all those nervous heartbeats should have warned him.

Hands clenched, he followed his father into the house.

All eyes swung in his direction.

Micah took a deep breath. "I guess those of you who weren't here know what happened," he said flatly.

There were nods here and there. His father said, "That awful woman, she fed on us."

Feeling sick to his stomach, Micah nodded.

"She told us she was a vampire."

Micah nodded again.

"And that you . . ." His father shook his head. "That you were one, too."

"It isn't true, is it?" His mother's face was pale, her eyes filled with despair. Guilt pierced Micah's heart. Like his father, his mother looked older, haggard.

"It's true." Micah glanced at his brothers and sisters and their spouses. Some looked at him in disbelief, some with horror, some with pity.

"How did it happen?" his oldest brother, Joe, asked.

"Why didn't you tell us sooner?" Sofia queried with a frown. She didn't seem too upset, but maybe that was to be expected, since she was a big fan of *Twilight* and *The Vampire Diaries* and all things Dracula.

"Is that why we haven't seen much of you lately?" his sister, Rosa, asked.

Micah held up his hand to stay their questions. As succinctly as possible, he told them about Lilith, how he had met her, and all that had happened afterward.

The room was silent when he finished.

And then his mother stood up. "It doesn't matter, Mikey." Hurrying across the room, she embraced him. "You're my son. This is your home. We are your family, no matter what."

"Ma . . ." Tears burned his eyes as he wrapped his arms around her.

The next thing he knew, the whole family was gathered

around him, his brothers hugging and punching, his sisters showering him with kisses.

Later, they inundated him with the usual questions.

Did he really drink blood? Yes.

What did it taste like? Warm and salty.

Could he fly? In a way.

Disappear? His sisters shrieked when he dissolved into mist.

Did garlic repel him? No.

Did silver burn him? Only weapons, although the metal also negated some of his powers.

Did he cast a reflection in a mirror? Yes.

Was he really immortal? Pretty much.

What had happened to Braga and her companion? They were dead. End of story.

And from his mother: "Where's Holly?"

Micah took a deep breath. "I think she went home, Ma. She had some things to sort out."

"She's a good girl," Lena said, patting his arm. "Don't lose her, Mikey."

Later, back in Morgan Creek, Micah decided that, all things considered, it was the best night he had spent with his family since he'd become a vampire. He had expected horror, revulsion, rejection. But as far as they were concerned, he was still Mikey, still family. Blood, he thought with a wry grin. It really was thicker than water.

He was thinking about Holly, wondering if he should call her, when his cell phone buzzed.

"Mikey, hi."

"Hey, Sofie. Is everything all right?"

"Fine. I always suspected you were a vampire."

"Is that right?"

"Well, not always," she admitted. "But I did wonder from time to time."

"Is that what you called to tell me?"

"No. I was wondering, that is, well . . ."

There was silence on the line. Micah grinned, imagining his sister twirling her hair around her finger the way she did when she was nervous, or when she wanted a favor. Like the time she'd wanted him to sneak her into an R-rated movie when she was twelve. Finally, he said, "Spit it out, Sofie. What do you want this time?"

In a rush, she said, "I want you to turn me into a vampire."

Micah groaned low in his throat. "You've got to be kidding me."

"No. I've done a lot of research into the subject, you know."

"Research?" he exclaimed. "Are you out of your mind? You can't research vampires like you're studying for a test. Trust me, little sister, you don't want this. There aren't any sparkly vampires in the real world."

"Well, duh, I know that."

"And I know you. Believe me, Sofie, this isn't the life for you. You can't try it on like a pair of shoes and change your mind if it doesn't fit. It's forever."

"But, Mikey, it looks like such fun! Being able to turn into mist. How cool is that? And staying young forever—"

"Even if I was willing to turn you, which I'm not, I wouldn't do it now. You're only eighteen. Way too young to make such a life-changing decision."

"But—"

"Just listen to me. If you feel the same when you're twenty-five, we'll talk about it some more."

"Twenty-five!"

"Like I said, we'll talk about it then."

"Fine," she said, the pout evident in her tone. "Love you."

"Love you, too." Micah shook his head as he disconnected the call. Of all the possibilities he had contemplated when he finally told his parents the truth, having his little sister ask to become a vampire had never been one of them.

Chapter Twenty-Three

It was almost 11 AM when Holly awoke. Turning onto her side, she stared out her bedroom window. The danger was past and she was home, in her own bed.

Where was Micah?

She shook the thought away as soon as it surfaced. She wouldn't think about him, not now. She needed a little space of her own. A little time to reflect on the events of the last few weeks. Time to sift through her jumbled thoughts and feelings when Micah wasn't there to influence her.

Throwing the covers aside, she headed for the shower.

A short time later, dressed in jeans and a T-shirt, she went into the kitchen, only then remembering that—like old Mother Hubbard—her cupboards were bare.

It seemed odd to go out alone during the day.

Holly pushed her shopping cart up and down the aisles, buying whatever caught her fancy. She stopped to shoot the breeze with a neighbor she met in the bread aisle, thinking how strange it felt to exchange idle chitchat with another human being after spending so much time among vampires.

She smiled at the cashier when he said he'd missed her.

"I was on vacation," Holly said, swiping her credit card.

"Did you have a good time?"

"Yes. And no. See you next week."

At home, while putting the groceries away, she let herself think of Micah. He would be resting now. Had he gone to see his parents? What had they said about being held by Braga? Had he told them that he, too, was a vampire? If so, what had their reaction been? Having met his parents, she was certain they wouldn't stop loving him, vampire or not.

Had he stayed home or gone back to Morgan Creek with Kadie and Saintcrow?

Was he missing her?

Was he angry because she had left without so much as a good-bye?

No matter where you go, I'll always be able to find you.

Of course, he wouldn't have to look very far, since he knew where she lived. Would he come here? Did she want him to?

When all the groceries were put away, she made a late breakfast of scrambled eggs, toast, and orange juice. She ate quickly, loaded the dishes into the dishwasher, then went into the living room, took a deep breath, and called Mr. Gladstone.

She crossed her fingers when he answered the phone.

He was polite, he was sympathetic, he was succinct.

She was no longer employed at the offices of Gladstone and Becket.

Hands shoved into the pockets of his jeans, Micah strolled the dark streets of downtown Los Angeles. He passed drunks and derelicts, gang members with shaved heads and leather jackets. This time of night, decent people stayed off the streets. He nodded to the officer behind the wheel of a black-and-white when the cop slowed to give him the once-over.

A week had passed since Saintcrow had destroyed Braga and Holly had hightailed it for home.

Holly. She was in his every waking thought. Time and again, he had contemplated going to her house. A few times, he'd made it as far as her front porch, but so far he hadn't found the courage to knock on the door.

Give her time, Saintcrow had said.

Easy for him to say. He didn't spend his nights wondering if the woman he loved had decided she never wanted to see him again. Or if she was going out with someone else.

But Holly wasn't his only worry. In the last week, he'd had several calls from Sofia asking questions about vampires. She seemed to think that being Undead was some kind of romantic fairy tale where everyone lived happily ever after. So far, nothing he'd said had changed her mind.

Tired of his own company, Micah went in search of a nightclub, hoping to drown his sorrows in blood and wine.

The first club he came to was a seedy tavern in a bad part of town, populated by a handful of disreputable-looking patrons, from the pasty-faced druggie slumped over a corner table to the hooker trying to persuade a john to take her home.

Micah ordered a glass of red wine, thinking that even if he was starving for nourishment, he would rather go hungry than prey on anybody in the place.

Muttering, "What the hell am I doing here?" he left the tavern in search of greener pastures.

Lost in thought, it took him a moment to realize someone was stalking him. Lifting his head, he opened his senses. Two men trailed behind him. Both had had too much to drink; one was armed with a snub-nosed pistol. They were spoiling for a fight.

Micah grinned into the darkness as he deliberately slowed his pace. *Bring it on*, he thought. *I could use the diversion.*

In the end, it was little more than a scuffle that the would-be assailants never had a chance of winning. Micah knocked out the gunman with a well-placed uppercut. The second man eased Micah's hunger before he was rendered unconscious.

"This is what it's like to be a vampire, little sister," he muttered, wiping his mouth with the back of his hand. "Walking the streets alone. Preying on the stupid and the weak. There's no way I'm letting this happen to you, Sofie. No way in hell!"

Holly spent a week feeling sorry for herself. She had lost a job she loved. She had lost a man she might have loved. She drowned her sorrows in hot fudge sundaes with double whipped cream, and cookies-and-cream lattes. When she wasn't wallowing in self-pity, she buried herself in housework and yard work.

When the allotted week was up, she went online and filled out job applications and resumes until she couldn't see straight.

Thanks to a downturn in the economy, no one was hiring.

Friday night, determined not to sink into a swamp of self-pity again, she showered, did her hair and her nails, dressed in a pair of black slacks and a silky white shirt, and went to a nightclub where one of her favorite bands happened to be playing.

She had hoped listening to music she loved and being

surrounded by people having a good time would somehow boost her morale. An hour later, she felt more depressed than ever.

"Another good idea shot to hell," Holly muttered, slipping into her coat. She seemed to be the only person in the crowd without a friend at her side or a date in her arms.

Why had she left Micah? she wondered, threading her way through the crowd toward the door. So, he was a vampire. So, he drank blood. At least he made her feel beautiful, desired. Happy. If she sent him a mental invitation, would he hear her? Would he answer?

The thought had no sooner crossed her mind than he was there, striding toward her. Had he always been that handsome, his hair that dark a brown, his eyes so mesmerizing? Just looking at him took her breath away. Tall, dark, devilishly sexy. He cut through the throng of people on the dance floor like a hot knife through butter, his gaze focused on her, oblivious to the number of women who turned to stare longingly at him as he passed by.

"Holly."

Just hearing her name on his lips made her heart skip a beat.

"You heard me." She couldn't stop looking at him. Just being close to him made her feel as if she had been sleepwalking through life since they'd parted.

"Did you think I wouldn't?" His gaze caressed her, so intense it was almost tangible.

"I didn't know. Micah . . ."

"Yes, love?"

"I just . . . I . . ."

"I know." He smiled down at her, his arms gently circling her waist, drawing her body close to his as he lowered his head to claim her lips.

This was what she wanted, she thought. What she had been missing. What she needed. Just Micah.

"I missed you, too. Are you ready to go?" he asked, taking her hand in his.

She nodded. She didn't care where they went, as long as they were together, as long as he would fold her into his embrace when they got there and kiss her again.

Outside, he wrapped his arms around her. "Hold on tight."

Holly closed her eyes. When she opened them again, they were in Shirley's house in Morgan Creek.

Micah set her on her feet. Moments later, a fire crackled in the hearth; soft music came from the speakers. A bottle of wine and two glasses waited for them on the coffee table, along with a plate of crackers and cheese.

Holly looked at Micah, her brow furrowed as she removed her coat. "When did you do all this?"

"I made a quick trip to the store when I heard you thinking about me, just in case you called for me." Taking her hand, he led her to the sofa. "How have you been, Holly?"

"Don't you know?"

He shook his head. "I blocked you from my thoughts for a while, hoping it would help me forget you. It didn't work. I started to call you a dozen times, but Saintcrow told me to give you some space, so . . ." He shook his head again. "If you hadn't called me tonight, I would have come to you. I need you in my life, sunshine."

"Oh, Micah." She leaned into him, lifting her head for his kiss. Right or wrong, she wanted him. Tonight or for always, she wanted him.

"Holly!"

He swept her into his arms, his mouth exploring hers in a searing kiss she felt all the way to her toes. It burned away every doubt even as it ignited her desire. He eased her back onto the sofa, his body tight against hers, his hand stroking up and down her side, lightly skimming her breast, cupping her buttocks to draw her closer.

She moaned softly when his tongue laved her neck, clutched his shoulders at the touch of his fangs.

"Holly?"

She nodded, then sighed when she felt the prick of his fangs. His bite heightened every sensation.

She wanted him desperately, felt bereft when he lifted his head.

"Tell me what you want."

"You," she whispered. "Now."

"Are you sure?"

Of course she was sure. Wasn't she? She gazed up at him, torn. There was only one thing more intimate than letting him drink her blood. Was she ready to cross that line?

As always, he knew what she was thinking. "It's okay, sunshine," he said, his voice thick. "When we make love, I don't want you to have any doubts."

"I'm sorry."

"Don't be." Taking it slow was the smart thing to do. She was young, innocent in many ways. When he took her, he didn't want her to have any regrets.

Later, wrapped in Micah's arms, Holly felt guilty. She hadn't meant to lead him on. She had been so certain making love was what she wanted. And yet, when it came right down to it, she had hesitated. Frowning, she stared at the flames, absently noting that the wood burned but was never consumed. She didn't really have anything to feel guilty about, she told herself. It was a woman's right to change her mind. And until she knew him better, until there was some kind of commitment between them, she wasn't risking her heart. And once she gave Micah her body, her heart would surely follow.

Remembering, too late, that he could read her mind, she bit down on her lower lip. Maybe he hadn't been listening.

She looked up at him, and frowned, thinking he looked far away. "Micah?"

"What?"

"Are you mad at me?"

"Of course not. Why would you think that?"

"No reason, except you seem so distant."

"Sorry. I was thinking about my sister. Sofia. She wants to be a vampire."

"What?"

"Yeah. She's been fascinated with vampires since she was a little girl. It's bizarre. When she found out I was one, she asked me to turn her." He shook his head. "After what happened to my folks, you'd think being a vampire would be the last thing she'd want. I told her we'd talk about it when she's older, but I'm afraid she won't wait."

"Is it that easy to just go out and find a vampire? And suppose she finds one . . . ?" Holly grimaced at the thought of his pretty little sister turning into a predator roaming the night in search of blood.

"I don't even want to go there." He raked his fingers through his hair. "I think I'd better sit her down and have another talk, explain to her about being sired and what it means before she does something stupid."

"What does it mean?"

"It's like the blood bond you and I share, only it's stronger, more compelling. Only death can break it."

"That's kinda scary."

A muscle twitched in his jaw. "It can be. Especially if you're turned by someone you don't like."

"Is there really no way to undo it once you're turned?"

"If there was, believe me, I'd have tried it a long time ago."

Holly rested her cheek against his chest, content to be in his arms. She tried to imagine what her life would be like if she stayed with him. She would go to work while he slept, but they would spend their nights together. She tried to imagine living with a man who could only share half her life. There would be no summer days at the beach. No picnics in the park on the Fourth of July, but at night they could watch the fireworks together. No Christmas mornings with his parents or hers, but they could spend Christmas Eve with family. What about kids? Somehow, she doubted children would be possible.

Holly sighed, then murmured, "Where do we go from here?"

"I guess that's up to you."

She had contemplated what it would be like to stay with Micah. Now, she tried to imagine her life without him, but it didn't bear thinking about. The past week had proven, beyond a shadow of a doubt, that she wanted—needed—him in her life.

"Before you make a decision, you should know that I can't father a child."

Holly nodded. Hadn't she guessed as much?

"Is that a deal breaker?" he asked. "I know kids are important to most women."

Holly started to say there was always adoption, but then she paused. What kind of life would that be for a child, having a father who was a vampire? A father who would never be able to attend school functions unless they were held after dark? Who would never be able to play ball with his son in the park, or spend summer vacations at the mountains or the beach or go to the zoo?

"So, what's it to be?" he asked quietly.

"Lots of couples can't have kids, and they manage to live happily ever after. And there are already plenty of kids in your family," she added, smiling. But she couldn't ignore a little pang of regret that she would never have a baby of her own.

"I will love you as long as you live," Micah said, his arm tightening around her.

As long as you live. Holly repeated the words in her mind. How long would that be? Another fifty years? Sixty? Seventy, if she was lucky. When she was old and wrinkled, he would still look twenty. She recalled asking Kadie if she had wanted to be a vampire, and Kadie's answer—*sooner or later, I'm sure I would have asked him to turn me because it was really the only way for the two of us to stay together.*

Holly closed her eyes. If she stayed with Micah, sooner or later, she would have to make that same decision. "There's just one thing," she said slowly. "If we decide to stay together, will you marry me?"

Chapter Twenty-Four

"You want to marry me?" Micah asked. "Seriously?"

Holly nodded. "I'm not comfortable having a long-time affair. I want a real relationship, something solid, with a future. I guess I'm old-fashioned, but I want a piece of paper that proves I'm yours and you're mine."

"Fine by me," he said, smiling down at her. "Tomorrow too soon?"

"I don't want to rush into marriage, either. I want to make sure that what I feel, what we have, is real. We haven't really had a chance to try living together under normal circumstances. Now that Braga is no longer a threat, and your parents know what you are . . ." She shrugged. "I want us to spend time together, like ordinary people." With anyone else, she wouldn't have suggested moving in together, but these weren't normal circumstances. Micah was a vampire, and she wanted to know what living with one was really like before making any lasting commitment.

"Ordinary," Micah repeated, chuckling. "All right, sunshine. I'm game if you are. Where do we start?"

Holly swallowed as his gaze met hers. He was so beautiful, and she wanted him so desperately. . . .

No more than I want you.

His words went through her like lightning.

"Make love to me, Micah," she murmured.

He arched one brow. "You sure this time?"

She nodded, too nervous to speak.

"Holly!" Wrapping his arms around her waist, he drew her down on top of him. Their clothes disappeared as if by magic as he murmured love words in her ear. She reveled in the touch of his bare skin against her, shivered with pleasure when he kissed her, his hands lightly stroking her back, delving into her hair. His tongue played over her lower lip before slipping inside.

Heat shot through her at his touch. Why had she waited so long for this? Her hands were impatient as they explored the broad expanse of his chest, the width of his shoulders, his hard, flat belly.

His kisses grew hotter, deeper, until she was afraid she might go up in flames.

With a low growl, he rolled over, carrying her with him, so that he was on top. When he gazed into her eyes, the most remarkable thing happened. She knew what he was thinking, feeling. Knew he loved her, as she loved him. Knew this was right. She sighed as he kissed her again, his body now a part of hers, carrying her away to places she had never imagined.

She was his now, she thought, really his, and there was no going back.

"Micah?"

"Hmm?"

"Where are we going to live?"

He brushed a kiss across her cheek. "I haven't thought that far ahead. Any preference?"

"Well, I don't have any income these days. Do you?"

"Not really."

She nodded. "Then it seems to me we only have two options—we can stay at my place or here, in Morgan Creek. You don't want to stay here, do you?"

Micah shrugged. "Saintcrow and Kadie are here. I know you're not crazy about him, but they're the only friends I've got."

Holly considered that a minute. She had friends at home, but maybe it was best to stay here, at least for the time being. "I need to find a job. Is there a town nearby?"

"Yeah, about twenty miles away."

Holly chewed on her thumbnail. Twenty miles wasn't that far. And staying in Morgan Creek might be best while they sorted out their relationship. If they lived here and it didn't work out, it would be much simpler for her to leave Morgan Creek and go home than to ask Micah to move out of her house. "I need to go back to my place and pick up some of my clothes and things, stop the mail delivery, and ask my neighbor's son to water the yard again."

"No problem. So, are we staying?"

"Yes," she said, smiling. "For now."

Saintcrow propped his elbows on the porch rail of Shirley's house, his chin resting on his folded hands "So, you're going to be here for a while?"

Micah nodded. "Yeah. If it's all right with you."

"I don't have a problem with it. How'd you talk Holly into staying? I was pretty sure she'd be eager to go back home."

"I thought so, too, but . . ." Micah made a vague gesture

with his hand. "She lost her job so we decided to stay here until she figures out what she wants to do next. Oh . . . she asked me to marry her if we decide to stay together."

"No shit?"

"Yeah, but first we're going to play house and see how that works out."

Saintcrow snorted softly. "Good luck with that."

"You think we'll need it?"

"A little luck couldn't hurt. Marriage isn't easy under the best of circumstances."

"And ours aren't the best. I get it." Micah paced the length of the porch, back and forth, then sat on the top step. "What would you have done if Kadie hadn't become a vampire?"

"I would have stayed with her as long as she lived. Kadie's the best thing that ever happened to me. She made me remember my humanity. All the people we kept here have her to thank for their freedom."

Micah nodded. "If something happened to her, do you think you'd ever fall in love again?"

"No."

"How can you be so sure?"

"I lived a long time before I met Kadie. Maybe too long. I've got no interest in going on without her."

"So, what are you saying? That you'd destroy yourself?"

"Yeah. But don't tell her that. She wouldn't like it."

Micah stared into the distance for several minutes, thinking about what Saintcrow had said. He hadn't lived nearly as long as his friend. Maybe he never would. But whether he lived another year or a thousand, he wanted Holly at his side. Another few minutes slid into eternity before he said, "Did I tell you my sister wants to be a vampire?"

Chuckling, Saintcrow dropped down beside him. "What brought that on?"

"She's always been into vampires. Funny ones, scary ones, it doesn't matter. She thinks it would be fun. Fun!" He shook his head in exasperation. "The woman I love doesn't want to be a vampire, but my little sister does. I get the feeling that fate's having a good laugh at my expense."

Rising, Saintcrow slapped him on the shoulder. "I think you're right."

Holly sorted through the piles of clothing on her bed, trying to decide what to keep and what to donate to the local homeless shelter. Moving in with Micah was the perfect excuse to clean out her closet and get rid of skirts, sweaters, shoes, and jeans that she hadn't worn in years.

Earlier, she had filled a box with a few of her favorite books and movies to take to Morgan Creek.

Holly folded one last sweater and dropped it into her suitcase, then went to the dresser and began sorting through her underwear. Spending a month or so in Morgan Creek had seemed like a good idea when she and Micah had discussed it. Now, she couldn't help wondering if she was doing the right thing. She had to work. She had to pay for the upkeep on her house, taxes, groceries. When she got a job, she wouldn't be able to keep Micah's hours. No staying up until three or four in the morning, not when she'd have to get up early and drive twenty miles to work. Assuming she could find a job. And then there was her house. She didn't want to sell it. She supposed she could rent it. . . .

Looking up, she frowned at her reflection in the oval mirror above the dresser. "Stop it. He loves you. You love him. No relationship is perfect. Every couple has problems to work out. So, Micah is a vampire. It could be worse," she muttered under her breath, then bit down on her lower lip when she saw him standing in the doorway.

"Yeah?" He lifted one brow. "What do you consider worse?"

"Someone who squeezes the toothpaste from the middle?"

Micah frowned. And then he laughed. Taking Holly in his arms, he kissed the top of her head, thinking that, as long as they could laugh together, everything would be all right.

"Are you about done here?" he asked.

"Yes, except for my toiletries."

It didn't take long to pack her toothpaste and toothbrush and cosmetics. She took a last look around to make sure she had everything she thought she might need. She had put a hold on her mail, asked Josh to water the yard and keep an eye on things until she returned.

One last turn through the house to make sure everything was closed and locked, and she was ready to go.

"We don't have to stay here if you'd rather not," Micah said when they arrived at Shirley's. "There are lots of other houses for you to choose from."

Holly shook her head. "I like this one. It feels like . . . like home." She carried her suitcase into the bedroom and dropped it on the foot of the bed.

Micah followed her, then stood in the doorway, one shoulder propped against the jamb as he watched her unpack.

"Do you think Saintcrow will rebuild the bridge?" she asked. Earlier, Micah had transported her and her belongings across the ravine. She hadn't realized how deep it was.

"I don't know. I doubt it."

"So, I'll be trapped here during the day." Why hadn't she thought about that before agreeing to stay? If she couldn't leave Morgan Creek, how would she find a new job? What would she do for fun or recreation on weekends when she wasn't working and the vampires were at rest? Of course, she could keep their hours on Saturdays, Sundays, and holidays. Lately, she had been doing that anyway. But she wasn't a vampire and she didn't want to spend the daylight hours in the dark. She needed something to occupy her time and her mind. And she liked working, feeling useful, meeting new people.

"I'll talk to Saintcrow about the bridge."

"Thanks."

"No problem." Taking Holly into his arms, he kissed her lightly on the cheek. "What would you like to do tonight?"

"Go grocery shopping."

"Not very romantic," he said with a wry grin, "but necessary, I suppose. Get your coat."

It took only moments for Micah to transport them to the store in the next town. He trailed behind Holly as she pushed her cart up one aisle and down the next. So many things he had once loved and would never eat again—lasagna, apple pie, ice cream, a good steak, spareribs, potatoes, cheese. He often caught a taste of some of his favorites on Holly's lips.

Micah paid the bill with a credit card Saintcrow had given him, then pushed the cart outside.

"I shouldn't have bought so much," Holly said. "How do you plan to get all this home?"

"Not a problem. Wait here. I'll be right back."

He was gone in the blink of an eye, taking the shopping cart with him. Holly glanced up and down the street. It seemed like a nice town, the stores and roads well maintained, the parkways green and neatly trimmed. When the bridge was rebuilt, she would come here and look for a job.

She jumped when Micah appeared beside her, the cart empty. "Would you like to take a walk?" he asked, taking her hand in his.

"I'd like that, but . . ."

"Don't worry, I put all the perishable stuff away."

"Well, then, what are we waiting for?"

It really was a nice town, Holly thought as they strolled down the sidewalk. People they passed nodded and smiled. Music spilled from an Italian restaurant.

Holly slid a glance at Micah, wondering if he had ever preyed on any of the men and women they passed, if any of the town's inhabitants had ever been held hostage by the vampires in Morgan Creek.

"You look worried," Micah remarked. "Is something wrong?"

Holly lifted one brow, surprised that he wasn't reading her mind. "No." She bit down on her lower lip, then blurted, "Have you ever hunted here?"

"Once or twice. We usually went farther afield. Never a good idea to hunt too close to where you live."

"That makes sense, I guess." She grinned inwardly, thinking her idea of "close" was probably a lot different from his. She glanced at the pretty young woman walking toward them. "What are you going to do about your sister?"

"I don't know. But if she's determined to become a

vampire when she gets older, I want to be the one to bring her across."

"You'd do that?" Holly exclaimed. "To your own sister?"

"Better me than some stranger. I need to talk to my family about this, let them know what Sofie's thinking. Somebody's got to keep an eye on her." He swore under his breath. "And it should be me. None of them can protect her."

"Micah . . ."

He shook his head. "I need to be there. I don't know why I didn't think of it sooner. She's eighteen. Technically, she doesn't have to answer to anybody but herself. And if she moves out of the house . . ." Micah came to an abrupt halt, his arm snaking around Holly's waist. "Dammit! I've got to go home! Now!"

"Now? But . . . we just bought groceries!"

"They'll keep for a few days. We can stay with my folks tonight. They've got lots of empty rooms since only Rosa and Sofia are still living at home. Come on."

Before she could argue, they were standing in front of the Ravenwoods' home.

Holly was a little hesitant at the idea of bursting in on Micah's parents unannounced, but Lena and Luciano welcomed the two of them with open arms.

"This is a surprise," Lena said when the four of them were seated in the living room. "Is something wrong, Mikey?"

"Yes and no, Ma."

Mr. Ravenwood leaned forward. "What is it?"

"It's Sofia."

"Sofia?" Mr. Ravenwood frowned. "What are you talking about?"

Micah blew out a breath. He was trying to decide whether to try to sugarcoat it or just spit it out when he noticed the books on the desk beside the fireplace. *Dracula—Fact or Fiction. So You Want to Be a Vampire. Fifty Myths About the Undead.*

"Is she in some kind of trouble?" Lena asked anxiously.

"Not yet," Micah replied. "The thing is, she wants to be a vampire. She asked me to bring her across."

His mother and father glanced furtively at the books on the desk and then at each other, leading Micah to believe that his news wasn't a total surprise.

"Has she mentioned it to you?" It seemed doubtful, but he had to ask.

"Not exactly," Lena said. "But she's been reading a lot about vampires and the occult, even more than usual. Last night, she had a date with a young man. She didn't invite him into the house."

"It wasn't until she was gone that I remembered we had to invite Holly's friend inside," Mr. Ravenwood remarked. "When I questioned Sofia about it later, she laughed it off, said it didn't mean anything. She'd just been in a hurry."

"She's in a hurry, all right," Micah muttered.

"You don't think . . . ?" Lena's face paled. "She wouldn't really . . . ?"

"Is she out with this guy now?" Micah asked.

"No. She went out with Rosa and a couple of their friends."

"Do you know where they were going?"

"They didn't say."

"I don't think she'll do anything rash as long as Rosa's with her," Micah said. "Tomorrow's Saturday. Holly, maybe you could ask Sofie to take you out and show you around, keep her occupied until I get up."

"I'll try."

"You never know. She might let something slip. Okay if we stay the night, Ma?"

"Of course. There are clean sheets on the beds. Take whichever rooms you want."

Micah didn't miss her emphasis on "rooms"—a subtle hint that there would be no hanky-panky under his mother's roof.

His parents and Holly went up to bed a short time later.

Micah sat in the living room, the TV turned down low, while he waited for his sisters to come home. Try as he might, he couldn't imagine Sofia as a vampire. She had always been squeamish where blood was concerned, always tenderhearted, unwilling to cause anyone pain.

It was well after midnight when he heard the sound of Rosa's giggle, followed by Sofie's hushed laughter as they tiptoed into the house.

"You two are as quiet as a herd of elephants," Micah said, switching on the table lamp.

"Mikey!" Sofia blinked against the light. "What are you doing here?"

"I'll tell you tomorrow night, when you're sober."

"I'm not drunk," she protested. "Just feelin' good."

"Yeah, a little too good. Go on up to bed, both of you."

"Yes, big brother," Rosa said, snickering. "Don't tell Mom."

"Have I ever?"

He hugged them both, shook his head as they staggered up the stairs, arm in arm.

With his preternatural hearing, he had no trouble discerning their movements as they got ready for bed. He listened as they changed into their nightgowns, brushed their teeth, slid under the covers. Minutes passed. And then the soft, even sound of their breathing told him they were asleep.

Micah turned off the lights and the TV, then went up to Sofia's bedroom. It was just as he remembered it. Half a dozen vampire movie posters covered the dark gray walls; a bookcase was crammed with paperbacks. A narrow shelf above the bed held a variety of vampire-themed knickknacks and a Dracula bobblehead. Sofia was asleep, snuggled beneath a black and gray quilt, one foot peeking out, her hair spread over her shoulders like a veil of black silk.

Sitting on the edge of the bed, he lifted her arm, his fingers lightly stroking the delicate skin. Then, murmuring, "I'm sorry," he made a shallow slit in her wrist. Her blood was warm and salty. He took only a little, just enough to form a bond between them so he would always be able to find her.

A flick of his tongue sealed the wound.

Whispering, "Sweet dreams, little sister," he left the house in search of prey.

Chapter Twenty-Five

Leandro Braga stood in the center of the condemned house where his sister had been destroyed. He hadn't truly expected to find the place. The blood link between them was fading fast, but, on a hunch, he had followed it to where it ended.

The lingering scent of her spilled blood mingled with the smell of violent death.

Of rotted wood and dust.

Of many humans.

And a single vampire.

Leandro took a deep breath, his nostrils filling with the distinctive scent of the vampire who had most likely destroyed his sister. It was not a scent he knew, but one he would not forget.

Returning to the empty warehouse he was currently using as his lair, he rummaged in his duffel bag for the pack of letters his sister had sent him over the years. Most were old, the ink fading, the paper yellowing. He put those carefully aside. Leticia had written him on a regular basis, even though he had never answered any of her letters. He read quickly through the most recent ones. Saintcrow's name came up often, but that was no surprise. . . .

Braga hissed an oath. Was it possible the scent he had picked up in the condemned house had been Saintcrow's?

His eyes narrowed, he perused several other letters. Leticia had mentioned a town in one of the recent ones. . . . Yes, here it was. Morgan Creek.

It wasn't much to go on, he thought, shoving the letter into his back pocket. But it was a start. A ripple in the air warned him that the sun would soon be rising. The hunt would have to start tomorrow night.

He sank down on the pile of old sacks he was using for a bed. Eyes closed, he thought of his sister. They had been close once. Raised in poverty by a widowed mother, they had roamed the village streets together, stealing bread and whatever else they could find. Leticia had grown up dreaming of becoming a fine lady; he had longed to be a knight.

He barked a humorless laugh. Dreams were for fools.

He would never forget the night that had forever changed her life. And his. Desperate for money, Leticia had tried to rob a gentleman of his purse. Only her mark had not been a gentleman at all, but a vampire who had turned her and abandoned her. And Leticia, alone and afraid, had run for home. He had been unable to wake her in the morning. She had risen with the setting of the sun, drained their invalid mother, and turned him into a vampire, for which he had never forgiven her.

And now she was dead. And he couldn't shake the feeling that it was all his fault. He had long felt her loneliness, her anger, her sense of betrayal. If he had not turned his back on her, if he had answered her letters, let her know he cared, she might still be alive.

"Forgive me, sister," he murmured.

But the words came too late.

Chapter Twenty-Six

Holly woke to the fragrant aromas of frying bacon and freshly brewed coffee. For a moment, she couldn't recall if she was in Morgan Creek or at home. And then she shook her head, remembering that she and Micah had spent the night at the home of his parents. She really had to stop bouncing around the country, settle down and find a job. What little money she had saved wouldn't last long.

She dressed quickly, made the bed, brushed her teeth and her hair, and then made her way downstairs. She couldn't help feeling a little ill at ease, sharing breakfast with Micah's mother and two of his sisters when he wasn't there. Not that his family didn't make her feel welcome, but they were, after all, little more than strangers.

Sofia and Rosa ate little at breakfast and said less. When the meal was over, Rosa said she had an appointment to get her nails done and hurried upstairs to get ready.

"I have some errands to run," Lena said, clearing the table. "Sofia, the dishwasher broke again last night. Do the dishes, please. I'll be back in an hour or so. Holly, you make yourself at home."

A moment later, Holly and Sofia were alone in the kitchen. Holly smiled at Micah's sister. "Do you have any plans for today? If not, Micah thought maybe you'd show me around."

Sofia shrugged. "There's not much to see," she remarked, filling the sink with hot water.

"Maybe we could take in a movie?" Holly suggested. "Or do a little shopping?"

"Shopping sounds like fun," Sofia said, her mood brightening. "I could use a new pair of shoes."

"Great." Holly grabbed a dish towel.

"I'd better leave Mom a note," Sofia said, rinsing a glass. "She'll have a fit if she doesn't know where we've gone."

"Are you in love with Micah?"

"What?" Holly stared at Sofia. They were waiting in line at Sofia's favorite department store, surrounded by people—hardly the place to discuss her love life.

"He's never brought a girl home before."

"Oh?" The thought made Holly smile.

"I was beginning to think he was gay."

"Definitely not," Holly said, laughing. "I hear you're dating someone new."

"Who told you that?" Sofia asked, immediately on the defensive.

"I heard somebody mention it last night." Holly swiped her credit card and signed the pad. "Would you like to go have lunch?"

"Sounds good to me," Sofia said as they left the store. "So, what did 'somebody' say?"

"Nothing, really. It was just some random remark. Where would you like to eat?"

"Here in the mall's fine with me. There's a great pizza place upstairs."

A short time later, they were seated at a small round table covered by a red-and-white gingham cloth, sharing a large ham and pineapple pizza and a pitcher of Coke.

"So, what's his name?" Holly asked.

"Jack." Sofia sighed dramatically. "My parents haven't met him, but it doesn't matter. They won't like him."

"Why not?"

"He's kind of wild. He rides a Harley and works nights as a bartender at a dance club downtown."

"What does he do during the day?"

"Sleeps, I guess." Looking suddenly thoughtful, Sofia took a sip of her Coke. "Does it bother you that Mikey's a vampire?"

"Shh!" Holly glanced around, hoping no one was listening. "That's not a word to be bandied about in public. But, yes, it's a little troubling." Lowering her voice, she said, "Sometimes it's still hard to believe he's a . . . you know. Doesn't it bother you?"

"Are you kidding? I think it's totally cool."

Micah shifted restlessly from one foot to the other as Holly related her conversation with Sofia later that evening.

"Do you think her boyfriend is a vampire?" Holly asked.

"I sure as hell hope not. Do you know when she plans to see him again?"

"She didn't say." Holly laid a hand on his arm. "I know you're worried about her and if you want to stay here, that's fine, but if we're not going back to Morgan Creek, then I really should go home. I need to apply for unemployment and look for a job."

"Right." Vampires were inclined to forget what it was

like to live a normal life, or to worry about mundane things like paychecks and debts, he thought. Most vampires tended to take what they wanted with little concern for those they took it from, whether it was money or blood. It was all too easy to steal from one's prey, or simply mesmerize waiters, clerks, and cashiers into believing you had already paid for whatever it was you wanted. "I'll take you home tonight."

Holly nodded. Now that he had agreed, why wasn't she happier about her decision? She knew he had to stay here and look after Sofia. Right now, that had to be his priority, because that girl wasn't thinking clearly. You didn't have to be a genius, or a vampire, to know that. And who knew how long it would take to make her see reason? The girl was looking for trouble. Maybe she had already found it in Jack.

Sensing Holly's distress, Micah took her in his arms. "You know I'd rather stay with you," he said, "but I need to be here until I'm sure Sofie isn't going to do anything stupid. Can't I talk you into staying here for another day or two, sunshine?" He brushed a kiss across the top of her head. "I know my family won't mind."

"Are you sure about that?"

"Very. I'll talk to Sofia tonight and see if I can't pound some sense into that hard head of hers."

Sighing, Holly rested her head against Micah's chest. What was another few days?

Micah blew out a sigh of exasperation. He had spent the last hour and a half trying to talk some sense into his sister, but instead of discouraging her, everything he had said so far only seemed to make being a vampire appear more attractive.

"Dammit, Sofie, why do you want this? You're young. You're beautiful. You've got your whole life ahead of you. Why do you want to give up half of it to be a vampire?"

"What do you mean?"

"You'll only be alive at night. From dusk to dawn."

She frowned, then shook her head. "I know that's what all the books say, but they must be wrong. When your friend, Saintcrow, came to the house and saved Mom and Dad, it was in the middle of the afternoon."

"Sofie, he's ancient. It takes centuries to be able to walk in the sun's light and even then, it's only possible for a short time. You won't be able to have kids. Or spend hours tanning in the sun. Or play tennis with Cassie, or do any of the hundred other things you like to do. If you're determined to be a vampire, at least wait a few years until you've done all the things you want to do."

"So the books are right, then. That's why we never see you during the day. Because you're not like your friend."

"Right."

"How long has he been a vampire?"

"I'm not sure, but he was a knight during the Crusades."

"The Crusades!" she exclaimed, eyes growing wide. "That's amazing!"

"Yeah."

Sofia glanced at her arms, which were both smooth and tanned to perfection. "I don't think I want to wait that long to see the sun again."

Micah felt a ray of hope. Maybe he was finally making some headway, after all. "You've got to promise me two things."

Her eyes narrowed suspiciously. "What things?"

"I want your promise that you'll call me before you do anything that can't be undone."

"What's the second thing?"

"If you're still determined to be a vampire when you're older, I want to be the one who turns you."

"Why?"

"Because the one who turns you, your sire, will always have power over you. Do you understand what that means? He'll be able to force you to do whatever he wants."

"I didn't know that. Where's your sire?"

"She's dead."

"Did you kill her?"

"No." But, given the chance, he would have done so gladly. "Do I have your promise?"

She sighed, then nodded.

"Do you mean it?"

"Pinky swear."

Micah laughed softly as they locked their little fingers together the way they had when she was a little girl, and then he pulled her into his arms and hugged her tight. "I love you, Sofie. Any time you need to talk about this, just let me know."

He rested his forehead against hers. If his sister was determined to become a vampire, he wanted to be the one to teach her how to hunt, how to protect herself. How to survive. He just hoped it never came to that.

Holly and Micah returned to Morgan Creek the following night. As soon as they arrived, Saintcrow and Kadie knocked at the door. Holly shook her head, still amazed that the couple had sensed their presence the minute they arrived. What would it be like, to have that kind of power?

Kadie hugged Holly. "Welcome home! I'm so glad you decided to stay here."

"For a while, anyway," Holly said, smiling. "Come on

in." She glanced past Kadie to where Saintcrow waited on the porch.

He lifted one brow expectantly.

"You, too," Holly said, stifling the urge to giggle.

Muttering his thanks, Saintcrow followed Kadie into the house. "So, how long are you staying this time?" he asked when they were all seated in the living room.

"I'm not sure," Micah said. "Does it matter?"

"Not to me."

"How would you feel about rebuilding the bridge?" Micah asked. "Holly wants to look for a job in the next town, but there's no way for her to get there with the bridge out."

"I'll order the materials we need tomorrow afternoon. Shouldn't take more than a week or two for the lumber to be delivered, a couple of days to build." Saintcrow looked at Holly. "That suit you?"

"That's very kind of you."

Saintcrow grunted softly. "Right. Just call me Mr. Kindness."

Chapter Twenty-Seven

Sofia smiled at Jack as he slipped his arm around her shoulders. They were at his place, just the two of them. It wasn't much, just a little three-room rental behind another house, but it was a place for them to be alone. She wanted to tell him about Micah in the worst way, but she had been sworn to secrecy. She could understand that. After all, there were a lot of people who were afraid of vampires, not to mention hunters and fanatics who would try to kill him if they could. She was certain Micah could defend himself. After all, vampires were strong and powerful and supernatural. The way she wanted to be.

But she had promised Micah she would wait. And sometimes, since talking to him, she wasn't certain that she still wanted to be a vampire. Mainly because of the blood thing. Next time she talked to Micah, she was going to ask him more about that. Considering her aversion to the mere sight of blood, it seemed odd she had never given *that* part of being a vampire much thought until now.

"What's wrong?" Jack asked.

"Nothing. Why?"

"You're awfully quiet. Did you have a fight with your old man or something?"

"No."

"Do you want to go dancing at the club? Cash said he'd be there tonight."

Cash was Jack's best friend. He owned a tavern on the other side of town. Sofia was a little afraid of him, though she would never admit it. There was something off about Cash, about the way he looked at her, even when she was with Jack. As though he was just biding his time. For what, she didn't know. Sometimes she had the unshakeable feeling that Jack and Cash were talking about her even when nothing was being said.

"Can't we just stay in tonight?" she asked. "It's nice, just the two of us for a change."

"Sure, if that's what you want." Drawing her closer, he ran his tongue along the length of her neck. "You smell really good."

"New perfume. I went shopping yesterday." She recoiled when she felt his teeth at her throat. "What are you doing?"

"Just taking a little nibble."

"Well, stop it." Feeling suddenly uneasy, she forced a smile.

"Something wrong?" he asked.

"No. I was just thinking, maybe we *should* go dancing."

Jack grinned as he stood and pulled her to her feet. "I knew you'd see things my way."

Sofia frowned as they entered the club. Usually, the place was packed on a Saturday night, with couples jammed together on the small dance floor, the music so loud you could hardly hear yourself think. Tonight, the jukebox was silent, the tables and booths empty.

A shiver skated down her spine. "Where is everyone?"

"We're having a private party tonight," Jack said. "Just you, me, and Cash."

With a shake of her head, Sofia backed toward the entrance. "I don't think so." She turned, intending to leave, only to find Cash blocking her path. She stared up at him. He was tall and broad and solid as a brick wall.

"You weren't going to leave, were you?" Grabbing her arm, he dragged her farther into the room. "That wouldn't be polite."

"Let me go!" She tried to twist out of his grasp, but he only tightened his hold, causing her to cry out as his fingers bit into her flesh. "What . . . what are you doing . . . ?" Her eyes widened when he smiled at her.

Terror shot through Sofia. She had seen fake fangs before. Lots of people who came here wore them. His weren't fake.

"Jack told me you wanted to be a vampire," Cash said, pulling her toward the door behind the bar.

"Not like this!" She sent a frantic look at Jack. "Help me!"

"I can't," he said, his voice subdued. "He's my master. I have to obey."

"Master?" Sofia blinked at him.

"Surely you've seen the movie *Dracula*," Cash said. "Jack isn't a vampire. He's my Renfield."

Fear settled in the pit of her stomach like a lead weight as Cash opened the door.

She knew what lay behind it—rooms where drugs were sold, among other things. "Are you going to turn me?"

His smile grew wider.

"No!" She screamed the word as Cash pushed her into

a small dark cubicle, then stood in the doorway, his bulk blocking the entrance.

"I was going to drain you," he remarked. "But if you please me when I return, you can be my number-two man."

Sofia shook her head as panic engulfed her. Be like Jack, a slave to a monster? That was a fate worse than death.

She screamed again when he wrestled her down on a narrow cot and strapped her arms to the bed frame. "Got a hot date, babe," he said with a wink. "But I'll be back for you soon."

She sobbed when he walked away, felt a cold chill run down her spine when he closed and locked the door behind him.

Tugging against her bonds, she screamed Micah's name, screamed until her throat was raw, for help she knew would never come.

Restless as a caged tiger, Micah prowled the streets of Morgan Creek. Holly was asleep. Saintcrow and Kadie had decided to go off somewhere for a few days—where, he didn't know. Saintcrow had promised to be back by the time the lumber for the bridge arrived.

Micah slowed, surprised to find himself standing outside the cemetery. Passing through the gate, he made his way to Shirley's grave. Standing there, his head bowed, he felt a shiver of unease, frowned when a pale, shadowy figure seemed to rise up from the earth. "Shirley?"

It hovered near him, its mouth moving. No sound emerged, but he heard the words in his mind. *She's in danger!*

A moment later, he heard Sofia's hoarse cry, sobbing, pleading for help.

There was no time to wake Holly and tell her he was leaving, no time to explain. Not with Sofia's life in the balance. Certain that Holly would understand his need for haste when she learned the details, he opened the blood bond between himself and Sofia and followed the link.

Micah followed the connection to a goth tavern on the outskirts of town. He paused outside the entrance, his senses alert. All was quiet inside, save for the muffled sound of his sister's tears. Unless he was mistaken, there was no one else in the place.

He tried the door. It was locked.

Going around to the back, he broke a window and climbed over the sill. Had this been a residence, he wouldn't have been able to enter. But no one lived here.

He waited a moment before padding silently down a dark corridor. He passed two doors before he came to the room he wanted.

This door was locked, too.

He heard Sofia cry out in alarm when he kicked it open. "Sofie, it's me."

"Micah!"

An instant later, he was at her side, freeing her from the restraints, gathering her into his arms.

Taking her home.

She sobbed the whole way. Not that he could blame her. She'd had a helluva scare.

When they reached home, he carried her around the back and into the kitchen.

After turning on the small light over the sink, he sat her on the counter. "Did he . . . ?" His gaze moved to her throat. There were no telltale marks. "Are you hurt?"

She shook her head.

"You're safe now." Opening a drawer, he pulled out a dish towel, wet it, and wiped the tears from her face. "Shh, stop your crying. Tell me what happened."

"I . . . I was out with . . . with Jack. . . ." Stammering, crying, she told him what had happened. "Oh, Micah, I was so afraid!"

"I know." He had felt her fear, her panic, as if it had been his own. He stroked her back, dried the fresh tears from her cheeks. "Come on, I'm going to put you to bed."

"No! Don't leave me!"

"I'm going to wake Dad and tell him what happened." Her eyes widened. "Do you have to?"

"Cash can't enter the house uninvited, but Jack can. If he tries, Dad's shotgun will make short work of him." Their old man knew his way around guns. The Ravenwood patriarch loved to hunt and he was a crack shot. "Come on."

Cradling Sofia in his arms as if she were a baby, he carried her up the stairs to her bedroom, turned on the light, then set her on her feet. "Get ready for bed. I'll get Mom to come and tuck you in."

Sofia grabbed his hand. "Thank you for coming after me."

He ruffled her hair. "So, little sister, do you still want to be a vampire?"

"No!" She shook her head vigorously. "Not anymore."

After waking his parents and explaining what had happened, Micah went hunting for Jack and his master. It was easy enough to track them. Their scents had been all over Sofia. All he had to do was follow their stink.

He found the pair bending over a young policewoman, Jack watching, wide-eyed, while Cash held her down, his fangs buried in her throat. The scent of fear and blood hung heavy in the air.

Micah broke Jack's neck, ripped the heart from the vampire's chest, before they even knew he was there.

For a moment, Micah feared the woman was dead, but then, detecting the faint beating of her heart, he scooped her into his arms and transported her to the nearest hospital. Depositing her on a gurney in the hallway, he shouted for help, then left as quickly as he'd arrived.

Returning to the bodies, he tossed Jack into a Dumpster, then carried the vampire to an open field where the morning sun would dispose of his remains.

Micah stood there for several minutes, feeling the rush of power flowing through his veins. He was stronger, faster, than he'd ever been before. And he owed it all to Saintcrow.

Congratulating himself on a job well done, he dusted off his hands, then returned to Morgan Creek.

A thought took him to Holly's bedroom. He had expected to find her asleep; instead, she was sitting up in bed, her expression tumultuous.

"Where have you been?" she asked.

"How did you know I was gone?"

"I . . . I don't know. I just woke up and I knew you weren't in the house. So where were you?"

"It's a long story."

She patted the bed. "Then you'd better sit down while you tell it."

"I was down by the cemetery when . . ." He shook his head. "You won't believe this, but I saw Shirley's ghost. She tried to talk to me, but I couldn't hear her. And then I heard her voice in my mind saying, 'She's in danger,' and then I heard Sofia's voice calling for help. I'd taken a little of her blood the last time we were there, and I followed the link to a goth club. I found her locked up in a room, tied to a bed."

Holly's eyes grew wide. "Is she all right?"

"She is now."

"But who took her? And why?"

"That guy she liked, Jack, took her to the club. Turns out he was a slave to a vampire. . . ."

"Was?"

"They won't be bothering any other young girls. They're both dead."

Holly tried to feel sorry for the young man who'd been in the vampire's power, but all she felt was relief that he wouldn't be putting any other people in danger. "Does Sofia still want to be a vampire?"

"No. After what happened with Braga and now this incident tonight, I think she finally realizes the reality isn't as romantic as the fantasy. What about you, Holly?" His gaze searched hers. "Is the reality of it going to scare you away, too?"

"I'm still here, aren't I?"

Nodding, he stretched out beside her and drew her into his arms. She was here, he thought, but for how long?

The next few days passed peacefully. Micah called home several times to check on Sofia. His mother said Sofia seemed to be holding up well, despite the fright she'd suffered. She had discarded all her black clothing and makeup, his mother went on, relief evident in her voice, and she was again dressing like any other normal young woman her age.

"Just one thing bothers me," Lena remarked. "She's only left the house twice since it happened, and she was home long before dark both times."

"Can you blame her, Ma?" he asked.

"No, of course not. I just worry about her. She's never been afraid of the dark before."

She had never been betrayed by a guy she thought she cared for, or kidnapped by a vampire, either, Micah thought, though he didn't say so. "Sofie's had a bad scare, but she's tough. She'll get over it," he said. "Just give her some time to put it behind her. I'll talk to you soon."

Micah disconnected the call. One good thing had come out of all this, he mused as he slipped his phone into the pocket of his jeans. His secret was out in the open, and his relationship with his family was stronger than ever.

Chapter Twenty-Eight

Saintcrow and Kadie returned to Morgan Creek two days later. Saintcrow picked up the lumber for the bridge the next morning, and they all met down by the ravine at sundown.

Holly and Kadie sat on lawn chairs, watching as their men hauled away the remains of the old bridge.

Holly shook her head in amazement. It would have taken mortal men several days—maybe a week or more—to dispose of the debris from the ruined bridge. Working with preternatural speed and strength, Saintcrow and Micah accomplished it in less than an hour.

Holly glanced at Kadie. "Has Saintcrow ever built anything like this before?"

Kadie nodded. "Once, during the Crusades."

"Does it ever just blow your mind, how old he is? I can hardly comprehend it."

"I know. Me, either. Imagine all the things he's done and seen. The places he's been. The women he's known." Kadie sighed. "I try not to think about that too much. And Rylan rarely talks about his past."

His past, Holly mused. What was it like, to watch the

world change before your very eyes? To watch the growth of civilization, to live through wars and plagues, to see the advancement of technology, to go from riding in a horse and carriage to traveling across the world in a jet? So many amazing inventions in his long lifetime. It was mind-boggling.

Holly's gaze settled on Micah. He had removed his shirt and his skin seemed to glisten in the moon's light. He was still a young vampire but, barring some bizarre accident or a fatal meeting with a hunter, he could live to be hundreds, maybe thousands of years old. No matter how long she lived, it would be like the blink of an eye compared to him. He loved her. She knew that. But when she was gone, he would still have centuries ahead of him. He might fall in love a hundred times with a hundred other women, and she would become nothing but a distant memory.

"Holly?"

She looked up when Kadie touched her arm. "Did you say something?"

"Are you all right? You look like you're about to cry."

"I . . ." Holly's gaze settled on Micah again. Her heart squeezed painfully when she thought of him with other women. She wanted to believe that he loved her so much he would never fall in love again, but besides being unrealistic, she knew it was grossly unfair to expect him to spend the rest of his life alone after she was gone.

Micah looked up abruptly, his gaze finding hers, his brow furrowing.

The next thing she knew, he was kneeling in front of her, his hands reaching for hers.

She was vaguely aware that Saintcrow and Kadie were no longer at the bridge.

"Don't go there, sunshine," Micah said quietly. "You don't know what the future holds. Nobody does. None of us can count on tomorrow. Not you. Not me. Not even Saintcrow. There's only today."

"I don't want to live without you," she whispered, her voice thick with unshed tears. "I don't want you to live without me."

"What are you saying?"

"I want you to turn me."

"Holly, this isn't a decision to be made on the spur of the moment or when you're overcome with strong emotions."

"Don't you think I've given it a lot of thought?"

"I'm sure you have, but . . ." Rising, he drew her to her feet and into his arms. "I heard your thoughts a few minutes ago. I don't think you're in any frame of mind to decide right now."

Sighing, Holly rested her forehead against his chest. "You're probably right."

"I know I am."

She nodded, and then she had a terrible thought. Maybe Micah no longer wanted to spend the rest of his life with her. Maybe he didn't want her to become a vampire. After all, eternity *was* a very long time.

"Holly." Placing his finger under her chin, he lifted her head. "Look at me. You don't really believe that, do you?"

"No, but I thought you'd be happier about my decision."

"I am. But there's no hurry, love. I just want you to be sure."

She smiled. And then she frowned. "Why is it you're all right with me becoming a vampire, but not Sofia?"

"For one thing, she's only eighteen, way too young to make an irrevocable decision like that, which is why I made her promise to wait until she was twenty-five. But it's a moot point now, since she doesn't want to be a vampire anymore."

Holly ran her fingernails down his chest and over his washboard stomach. "Twenty-five, huh?" she said with an impish grin. "Well, then, I guess it's lucky that I'm almost twenty-six!"

They were all back at the ravine at sundown the next evening. As she had the night before, Holly watched Micah and Saintcrow. She envied the easy camaraderie between them, the way they laughed and joked as the new bridge took shape. They didn't seem to be in as much of a hurry to put up the new one as they had been to get rid of the remains of the old one.

One more night, and it would be done.

She couldn't stop watching Micah. The way he moved, muscles flexing and bunching, the power in his arms as he lifted heavy pieces of wood as if they weighed nothing at all. What was it like, to be that strong? Not to worry about getting seriously hurt if something went wrong?

"It's the best show in town, isn't it?" Kadie remarked, grinning. "All that male muscle and beauty. Too bad we can't charge admission."

Holly laughed, thinking how lucky she was to have Kadie for a friend. At times like this, it was easy to forget that her three closest companions were vampires. In movies, vampires were either monsters ravishing the countryside, or brooding heroes who yearned to be human again. Saintcrow and Kadie seemed happy enough with the way things were, but how was she to know how they really felt, what they really thought?

She had asked Micah if he was happy as a vampire, whether he would be human again, if he could. He had never answered her.

Did she really want to become a vampire, to live by night and drink blood to survive? Did she want to have to worry about hunters? And what about her parents? Would they be as accepting as Lena and Luciano? Or would they be horrified? Did she want to spend the rest of her life just drifting from night to night, contributing nothing to society, not really being involved in the world around her?

So many questions, she thought. Questions to which she had no answers. But the real question was, did she love Micah enough to give up her old way of life and embrace his? It didn't matter if Kadie and Saintcrow were happy being vampires or not. Didn't matter if Micah wanted to be human again or if he was happy as he was.

It was her life. What mattered most was what she wanted.

She just wished she knew what it was.

"The bridge will be done tonight," Micah said as they left the house the next evening. "When you get ready to go job hunting, Saintcrow has a car you can use."

"He's really a nice guy, isn't he?"

"Why do you sound so surprised?"

"I don't know. I guess because he always seems so stern and unapproachable."

Micah shrugged. "He is what he is."

Saintcrow and Kadie waved as they neared the ravine.

"I'll work on this side," Saintcrow said. "You take the other. Once we get the supports in place, the rest should be a breeze."

At her request, Micah carried her across the ravine so she could keep him company while he dug a hole for one of the posts and filled it with concrete. It would have taken her days to dig a hole that deep; he was finished in minutes.

Saintcrow was doing the same on the other side, while Kadie looked on.

Holly smiled inwardly, thinking how much better it would be if she, too, was a vampire. She would be able to leap across the ravine on her own, hear what Saintcrow and Kadie were laughing at, help Micah with the heavy lifting and set the post in place, though he didn't seem to need any help.

It would likely take some getting used to, being a vampire, but there was really no other alternative if she wanted to spend the rest of her life with Micah, because there was no way she was going to burden him with having to care for her when she grew too old and feeble to care for herself. And if she was going to be a vampire, then she wanted to make the transition while they still looked the same age.

Holly was about to climb down the rocky hillside to tell Micah she had definitely made up her mind when she caught a sudden movement out of the corner of her eye. Before she had time to register what was happening, a strong arm snaked around her throat. She dug her nails into the arm that was cutting off her breath, twisted and fought as best she could but to no avail.

She cried Micah's name as the world faded to gray and then went black.

"Holly!" Micah leaped effortlessly to the top of the ravine in time to see a tall man in a long black coat drag Holly across the road and vanish from sight.

"What the hell?" Saintcrow appeared beside Micah, his nostrils flaring. "Damn, if I didn't know it was impossible, I'd think Braga had been here."

"I'm going after her." Honing in on the blood link that bound him to Holly, Micah took off after the vampire who had taken his woman.

Chapter Twenty-Nine

Holly stared at the vampire who had abducted her. He could only be Leticia Braga's brother. There was no mistaking the strong family resemblance between the two. The same sharp features, the same pale blond hair. The same intense hatred in his eyes.

She tried to still her trembling, tried to keep her voice even as she asked, "What are you going to do with me?"

Fangs bared, he glared at her, a faint red glow visible in his close-set eyes. No one, seeing him for the first time, would ever mistake him for anything but what he was.

Holly lifted her head in hopes of staring him down. "Micah will kill you for this."

"Micah?" His eyes narrowed. "Who the hell is Micah?"

"You'll find out soon enough!" she snapped, with far more bravado than she felt.

He snorted disdainfully. "Doesn't matter who he is. I'm just waiting for Saintcrow to come looking for you. We have a score to settle."

His hand tightened around her waist, holding her in

place as he lowered his head and buried his fangs in her throat.

"No!" She hissed the word through clenched teeth as pain splintered through her. *No, not now! Not like this!*

He was drinking from her. Not sipping a few drops the way Micah did, but drinking with great slurping noises. She could feel the warmth of her blood dripping like rain down her neck. There was a peculiar buzzing in her ears followed by a sudden light-headed feeling.

She was dying.

She sagged in his arms as the strength went out of her legs.

Time lost all meaning. She felt lighter than air, as if she were floating away, no longer subject to gravity.

And then, somehow, Micah was there.

But he was too late, she thought dully. Eternally too late. It was her last conscious thought before she pitched headlong into a narrow black tunnel that spiraled down, down, into an endless black void.

Rage exploded through Micah as he watched the vampire toss Holly aside. Limp as a rag doll, she skidded across the ground and lay still. He stared at her, certain she was dead. He detected no heartbeat, no sign of life.

With a snarl, Micah launched himself at the man who had dared lay hands on the woman he loved.

The other vampire, older and stronger, fought silently, confident of his ability to emerge victorious. They traded blows, teeth and claws ripping and tearing. There were only a few ways to destroy a vampire, but a loss of blood could weaken them.

Micah was confident he had the upper hand until Braga got in a lucky blow that sent him reeling backward.

With a howl of triumph, Braga grabbed a long thin metal stake and drove it into Micah's chest, missing Micah's heart by inches, pinning him to the ground.

Weak with pain and blood loss, Micah waited for the killing blow, but it never came.

And then Saintcrow was there. "This is going to hurt like hell," he said, and ripped the metal bar from his chest.

"Braga," Micah gasped.

"He's gone."

Struggling to his feet, Micah crawled toward Holly. She lay sprawled in the dirt, her hair and neck and clothing stained crimson with her own blood.

With a cry of denial, he cradled her in his arms. Her skin was fish-belly white, her lips turning blue, her skin already cold to the touch. Was he too late? He placed his fingertips to her throat, murmured a prayer of thanks when he felt the faint beat of a pulse. Concentrating, he heard the equally faint, thready beat of her heart.

Bending his head to her neck, he drank what little remained of her life's blood, felt it flow into him, healing the ragged wound in his chest. He took a deep breath, then bit into his wrist and held the bleeding wound to her lips. "Drink, Holly," he coaxed, his voice tinged with desperation. "Drink, love, and stay with me forever."

When she didn't respond, he stroked her throat. "Drink, dammit! Don't you dare leave me here in the dark, sunshine."

Just when he feared he had arrived too late, that she lacked the strength or the will to save herself, she lapped at his blood. Then, gripping his wrist with both hands, she covered the wound with her mouth.

A moment later, she sagged in his arms.

"What's wrong?" Alarmed, Micah looked up at Saintcrow. "What happened?"

"It's perfectly natural. Nothing to worry about. She'll sleep the rest of the night, and when she wakes at sunset tomorrow, she'll be one of us."

Cradling Holly to his chest, Micah rose to his feet and willed the two of them back to Shirley's house.

Inside, he laid Holly on the bed, removed her stained clothing, washed her from head to foot. After changing the sheets, he tucked her under the covers.

"I'm sorry it happened this way, sunshine," he murmured, lightly stroking her cheek. "So damn sorry."

She had wanted to be a vampire, he thought, watching her sleep.

Would she feel the same when she woke tomorrow night?

"Who was it?" Kadie asked. They were in the living room, sitting on the floor in front of the fireplace. Micah was looking after Holly in their bedroom. He hadn't left her side since they brought her home.

"I'm not a hundred percent sure, but from the glimpse I got, I'd say it had to be Leticia's brother."

"Did you know she had a brother?"

"No."

"Why did he run?"

"Who the hell knows? Maybe he knew he couldn't win and he lost his nerve. I'm pretty scary, you know."

"Oh, yes, I know." She shivered all over. "Why, I'm terrified just being in the same room with you."

Saintcrow snorted. "Yeah, right."

Kadie sighed. "So what do we do now? Do you think he'll come back? He knows where we are."

"That's a worry for another day."

"Do you think Holly will be okay?"

"She's Micah's worry, not mine."

"Rylan! What a thing to say!"

"I don't want to talk about Braga or Holly or Micah, or anything else," he said, drawing her into his arms.

"No?" she asked, batting her eyelashes at him. "What do you want to talk about?"

Flashing a wicked grin, he stretched out on the rug and drew her down beside him. "I don't want to talk at all, darlin," he drawled, nibbling her earlobe. "I had other things in mind."

Chapter Thirty

Leandro Braga paced the outskirts of Morgan Creek. His physical wounds had healed. But the blow to his ego remained open, like a raw wound in his chest. He had run from Saintcrow. The fact that the other vampire was ancient, stronger, did nothing to alleviate his anger or his shame.

He glared at the town. They were all there   Saintcrow and Micah and the women. Braga gnashed his teeth as his rage built inside him. He was strong, but even he couldn't go up against four vampires and hope to survive.

He would bide his time. Feed his hunger. He had consumed the woman's blood. When the time was ripe, he would follow the link between them. She would lead him to Micah. Micah would lead him to Saintcrow. They would all die, one by one. Saintcrow last of all.

"I will yet avenge you, my sister," he vowed. "I swear it on your life and my own."

Chapter Thirty-One

Holly woke feeling wonderful. Sitting up, she stretched her arms over her head, then frowned when she saw Micah standing at the foot of the bed, his expression guarded.

"What's the matter?" she asked. "Why am I naked? Why do you look so serious? Is something . . . ?" Her voice trailed off as she glanced around the room. It looked the same as always, yet the colors seemed brighter. She blinked as she realized she could see everything in the room clearly—the pictures on the wall, the furniture, each item on top of the dresser—even though the lights were off. That was odd, she thought. Odder still, she could detect every thread, every stitch, in the sheet pooled around her bare legs. Not only that, she could hear the low hum of the refrigerator in the kitchen.

She pressed a hand to her stomach. She was hungry. Ravenous. "Micah, say something. You're scaring me."

And still he just stood there, watching her.

She frowned. And then felt her eyes widen. "That vampire. He fed on me. He drained me. . . ." She licked her lips and tasted blood. Micah's blood. "I drank from you."

He nodded, his hooded gaze searching hers.

"Am I . . . ? I am, aren't I? I'm a vampire now."

He nodded again.

Vampire. It was what she had wanted. Wasn't it? She searched her feelings as reality set in. She was no longer human, but a supernatural creature. She should have been more upset, she thought, but it was hard to be angry or resentful when she felt so good. When she was still alive . . . sort of. When it meant she could be with Micah for centuries instead of decades.

And then she frowned.

"Holly?"

"Darn, darn, darn!"

Micah lifted one brow. "Is that all you've got to say?"

Sighing, she swung her legs over the side of the bed. "You don't understand. I had it all planned out. I was going to get a manicure and a pedicure and then indulge in one last gigantic meal before you changed me, you know? Gorge on salty French fries and greasy bacon. Have chocolate fudge cake and buttermilk doughnuts for dessert and wash them down with a glass of ice-cold milk. Have one last cheeseburger and a hot fudge sundae smothered in whipped cream . . . and now I'm starving and I can't have any of it."

"So, you're not mad at me?"

"Why would I be mad? I told you this was what I wanted. What happened to that horrible man who bit me?"

"He saw Saintcrow coming and he ran."

"He was related to Leticia Braga, wasn't he?"

"Her brother, I'm guessing. They were both butt-ugly."

"He'll come back, won't he?"

Micah shrugged, torn between the hope that he'd never see Braga again and the overwhelming desire to rip the bastard's heart from his chest.

"Well, if he shows up again, we'll fight him together."

"Already spoiling for a fight, are you?" Micah asked, chuckling.

"Let's not talk about what happened. Not now." She looked up at him, a smile teasing her lips. "Aren't you going to kiss me?"

With a shake of his head, Micah pulled her to her feet and into his arms. "You beat everything, you know that?"

"I'm still starving," she reminded him, lifting her face for his kiss.

"You can't go out like that," he muttered. "Put some clothes on and I'll take you hunting."

"I'm not really hungry for food anymore," Holly murmured, slipping her hands under his shirt, sliding her palms up and down his back.

"No?" He grinned at her, his dark eyes twinkling with merriment. "I'm not sure I want to bed a hungry fledgling. It could be hazardous to my health."

Standing on tiptoe, she ran her tongue across his lower lip, then nipped it hard enough to draw blood. "It might be more hazardous if you don't." She wiped the blood away with her fingertips, then licked it off.

"I'll take that chance." He brushed a kiss across her lips. "Seriously, sunshine, you need to feed before we do anything else. Trust me."

"What am I going to tell my parents?" Holly glanced at Micah. Earlier, she had showered and dressed, and now they were in a nearby town, searching for prey. It was a bit startling, how quickly she had accepted the idea of feeding on another human being.

Only she wasn't really human any longer. She was a vampire. She should have been shocked, alarmed, maybe.

Even scared. Yet she was none of those things. It seemed like the most natural thing in the world to be able to see and hear everything around her—and beyond—with such crystal clarity.

"No need to tell your folks anything if you don't want to," he said.

"But they'll know something's wrong eventually. I mean, how many excuses can I make for missing family get-togethers that aren't held at night, and . . ." She laughed softly. "Look who I'm asking. You've been doing it for years. Did it ever get easier?"

"Not really. But you'll be surprised how inventive you can be when you have to." He jerked his head toward a man walking ahead of them, alone. "No sense worrying about it now. I've spotted our prey. Are you ready?"

With some trepidation, she said, "I guess so." But she couldn't help feeling a little apprehensive. Accepting her new preternatural vision and hearing abilities was one thing. But could she really drink some stranger's blood? "What do I do?"

"I'll show you. Nothing to it."

She watched as Micah mesmerized the young man, then bit him lightly, just enough to draw blood.

The rich, coppery scent of it flooded Holly's senses and quickened her hunger. There was a slight pain as her fangs—her fangs!—ran out, but the pain was forgotten when she got her first taste of human blood. It was warm and salty and more satisfying than anything she had ever known. She might have drained the man dry if Micah hadn't warned her to stop.

Micah showed her how to seal the wounds in the man's neck, then he wiped the memory from the man's mind, and sent him on his way. "You see?" he said, smiling at her. "Nothing to it."

Holly nodded, thinking about the way the vampires fed on one of her favorite TV shows. They always had blood dripping from their mouths and smeared over their faces. Was that how she looked? She had often wondered why they were so untidy.

"You okay, sunshine?"

"Is there blood all over my face?"

"What?"

She lifted her hands to her cheeks, relieved that there was nothing there.

"Holly?"

"I thought it would be repulsive."

"Yeah?"

"But it wasn't."

He looked at her askance.

"It's kind of troubling that it wasn't. That it was so easy."

"That's because you're trying to look at it from a human point of view. You need to stop thinking like a mortal and let your vampire nature take over."

"Is that what you did?"

"Not at first. I told you about Saintcrow. If not for him, I'd probably be some kind of mindless monster. But that's not going to happen to you, sunshine."

"How can you be so sure I won't suddenly go off the deep end?"

"I had Saintcrow to keep me in line." Drawing her into his arms, he brushed a kiss across her lips. "You've got me."

"I love you."

"I know. So, now that you've had dinner, so to speak, what do you say we go home and have our dessert in bed?"

I'm a vampire. It was Holly's first conscious thought when she awoke the following night.

Vampire. Creature of the night. Undead. Nosferatu.

"Daughter of Dracula," she murmured, and then laughed, because being a vampire was totally amazing, as was making love to Micah. It had been the most incredible experience of her life. He had been warm and tender, as if he'd been afraid of hurting her. And that had been fine, the first time. But the second time . . . she blushed at the memory. What had started in bed had ended in a tangle of arms and legs and blankets on the floor.

She bolted upright when the doorbell rang, then laughed self-consciously. It was only Saintcrow and Kadie come to call.

Holly frowned. How had she known that? Their scents, of course. Plus, she easily detected the slow, barely audible beating of vampire hearts.

Slipping out of bed, she quickly pulled on a pair of jeans and a T-shirt; then, feeling suddenly shy at facing them as a new vampire, she paused.

In the living room, she heard Micah open the door and invite their guests inside.

Taking a deep breath, Holly walked down the narrow hallway into the living room.

A wry grin crossed Saintcrow's face when he saw her. "I guess we won't have to finish that bridge now."

Muttering, "Be nice," Kadie punched her husband on the arm, then hurried forward and clasped Holly's hands. "You look wonderful! Welcome to our world, fledgling."

"Thank you."

"I'm so glad you're one of us now!"

"Me, too," Holly said, and meant it. She frowned as Micah, Kadie, and Saintcrow exchanged sly glances. "What's going on?"

"We were thinking we should go out and celebrate this

awesome, once-in-a-lifetime occasion," Saintcrow said. "Dancing," he added with a flash of his fangs. "Dining."

"Maybe Holly isn't ready to *dine* with us," Kadie said, glancing at Holly. "And maybe she'd like to be alone with Micah."

"They've got eternity to be alone," Saintcrow said, dismissing Kadie's objection with a wave of his hand. "How about it, Holly? Are you ready to go hunting with the pros?"

"We don't have to go if you'd rather not," Micah assured her.

"I am a little hungry," Holly admitted. "So I'm game if you are."

"It's game we're after," Saintcrow said, with a wolfish grin. "Let's go!"

"Um, if you don't mind," Holly said, gesturing at her jeans. "I think I'd like to change into something more appropriate for a night on the town."

Holly's head was still reeling when they arrived at the destination Saintcrow had chosen as their hunting ground. Vampire or not, she mused, hurtling through time and space took some getting used to.

Luigi's turned out to be an intimate nightclub in Boston's Little Italy, located in the North End. The tables were covered with fine damask, matching cloth napkins, crystal vases filled with fresh flowers, and gleaming china and silverware. A three-piece band provided music for dancing.

Saintcrow guided them to a curved booth along the back wall, where he perused a drink menu, then ordered a bottle of wine.

Holly almost choked when she saw the price. "Two thousand dollars!" she exclaimed. "For a bottle of Cabernet Sauvignon?"

"It's good stuff," Saintcrow said with a shrug. "Besides, we're celebrating your transformation, remember? Now, look around. Do you see anything that appeals to you?"

"Any*thing*?" Holly repeated, emphasizing the last half of the word.

"My mistake," Saintcrow said dryly. "Any*one*?"

Holly glanced around the room, her nostrils filling with the mingled scents of perfume and cologne, perspiration, and the myriad aromas of food and drink. But it was the smell of blood that overwhelmed her senses. Surprisingly, it didn't all smell the same.

Leaning close to her, Micah whispered, "Different types. They all taste and smell just a little different. You know what they say. Variety is the spice of life."

"I like him," she decided, gesturing at a tall, blond young man seated with three other men at a table across the room.

Saintcrow nodded. "Good choice, fledgling. One for each of us."

The bottle of Cabernet was empty by the time the four men rose to leave.

Saintcrow paid the bill—in cash—and they left the club.

The four men stood outside near the curb, laughing and talking as they waited for the valet to bring their car around.

Holly watched, fascinated, as Saintcrow approached their intended prey. He spoke a word and, as one, the four men turned and followed him down the street and into a parking lot behind a large hotel.

The rest was all too easy.

* * *

That night, at home in bed, Holly burrowed deeper into Micah's arms. It had been fun hunting with Micah and Kadie and Saintcrow, she thought, and then grimaced, thinking "fun" was probably a poor choice of words. Still, she hadn't really hurt the young man she had chosen; she had taken less than he would have given if he'd been donating to the Red Cross.

"Happy?" Micah asked.

"Oh, yes."

"No regrets, sunshine?"

"That's a silly question!" Exerting her newfound strength, she flipped him onto his back and straddled his hips. "Do I look unhappy?"

"Do you remember what you said?" he asked.

"What do you mean?"

"You said if we were going to stay together, you wanted to get married."

"Oh, that. Of course I remember."

"So, are we? Going to stay together, I mean? Or have you changed your mind?"

"Of course not." Her gaze searched his. "Have you?"

"No, but . . ."

"But?"

"Well, now that my family knows what I am, I was wondering . . ."

"If we could invite your family to the wedding."

"Yeah."

"Will they be able to tell that I'm . . ."

"A vampire now? No."

Holly frowned at him. "Why are we finishing each other's sentences?"

"I don't know," Micah said, laughing. "It's kind of neat, though, don't you think?"

"I think it's kinda creepy."

"I'm sure it's partly because I'm your sire and partly because I've got Saintcrow's blood in me. It makes the link between us stronger. So, about the wedding? Are you sure you don't want to tell my folks the truth?" he asked. "I mean, they're sure to guess when you sleep all day and don't eat anything. On the other hand, it might be best if we keep it a secret. If Sofia sees how happy you are, she might start rethinking her decision."

"If I'm happy, it's because of you, you idiot, not because I'm one of the walking dead."

"Speaking of the walking dead, we've got to invite Saintcrow and Kadie."

"Of course. And considering the size of your family, it would probably be easier to have the ceremony in your hometown."

Micah grinned. "My mother and sisters would love that."

"Well, maybe you should call them tomorrow and let them know we're getting married. They might not be as thrilled as you think."

"Are you kidding? My parents both love you already."

Holly stroked his cheek. "I love you."

"Do you?"

"Don't you believe me?"

"Actions speak louder than words." Pulling her down on top of him, he murmured, "Show me, sunshine. Show me how much."

Chapter Thirty-Two

Sated and spent, Holly snuggled against Micah. Why had she waited so long to let him make love to her? Being in his arms, touching him, knowing he was hers, was the most wonderful thing in the whole world. Soon, she would be his wife, and how awesome would that be?

"Awesome?" As usual, he was eavesdropping on her thoughts.

"It's a good thing I never think bad thoughts about you, isn't it?" she muttered. But she wasn't really mad. She was a vampire now, able to shield her thoughts if she really wanted to.

"How could you, when I'm so awesome?"

She stuck her tongue out at him. "No, you're not. I changed my mind."

"Too late." Holding her down with one hand, he tickled her feet.

"Stop!" She bucked and twisted, but, of course, he was too strong for her.

"Change it back."

"All right, all right, I give up! You're the most awesome man on the face of the planet."

"That's better." Drawing her into his arms, he kissed her, a lazy, we've-got-all-the-time-in-the-world kind of kiss that drove everything else from her mind. Everything but the wonder of his touch, the magic of his love.

Holly called her parents while Micah showered. Only her mother was at home. After asking about their vacation, Holly announced her engagement. Her mom was more than a little surprised to learn Holly was getting married as soon as possible to a man she had known such a short time, someone her parents had never met.

"Is there a reason you're in such a rush?" her mother asked. "I mean . . ." She cleared her throat. "Are you in trouble, Holly?"

"No, Mom, nothing like that. You and Dad will come to the wedding, won't you?"

"Yes, of course. Is there anything we can do to help?"

"I'll let you know. Give my love to Dad. Talk to you soon."

With a sigh of relief, Holly tossed her phone aside. She couldn't help smiling when Micah came out of the bathroom a moment later, a towel wrapped around his lean hips. He was gorgeous. And he was all hers. Forever.

"How'd it go?" he asked.

"She thinks I'm pregnant."

Micah grunted softly. There was no chance of that.

He dressed, then called home while Holly went in to shower. As he'd predicted, his mother was thrilled.

"That's wonderful!" she exclaimed. "I'll talk to Father Anthony about setting a date and reserving the church, and . . ." She paused. "Of course, you and Holly should decide where to be married. And her parents should probably make arrangements. . . ."

"It's okay, Ma. It's easier for us to go there for the wedding, than for you and Dad and the rest of the family to come here." *In more ways than one*, he thought. Morgan Creek was no place for a family gathering. "Holly's parents have offered to help, too. So, get in touch with the priest. We'll be there in a day or two to talk things over."

His father was equally happy with the news. Sofia and Rosa were delighted. He had to laugh when Sofia asked if it was safe for him to enter a church, or if he'd go up in smoke.

He was still laughing when he disconnected the call.

Holly opened the bathroom door, her brow furrowed. "What's so funny?"

"Sofie was afraid I'd burn up if I went to church."

Holly's eyes widened. "Will we?"

"No, love." Drawing her into his arms, he kissed the tip of her nose. "All we need to do now is set a date."

They broke the good news to Saintcrow and Kadie later that night.

"I'm so happy for you both," Kadie said. "Holly, you'll make a beautiful bride."

"Thank you. I'm a little nervous about seeing my folks."

"Don't worry. They won't notice anything. Well, maybe a few things, but they'll just chalk it up to your being in love."

"I hope so."

"All right," Saintcrow said, "My turn." He put his arm around Micah's shoulder. "I've never had a son, but if I did, I'd like him to be just like you." Turning to Holly, he gave her a quick hug. "Take care of each other."

Holly nodded. "I don't have any sisters, but, Kadie, I'd love it if you'd be my matron of honor." Glancing at

Micah, she said, "I thought I'd ask your sisters to be my bridesmaids."

"They'll love it," he said. "Saintcrow, since we're talking about the wedding, I'd like you to be best man."

"I always have been," he said with a wry grin. "Seriously, I'd be honored."

"Thanks."

"Just let us know when and where," Kadie said, "and we'll be there."

Three nights later, just after dinner, Holly and Micah arrived at his parents' home. She was nervous about telling his family that she was now a vampire, but trying to hide the truth, now that they knew about Micah, seemed ridiculous.

His parents welcomed them with open arms. Luciano opened a bottle of wine and offered a toast.

"To your health and happiness, my children," he said, raising his glass. "May you find as much joy in your marriage as Lena and I have found in ours."

"Here, here!" Micah said.

"Have you set a date yet?" Sofia asked.

"I'd like to make it as soon as possible," Micah said, squeezing Holly's hand.

"I'll bet you would!" Sofia exclaimed with a knowing grin.

Feeling herself blush, Holly said, "I'd love for you and Rosa to be my bridesmaids."

"Oh!" Sofia squealed. "I was hoping you'd ask."

"Me, too," Rosa said.

Sofia cocked her head to the side. "So, Holly, how long have you been a vampire?"

Lena gasped, her empty glass falling from her hand. It rolled across the carpet, but she didn't seem to notice.

Luciano simply stared at Holly, as did Rosa.

Caught completely off guard, Holly glanced at Micah.

He laughed as he put his arm around her. "It happened recently," he said. "She's still getting used to the idea."

"But how?" Lena asked. "Why?"

"It's a long story," Micah said. "Why don't we sit down and I'll tell you all about it."

Holly wasn't surprised when Sofia took her aside later that night. As she followed her outside, she was pretty sure Micah's sister didn't want to talk about the wedding, and she was right.

Sofie gestured at an iron bench. "Shall we sit here?"

"If you like."

Sofia bit down on her lower lip, then said, in a rush, "Tell me the truth. What's it really like? Micah makes it sound horrible, but you wanted it."

Holly sighed as she pondered how best to answer. "I love Micah," she said, remembering a similar conversation with Kadie. "He's the only reason I ever considered becoming a vampire. Because of what happened with Braga, it happened a little sooner than I'd planned, but I'd already made the decision to ask Micah to bring me across if we were going to stay together."

"So, what's it like? Is it wonderful? Horrible? What?"

"I don't know how to describe it. There are so many things I miss—my favorite foods—mainly chocolate and coffee—being awake during the day. Dreaming. Just being normal. Human. Some things are good, like not having to worry about getting sick or growing old. But I'll never have Micah's baby, never have grandchildren. You're so young, you're probably not thinking about any of that now. . . ."

"You're not that much older than I am."

Holly nodded. "I know. At your age, I never thought about having a family. To tell you the truth, I never really gave it much thought until I knew it would never happen. Like being human, being a vampire has its advantages and its drawbacks."

"What about the blood thing?"

"It's a big part of it. You can't go without it. I hear it's very painful if you do." Holly placed her hand on Sofia's arm. "I thought, after what happened to you, that you'd given up the idea of being a vampire."

"I did, but you seem so happy."

"Sofie, I was happy before. It isn't being a vampire that makes me happy. It's being with Micah."

Sofia nodded, her expression pensive.

"Micah was right. If you decide you want to be one of us, you need to wait until you're a little older. I know you feel all grown up at eighteen, but you don't want to be eighteen forever. Trust me. Twenty-five is the perfect age. Old enough to have some wisdom, but still young."

"Do your parents know?"

Holly shook her head. "Not yet. I'm afraid to tell them."

"Why? Don't you think they'll still love you?"

"I don't know. I haven't told Micah, but my father is very rigid in his thinking. He's convinced vampires are the devil incarnate. A good friend of his died mysteriously. To this day, my dad is convinced a vampire killed him. Who knows? Maybe he's right. As for my mom . . ." Holly made a vague gesture with her hand. "I just don't have any idea how she'd react to the news that her only child is a vampire."

"Well, I'm sorry I blew your cover tonight."

"It's all right," Holly said, grinning. "Micah said it would be hard to keep my secret, since you guys already knew about him." Squeezing Sofia's hand, she said, "Please think about what I said."

"I will. Thanks for being honest with me. I'm glad you're going to be my sister."

"Me, too. You know, if you were a little older, I could fix you up with my cousin Ethan. He's really cool. I think you'd like him."

"How old is he?"

"Twenty-six."

"Hmm. Is he cute?"

"Very. Tall, Blond hair, dark brown eyes. Played football in college."

"Sounds dreamy. Do you think an eight-year age gap is too big?"

"I don't know. If he's at the wedding, I'll introduce you, assuming he's still single. We've kind of lost touch over the years."

"I'll hold you to it," Sofia said. After giving Holly a quick hug, she went back inside.

Holly gazed up at the night sky, wondering if her talk had done any good. She wasn't unhappy as a vampire. There were, as she'd said, things she liked about it, though, given a choice, she would choose to be human again. But if that choice meant being without Micah, then she would choose to be a vampire every time. Because she loved him more than life itself.

Holly changed her phone from one ear to the other as she tried—and failed—to staunch her mother's tirade.

"We're your parents. If anyone is going to plan your wedding, don't you think we should be involved? I'm sure

Micah's family is very nice, but it's traditionally the bride and her family that arrange the wedding, not the groom's."

"I understand that, Mom," Holly said patiently. "But since we're getting married here, I just thought it would be easier to let Micah's mother help, since she attends the church where we're being married, and . . ."

"Well, of course, it's up to you," her mother said, her voice frosty.

"I was planning to come home to look for a dress. I'd love for you to go with me."

There was a distinct thaw on the other end of the phone. "Well, of course, I'd love to."

"That's great. I'll be there Friday night, around six."

"Wonderful. We can shop all day Saturday."

Holly bit down on her lower lip. She should have seen that coming.

"Holly?"

"Mom . . ."

"Is something wrong?"

"It's just going to be a quick trip. I have to be back Saturday morning to . . . to go with Micah's sisters to pick out their bridesmaids dresses."

"I see." The frost was back. "Do you think you can find a dress in one night?"

"I hope so. I just need something long and white, you know," she said, hoping to lighten the mood.

"Very well. I'll see you Friday night. Do you need us to pick you up at the airport?"

"No, we'll just rent a car. Thanks, Mom. See you then."

She disconnected the call with a sigh of relief. At least that old saw about vampires not casting a reflection wasn't true. She didn't know how she would have explained that to her mother!

"Everything okay?" Micah asked, stepping into the room.

"I guess so." She fell back on the bed, arms thrown wide. "Maybe we should have just eloped."

Micah stretched out beside her. "Your mom giving you a hard time?"

"Sort of. She's feeling left out. Not that I blame her. Ever since I was a little girl, she's had this idea of what my wedding would be like. You know, about a dozen bridesmaids, me in a Cinderella dress, a reception fit for a queen."

"Is that what you wanted?"

"No. I've never liked being the center of attention."

"It's not too late to elope."

"It would break my mother's heart. And what about your mom? I know she wants to be there. And your sisters and your brothers."

"Yeah."

"So, I told my mom I'd be there Friday night to go look at dresses. Is that all right?"

"Sure."

"Will you zap me there? I don't feel comfortable trying to transport myself that far."

"You know I will."

"I just . . ."

Micah covered her mouth with his hand. "No more wedding talk tonight," he said. "I had something else in mind."

She looked up at him, brows raised.

"Like what?" he asked, reading her mind. "Like this."

Removing his hand, he kissed her, a slow, gentle kiss that made her toes curl with pleasure. He loved her. The thought flooded her with warmth and a sense of belonging that brought tears to her eyes as he drew her close, closer. All borders and boundaries fell away as he kissed and caressed her. She made no protest as he slowly undressed her, then shed his own clothing in a blur of movement.

She slid her fingers into his hair. He was beautiful. She ran her hands over him. His body was ripped, muscular. She reveled in the heat and hardness beneath her palms.

She sighed as he caressed her in return, his dark eyes filled with love and desire as he aroused her. She knew his thoughts, his hopes, his dreams, as intimately as he knew hers. Every touch was intensified, every wish fulfilled, until sated and complete, she drifted to sleep in his arms, always and forever his.

Holly was a nervous wreck when they arrived at her parents' house in Sacramento. What if her parents took one look at her and shrieked, "Vampire!" She knew she was probably worrying for nothing, but she just couldn't help it.

She was giving serious thought to making some excuse and going back to Micah's place when he exclaimed, "Hot damn, girl!"

"What?"

"You didn't tell me you grew up in a mansion."

Holly looked at the house at the end of the long, curved driveway. A mansion? It was just home. But she had to admit that, if she hadn't grown up here, she might think the same thing. It was a beautiful house. The white stone glistened in the moonlight. A bay window looked out over the rolling lawn. Tall trees grew on both sides of the house, offering both shade and privacy.

Micah parked the rental, then got out to open her door. "Text me when you're ready to leave."

"Oh, no you don't," she said, grabbing hold of his arm. "You're coming in to meet my folks."

"I was thinking I'd do that at the wedding."

"Chicken?"

"Who, me?"

"Come on," she said, tugging on his arm. "I survived meeting *your* parents."

"Okay."

Holly opened the door, calling, "Hey, Mom? Dad?"

A woman in a pair of gray slacks and a white sweater swooped down on Holly. It was, Micah thought, easy to see where Holly got her good looks. The woman was beautiful. Elegant.

Holly grinned at Micah over her mother's shoulder.

Mrs. Parrish took a step back, holding her daughter at arm's length. "Let me have a look at you!" It was then she saw Micah for the first time. "You must be Micah," she said, extending her hand. "I'm Vivian."

"Pleased to meet you, Mrs. Parrish."

"Vivian, please. I'm sorry Arthur isn't here to meet you. He had a late board meeting."

"Next time," Micah said, smiling. "Holly, call me when you're ready."

"I will."

With a nod, Micah took his leave.

"He's quite handsome, isn't he?" her mother murmured.

"I think so. Shall we go?"

"Just let me grab my bag."

Holly's nervousness left her as they drove to the bridal shop in the mall. Talking to her mother had always been easy. How had she forgotten that? They chatted like best friends as her mom brought her up-to-date on the girls

Holly had gone to school with, who was getting married, who was getting divorced, who was having kids.

Inside the shop, her mother told the consultant that money was no object, and the next thing Holly knew, she was up to her eyeballs in wedding dresses. So many gowns to choose from—plain and fancy, short and long, modest and not so modest. Beautiful gowns of satin, lace, silk, taffeta, chiffon, and tulle. And the colors—white, ivory, blush. Even black.

"I don't know how I'll ever decide," Holly declared. "I love them all!"

And then she tried on a gown of satin and lace that drove all the others from her mind. The bodice was fitted, then flared at the hips, with a short train behind. The consultant brought in a floor-length veil, and the decision was made.

"It fits perfectly," the consultant remarked. "You can take it with you, if you like."

"We'll do that," Vivian said. She smiled at Holly when the consultant left the room. "I didn't think you could find a dress in one night," she said, "but you did. And it fits as if it were made for you."

Her father was home when they got there.

"So, how'd the shopping go?" he asked. "Did you find anything you like?"

"It's being delivered to Micah's house," Holly said.

"What? You mean I don't get to see it? I paid for it!"

"Sorry, Dad," Holly said, kissing his cheek. "You'll get to see it before anyone else except Mom."

"Well, I guess that's okay," he said. "Where's this man you're marrying?"

"I texted him on our way home. He should be here any minute."

"What does he do for a living?"

Holly hesitated. This was something else she should have seen coming. Her father would never approve her marrying a man who didn't work. "He's an actor." It was the only thing she could think of.

"An actor! I've never heard of him."

"Well, he's just starting out."

"I'm sure he'll be a star if he gets a break," Vivian said. "He's very handsome."

"Handsome! Humph!"

When the doorbell rang, Holly ran to answer it.

"How'd it go?" he whispered.

"Better than I expected. Come on in. Be charming."

"Charming? Right."

Hand in hand, they entered the living room.

"Dad, this is Micah. Micah, my dad, Arthur Parrish."

She stood back as the two men shook hands.

"Let's sit down and get acquainted, shall we?" Vivian suggested.

Holly smiled at Micah as she led him to an elegant white sofa. The whole room was elegant, he thought, from the matching white sofas that faced each other over a black lacquer coffee table, to the plush white carpet. He figured the furniture alone cost more than everything he'd owned—or would ever own—in his life.

Arthur sat back, one leg crossed over the other. "So, Mr. Ravenwood, Holly tells me you're an actor."

"Not yet," Micah said.

Arthur's disapproval was palpable.

Vivian broke the taut silence. "Can I get you two something to drink?"

"A glass of red wine, please," Micah said.

"I'll have the same," Holly said.

Vivian's delicately arched brows lifted slightly. "You've never cared much for wine."

"I know," Holly said, smiling. "But since Micah introduced me to it, I rarely drink anything else."

"Well, I'm glad that's over," Micah remarked as they returned the rental car to the agency. "Your old man hates me."

"I should have told him you were a stockbroker or something."

"Good thing you didn't. He would have asked me questions I couldn't answer. Did you find a dress you liked?"

"Oh, Micah! Wait until you see it."

"Did you and Vivian set a date?"

"No. We need to talk to your mom and find out what days the church is available."

Sweeping her into his arms, he murmured, "It can't be soon enough for me."

"Me, either. Micah?"

"Yes, love?"

"I'm hungry."

"Me, too," he said, his dark eyes suddenly hot with desire.

"Not *that* kind of hungry."

"Another hope crushed," he said with a woebegone expression.

Holly poked him in the chest with her forefinger. "You turned me, Mr. Ravenwood," she reminded him. "Now you have to feed me."

"I guess you're right. I've never hunted in Sacramento

before," he said, taking her hand. "Let's go see what the city has to offer."

One of the things Holly liked about being a vampire was that it didn't take long to get from one place to another. Most of the shops were closed, but at this time of night, prey could be found in restaurants, bars, hotels, and theaters.

They strolled hand in hand down restaurant row. Holly's nostrils filled with a myriad of scents—fresh baked bread, fried chicken, fish, shrimp, and rice. Once, it would have made her mouth water. Now, it was the scent of blood that enticed her.

"How about those two?" Micah asked, gesturing at a young couple exiting one of the restaurants.

Holly nodded.

With practiced ease, Micah called the couple to them and led them into the shadows. "A boy for you," he said with a grin. "A girl for me."

Holly placed her hands on the man's shoulders and bent her head to his neck, then hesitated. *Take him. He's just prey.*

She jerked her head back. *Just prey?* What was she thinking? People were more than prey. They were men and women with homes and families, hopes and dreams. Would the day come when she would see her parents as nothing more than prey?

"Micah? Have you ever wanted to feed on your family?"

He looked up, his hand wiping his mouth. "Hell, no. What brought that up?"

"It bothers me that I'm starting to think of the people we hunt as prey."

"Ah. I guess that's something every new vampire has to

come to terms with. It's a line you either cross or you don't. I never want to cross it again."

"I never knew being a vampire was so complicated," Holly remarked.

"It's easy to turn off your humanity," he said quietly. "To forget you were once human. To just think of people as food, here to satisfy your hunger and nothing more. It's easy to mesmerize them, to turn them into slaves willing to do whatever you ask. To just go rogue."

"Do you know anyone like that?"

"No. I never sank that low. But the ones who do are a menace, not only to humanity but to our kind, as well. I know Saintcrow's destroyed a few of them."

"Was Braga that way? A rogue?"

"Pretty much."

"If I ever get like that . . ."

"You won't. I'll never let that happen. What's wrong?"

"Braga. He's still out there somewhere. It's horrible to wish anyone dead, yet we'll always be wondering where he is, won't we?"

"I've got his scent. If he's around, we'll know it. Saintcrow, too." Micah looked from her to the young man, one brow raised, a silent query in his eyes.

Holly eased her hold on the man's shoulders and again bent her head to his neck. She drank quickly and took only a little, feeling guilty all the while.

When she stepped away, Micah wiped the memory from the couple's minds, then took Holly's hand in his. "Come on, sunshine. Let's go home."

Holly had assumed Micah meant Arizona when he mentioned home; instead, he transported them back to Shirley's house in Morgan Creek.

He made love to her that night, as gently and tenderly as

ever a man had loved a woman, making her feel cherished, desirable. In some way she couldn't explain, it made her feel human again. And though she couldn't put it into words, he knew what she was thinking, feeling.

That morning, when the dark sleep carried her away, she was still smiling.

Chapter Thirty-Three

Micah and Holly went to see his parents the next night.

Holly sat at the big dining room table with his whole family present while they went over the list of days the church was available. When they had the dates narrowed down to four, Holly called her parents to see which date worked best for them.

They settled on a Saturday night the second week in November, just two weeks away.

Holly's father insisted on paying for the flowers and the limo and the reception.

"I won't take no for an answer," Arthur said. "Just send me the bills."

Lena invited Holly's parents to stay with them, but when Holly extended the invitation, her father declined, saying they would rent a hotel room.

Holly breathed a sigh of relief when she disconnected the call.

"So, we're all set then?" Micah asked.

"Except for bridesmaids' dresses for the girls," Lena said. "And something for the mother of the bride, and a tux for your dad and your brothers."

"I guess we're not quite all set," Micah muttered.

"What color were you thinking of for the bridesmaids?" Sofia asked. "I was thinking red."

"Bloodred?" Micah asked dryly, and everybody laughed.

"Actually, I think red would be wonderful," Holly said. "After all, Christmas is right around the corner."

"Two weeks," Micah grumbled as he crawled into bed beside Holly. They had returned to Morgan Creek late last night. His parents had wanted them to stay, but Micah had declined.

"It's not that long. If we were having a traditional wedding, with all the trimmings, it would take months to plan. You're lucky we're just having family. What's the rush, anyway?"

"I want to make you mine."

"I'm already yours."

"I want it in writing," he said, nuzzling her neck. "Written proof to show the world."

Holly brushed a lock of hair from his brow. "That's very romantic."

"Well, I'm a very romantic kind of guy." He rained a trail of kisses along the side of her neck. "Haven't you noticed?"

"Not lately," she teased.

"No?" With a ferocious growl, he tucked her beneath him, his clever hands, his fiery kisses, branding her his in a way a piece of paper never could.

Hands shoved in the pockets of his jeans, Rylan Saintcrow strolled along the deserted streets of Morgan Creek. He loved this time of the night, when the world around him lay asleep. And quiet. He had been a vampire long enough that it was now second nature to shut out the barrage of noise that had once threatened to drive him insane. Vampires tended to move silently, to speak in low tones so as not to draw unwanted attention. Humans were a noisy bunch.

He wondered how Holly was adapting to her new life. He had made few friends in his time, but he counted himself lucky to have Micah and Holly among them.

He paused, surprised to find himself nearing the cemetery. He had buried a lot of people there. But for Kadie, the number would have been a lot higher. She had reawakened the humanity within him, guilted him into freeing the men and women the vampires were preying on.

But there were times, though few and far between these days, when he just wanted to surrender to the hunger inside, to hunt some mortal and take what he wanted, to drink and drink until he was sated. But he wouldn't, because Kadie would never forgive him. And he didn't want to live without her.

Stepping through the gate, he wandered among the graves. He remembered all of the deceased, some more than others.

Saintcrow lifted his head when he caught Micah's scent. He found him standing by Shirley's marker, hands shoved into his pockets.

"What are you doing out here?" Micah asked.

Saintcrow shrugged. "I could ask you the same question."

"I stopped by your place. Kadie said you'd gone for a walk. She said you seemed troubled about something."

Saintcrow frowned at Micah. "You looking out for me now?"

"Do I need to?"

"No. I was just reminiscing."

"A man as old as you are, I guess you've got a lot to remember."

"A hell of a lot more than I want to." Saintcrow made a gesture that encompassed the cemetery. "I've got a lot of blood on my hands."

"Don't we all?"

Saintcrow nodded. "All but Kadie and Holly. We spared them that, you and I. Maybe that will count in our favor on the day of judgment." He slapped Micah on the shoulder. "This is no time for morbid recollections. You're getting married."

Micah thought about his conversation with Saintcrow while strolling back to Shirley's house. He had a lot of blood on his hands, too. Oh, not nearly as much as Saintcrow, but enough. Kadie had saved Saintcrow. Saintcrow had saved him. He had saved Holly's life. And she had saved him, he thought. Saved him from a lifetime of regret and loneliness.

"What goes around comes around," he murmured, thinking he would be forever grateful that Holly had mistaken him for the late Joseph Burke.

But that was all in the past. Undressing, he climbed into bed beside his bride-to-be and slipped his arm around her. He'd come so close to losing her. Thirteen days to the wedding. Thirteen. Not a lucky number. Where was Braga? Micah cursed softly. The vampire was still out there, somewhere. Micah could almost feel him lurking in the distance, waiting for just the right moment to strike again. Next time they met, one of them would die.

* * *

For Holly, the next two weeks passed in a flurry of activity—at least from 5 PM to 9. There were bridesmaids dresses to decide on, new lingerie for Holly to wear under her gown, a sheer, sexy nightgown for the wedding night. Since she couldn't sample any of the wedding cakes, Rosa and Sofia were given that task. They chose a four-tier cake, with each layer a different flavor—chocolate, strawberry, white, and carrot. Holly decided on a buffet for the reception and left the menu to Lena. Knowing that her mother felt left out, Holly asked her to select the flowers for the bridal party and for table decorations, and asked her father to choose the wine and the champagne for the bridal toast.

Micah was less busy. His only duty was to find a tux and make sure his father, his brothers, and Saintcrow coordinated with him. His brother Sergio was in charge of finding a band, Enzo in charge of renting limos for the bridal party.

To Holly's amazement, everything came together beautifully.

The night before the wedding, lying in Micah's arms, she confessed, "I never thought we'd pull it off."

"With our mothers in charge?" he said, chuckling. "Never a doubt."

"I love your family. They're so open and outspoken about everything. I always wanted brothers and sisters, but . . ." She blew out a sigh. "I've wondered my whole life if having me was so awful that my parents decided they didn't want any more kids."

"Holly! I'm sure that's not true. Maybe your mother couldn't have any more."

"Maybe. I almost worked up the nerve to ask my mom about it once, but I chickened out."

"Well, by this time tomorrow night you'll be part of the Ravenwood clan. Try not to get lost in the crowd."

"I love you, Micah."

He stroked her cheek, then kissed her lightly. "I love you, too, sunshine. You're the best thing that's ever happened to me."

Holly came awake with a start, as she had every evening since becoming a vampire. As always, the assault on her senses was a little disconcerting. She knew that it was a little after five, that the moon was full, that it was sixty-nine degrees, that Micah was awake, his body curled around hers.

Smiling, she rolled over to face him. "Hello, groom."

"Hello, bride."

"We need to get up."

"I'm already up."

Stifling a grin, she said, "So, I see. You can stay in bed if you want. I have a lot to do before seven." Swinging her legs over the edge of the bed, she headed for the bathroom. "Your mother's probably wondering where I am."

Groaning softly, Micah let her go. The female half of the wedding party was getting ready at his parents' house; the male half was meeting at Sergio's.

Holly emerged from the bathroom twenty minutes later. She grabbed the garment bag that held her dress and a small makeup case. "Don't be late," she warned.

"Not a chance."

"Good." A quick kiss and she was gone.

* * *

Chaos reigned at the Ravenwood home. The house was crowded with Micah's sisters, nieces, and nephews, all talking at once.

Rosa grabbed Holly's hand. "This way. We reserved a room for you upstairs. Sofie's already up there."

Holly followed Rosa up the stairs into one of the bedrooms. Sofia sat at a dressing table applying her makeup.

"Are you nervous?" Sofia asked, meeting her gaze in the mirror.

"Terrified," Holly said.

"Well, you're marrying Micah," his sister, Delia, said. "Who could blame you?"

Laughing, Holly unzipped her garment bag and carefully removed her gown. A few minutes later, her mother and Lena burst into the room. Holly thought her head might explode as the five women fluttered around her, helping her into her dress, arranging her hair, setting the veil in place. An hour and a half later, everyone was dressed and ready to go. Micah's four sisters looked lovely in their tea-length red dresses and matching heels. They wore fingertip veils and carried bouquets of red and white roses.

"Where's your maid of honor?" her mother asked.

"She's meeting us at the church." Kadie's dress was the same as the bridesmaids', except it was floor-length.

Vivian gave her daughter's hand a squeeze. "You make a beautiful bride, Holly. I've never seen you looking so radiant."

"Thanks, Mom."

"I wish you every happiness."

"I don't think I could be any happier."

"I'm so glad you're going to be part of our family," Sofie said.

"Me, too," Holly said.

"Okay," Lena said briskly. "If we don't leave right now, we'll be late!"

Micah stood in the middle of a circle of his brothers, enduring their juvenile jokes about married life, the whole "happy wife, happy life" speech, and warnings to remember to put the toilet seat down, to take out the trash, to beware of PMS.

Micah snorted, then frowned. Did female vampires suffer from PMS? If so, he could be in a world of hurt.

"All right, you idiots," his father said. "It's time to go. One thing I do know is that being late to your own wedding is no way to start a marriage."

"You speaking from experience, Dad?" Mario asked.

"Of course," Luciano said with a broad grin. "That's how I know. Let's go."

Saintcrow met Micah on the steps of the church.

"Where's Kadie?" Micah asked.

"She's in the bride's room with the rest of the women. You ready, bridegroom?"

Micah took a deep breath. "I wish we'd gone to Vegas."

"I hear ya." Saintcrow clapped him on the shoulder. "Let's get it over with."

Micah followed his brothers and Saintcrow through the side door into the chapel, felt a rush of nervous tension as they took their places in front of the altar.

His gaze swept the room. He had expected family only, but his side of the church was crowded with old friends and neighbors. There were maybe a dozen people on the bride's side. His mother smiled at him through her tears while his sister Angela patted her on the shoulder. His nieces and nephews, all dressed in their Sunday best, wriggled in their seats.

Saintcrow nudged Micah. "This is it," he whispered, so low no mortal ear could hear.

"Yeah."

"Not too late to change your mind."

"It was too late from the first time I saw her." Micah frowned as Saintcrow went suddenly still. "What's wrong?"

"Do you smell that?"

Micah lifted his head, nostrils flaring. It was hard to smell anything but flowers and perfume. He opened his preternatural senses. . . . Braga. He'd know that stink anywhere. "You don't think he'd . . ." Micah's voice trailed off as the organ began to play the wedding march.

When Holly and her father appeared in the doorway, he forgot all about Leandro Braga. Never, in all his life, had he seen anything as beautiful as the woman who would soon be his wife. Cheeks flushed, her golden hair framing her face, she was a vision to behold, an angel clad in silk and sunshine. A veil as delicate as a spider's web trailed behind her.

He couldn't stop looking at her, couldn't believe she was really here. Really his.

"Who giveth this woman to be married to this man?"

"Her mother and I do." Arthur spoke clearly as he placed his daughter's hand in Micah's.

Micah was hardly aware of the priest's words until he said, "Repeat after me. I, Micah, take thee, Holly, to be my lawfully wedded wife, to love and to cherish, from this day forward, so long as we both shall live."

Taking both of Holly's hands in his, Micah repeated the words.

Holly gazed deep into Micah's eyes as she repeated the words that made her his wife, thinking that her marriage was every bit as life-altering as becoming a vampire. She was bound to him now, not only by blood, but by the vows they had exchanged.

"I now pronounce you man and wife," the priest said solemnly. "You may kiss the bride."

Micah smiled at her as he drew her into his arms. "I will love you forever," he murmured.

"And I you."

Her eyelids fluttered down as he claimed his first husbandly kiss.

Holly couldn't stop smiling as they left the church. Mrs. Micah Ravenwood, she thought. As long as they lived. Little did the priest know how long that might be.

Outside, they were surrounded by their families, all eager to wish them well.

Holly breathed a sigh of relief as they climbed into the limo. She looked at Micah, eager to be in his arms, frowned at the tight lines around his mouth. "Are you all right?"

He glanced out the window. Should he tell her there was a chance Braga was in the area? He hated to worry her on this, of all days. But she needed to know. "Braga might be here."

"Here?"

Micah nodded. "Saintcrow caught his scent. So did I."

"What are we going to do?"

"Just stay close to me and keep your eyes open." He took her hand in his and gave it a reassuring squeeze. "I can't imagine he'd be dumb enough to try anything at the reception. Not with that many people around."

"I guess you're right." She chewed on her thumbnail, then muttered a very unladylike word. "Well, if he's here, tell him to bring it on!"

Micah folded his hands over her shoulders and kissed her soundly. "That's my little hellcat."

"I mean it. I'm tired of waiting and wondering when he's going to strike again." She flashed her fangs. "I'm not afraid of him."

"Good," Micah said. "Because I am."

"You are?" She stared at him. "I don't believe it."

"Good. Because I aim to rip out his heart and feed it to him."

"My hero."

"Damn right."

When they reached the site of the reception, Holly pushed all thought of Leandro Braga into a compartment in the corner of her mind and shut the door. If he was here, they would deal with it. In the meantime, she was going to enjoy this night. After all, she was only going to get married once, and she wanted to enjoy every minute of being a bride.

The room was beautiful. Pristine white cloths covered the tables. There were flowers everywhere. Tiny colored lights flickered from the ceiling, casting rainbow shadows. Several long buffet tables lined the back wall. Soft music filled the air.

"There's a lot of people here," Micah remarked as they made their way to the receiving line. "What happened to the whole 'family only' thing?"

"I don't know. It just sort of got out of hand."

Holly stood beside Micah in the receiving line as they greeted their guests. Most were friends and relatives of the Ravenwoods; the rest were from Holly's side of the family, including a few of her mother's friends who lived in the area.

She hugged Sofia, who leaned forward and whispered, "Where's that good-looking cousin of yours? You promised to introduce me."

Holly shrugged. "I know. I'm sorry, but I guess he couldn't make it."

"You owe me one," Sofia said, grinning. "You look beautiful."

"Thanks, sweetie. So do you."

Holly's cheeks were tired from smiling by the time the last person made it through the reception line. "Most of the people here are going to wonder why we don't eat, or do the cake-cutting thing."

Micah glanced around. The guests stood around in clusters, waiting. Taking Holly by the hand, he headed for the buffet table. "Come on. Let's get this over with. No one's going to eat until we do."

Holly frowned as Micah filled his plate. "What are you doing?" she whispered, conscious of the people who had lined up behind them. "You can't eat that."

"Not to worry. Saintcrow's going to work a little vampire magic."

"Ah."

Holly followed Micah to the bride's table. She didn't miss the knowing look that passed between Micah and Saintcrow.

Later, as the waiters began to clear the tables, the band played Holly's favorite song and Micah's father invited the bride and groom onto the dance floor for their first dance as husband and wife.

"You look wonderful," Micah said as he took her in his arms.

"So do you." She glanced around the room, her gaze lingering on the exits. "Do you think he's here?"

Micah closed his eyes and opened his senses. It took a moment to filter out the scents of perfume, flowers, cologne, and the food and drink from the buffet table. But Braga's scent was there. Faint, but there.

"He's here, isn't he?" Holly asked.

"Yeah. Outside, I think. Not too close." Micah looked around for Saintcrow, saw him dancing with Kadie on the other side of the room.

Feeling his gaze, Saintcrow looked up. He spoke a few words to Kadie, then circled the floor. "He's here."

"We know."

"So, how do you want to play this?"

"I don't think he'll come inside."

"Not if he's smart."

"Shh." Holly tugged on Micah's hand. "My mom's headed this way."

"It's time to cut the cake," Mrs. Parrish said, beaming at her daughter.

"We'll be right there, Mom."

"Don't be long."

Holly's mother had no sooner moved away than Micah's mother hurried toward them. "What's wrong?"

"Ma . . ."

"Don't 'ma' me, Micah Ravenwood. Something's wrong. I can feel it."

Micah glanced at Holly, who shrugged.

"There's a man outside. He might cause a little trouble later."

"A man?" Lena's eyes narrowed. "You mean a vampire, don't you?"

Micah nodded. "Just stay inside and try to see that no one leaves."

Hand in hand, Micah and Holly approached the table holding the wedding cake. Holly forced a smile as friends and family snapped photos.

She cut a small piece of cake and offered it to Micah, who chewed it but didn't swallow. She did likewise when he fed a piece to her. Then, while everyone was busy at the cake table, Holly grabbed a couple of napkins to hide the uneaten bites and tossed them in the trash.

Micah didn't miss her nervous glance at the nearby exit.

"Come on," Micah said. "It's our big day. Don't let him spoil it. Let's dance."

Holly put thoughts of Braga out of her mind as Micah drew her into his arms.

"Husband," she murmured. "What a beautiful word."

"Mrs. Micah Ravenwood sounds mighty good, too."

She smiled up at him, thinking how much she loved him, how handsome he looked in his tux, and how anxious she was to get him out of it.

His laughter told her he was reading her mind, but she didn't care. Pulling her closer, he asked, "How much longer do we have to stay?"

"I think we can leave any time."

"So, what do we do?" Micah asked. "Just sneak out?"

"Or we could just dissolve into mist and disappear," she said, giggling.

"I'm game if you are."

"Probably not a good idea. Let's go start our honeymoon."

"We never decided where to go."

"I don't care, as long as we're together," Holly said.

"Go tell your mom we're leaving, and I'll tell mine. Then we'll sneak out and meet by the back door."

"Sounds very James Bond, wife." He twirled her around, kissed the tip of her nose, then escorted her off the dance floor.

Holly paused to speak to Micah's brothers and sisters as she made her way through the crowd toward her parents. "Mom, Dad, Micah and I are leaving. Thank you for everything."

"You're welcome, darling," Vivian said. "Where are you going on your honeymoon?"

"We haven't decided." Holly hugged her mother, then turned toward her father. "I'll call you when we get back," she promised.

"Holly, I'm sorry to intrude," Kadie said, coming up behind her. "But . . . um . . . we're not quite ready to go yet if it's all right with you."

Wondering what was going on, Holly said, "Sure, no problem."

Holly's father frowned. "Are they going with you on your honeymoon?"

"No. They're . . . uh . . . they don't have a car and we said we'd drop them at their hotel on our way out of town." It was a lie, of course, but the only one she could think of.

Holly waved to Micah, who hurried toward her.

"Ready?" he asked.

"Yes." Holly hugged her parents again, then took Micah's hand. "He's here, isn't he?" she whispered.

He nodded. "You stay here until it's over."

"Oh, no you don't. I'm going with you."

Micah glanced pointedly at her wedding gown. "You're really not dressed for a fight, sunshine. Besides, I need you to stay in here with Kadie and make sure no one goes outside until I get back. Get my dad to stand at one of the doors, and you and Kadie guard the other one."

Seeing the protest rising in her eyes, he kissed the tip of her nose and hurried out the door.

Saintcrow was waiting for him outside.

Chapter Thirty-Four

"I'll handle this," Saintcrow said. "It's me he wants. You go back inside and look after your bride."

Micah shook his head. "No way. After what he did to Holly, he's mine."

"You really think you can beat him?"

"I don't know, but I'm sure as hell gonna try. If I fail . . ." Micah shrugged. "Then he's yours."

"It's your funeral."

"Thanks for the vote of confidence," Micah muttered, and willed himself to the back of the building.

Braga wasn't hard to find. He stood in a pale shaft of moonlight, eyes narrowed, meaty hands balled into fists. He snorted when Micah rounded the end of the building. "Didn't you get enough last time?"

"Let's get on with it. Or are you gonna talk all night?"

Fangs bared, Braga shambled forward.

Micah took a deep breath. This was the man who had attacked Holly. His rage rose swiftly to the surface, strengthening his resolve as he gathered his power. When Braga struck, he was ready.

As before, it was a silent, bloody battle. Braga was

bigger, physically, but Micah was faster, more flexible. He darted in and out, striking hard and fast, then dancing out of the way. Power flowed through him and with it a kind of exhilaration he had never known before. Braga had defeated him the last time. Tonight, the victory would be his.

Time lost all meaning as they came together again and again, claws and fangs rending flesh.

Micah slipped out of Braga's grasp and the two men glared at each other across six feet of concrete stained with blood.

"You're dead!" Braga hissed the words as he pounded his fists together.

Micah shook his head. "Not tonight." He flexed his arms and shoulders, then flew at Braga, a wild cry erupting from his throat as his claws sank deep into Braga's chest and ripped out the vampire's heart.

Breathing hard, he stared at the body at his feet, then dropped the heart beside it.

A moment later, Saintcrow appeared beside him. "Hell of a fight." He clapped Micah on the shoulder. "For a while there I wasn't sure you'd survive."

"You watched it?"

"Hell, yeah." He cleared his throat. "We have another problem. Let's get the girls and get out of here and I'll tell you all about it."

Holly knew something was wrong the minute she saw Saintcrow's face. "Where's Micah?"

"He's fine. He's waiting outside."

"Is he all right?"

"Yeah, just a little bloody."

"What about Braga?" Kadie asked.

"He's dead." Saintcrow looked at Holly. "We need to talk. Go tell your folks good-bye and let's get out of here."

"You what?" Holly stared at Saintcrow. "How could you?" They were in the back of the limo. Saintcrow had instructed the driver to just drive around for an hour.

"I found a young man in the alley, bleeding out. Apparently Braga waylaid him when he got out of his car, dragged him into the alley, and had a little snack. Turns out the kid is your cousin. Ethan?"

"And you turned him?" Holly shook her head. She couldn't begin to imagine her cousin as a vampire.

Saintcrow shrugged. "It seemed like the thing to do at the time."

"Where is he now?"

"I took him to Blair House and locked him inside."

"But . . . you can't just let him wake up tomorrow night with no idea what happened!" Holly exclaimed.

"I wouldn't do that to him," Saintcrow said. "I'll be there when he wakes up."

Holly nodded. Saintcrow's sire had abandoned him. He knew all too well what it was like. "I don't know what to say, what to think. He's the most unlikely person in the world to be a vampire. Well, I guess I won't be introducing him to Sofia now."

"Why not?" Micah asked with a wry grin "My sister's crazy about vampires."

An hour later, the limo driver parked in front of the Ravenwood house. Micah retrieved their luggage while Kadie and Holly hugged.

Saintcrow slid out of the car. Reaching into his pocket,

he pulled out a wad of cash that would have choked a horse. "Have a good time on me."

"I can't take all that!" Micah exclaimed. "There must be a couple thousand dollars there."

"Consider it a wedding gift. See you when you get home."

Holly and Kadie hugged one last time, and then the limo pulled away from the curb.

"I need to get out of these clothes," Micah remarked, opening the front door. "How about you?"

"No way. I'll only wear this dress once, and I'm not ready to take it off."

"No?"

The look in his eyes sent a rush of heat spiraling through Holly. Batting her eyelashes at him, she said, "Maybe when we get to wherever we're going."

"Maybe?"

"Where are we going, Micah? We never decided."

"Any place you want is fine with me, as long as they've got a big bed."

"I've always wanted to see New York City," Holly said. "Visit Times Square and the Empire State Building. Climb the Statue of Liberty. Go to a Broadway show. Shop at Bloomingdale's."

"I think I can arrange that." He took her hand in his and pulled her close enough to kiss her without getting blood on her dress. "Don't go away, sunshine. I'll be back in a flash."

Pulling away from the Ravenwood house, Kadie rested her head on Saintcrow's shoulder. "So, what are you going to do about Holly's cousin?"

"Keep him in Morgan's Creek? Find him a live-in snack? We've got lots of empty houses."

Kadie elbowed him in the ribs, hard. "You're not going to start that all over again, Mr. Saintcrow."

"Yeah," he muttered. "What was I thinking?"

"You tell me."

"I don't know. He's Holly's cousin. I couldn't just let him die. He was too far gone for a doctor to do any good." He shrugged. "What's done is done."

"You know he's probably going to hate being a vampire."

"I know. Dammit!" He blew out an exasperated sigh. "What do you say we go grab a bite before heading home? I'm thinking we'll need all of our strength when Cousin Ethan wakes up tomorrow night."

It took less than ten minutes for Micah to shower and dress in clean clothes.

"Much better," Holly said as he came down the stairs.

"Ready?" Micah asked.

When she nodded, he picked up their suitcases, then took her hand in his. The next thing Holly knew, they were in front of the Crowne Plaza.

"You said you wanted to see Times Square," Micah said, grinning. "Here we are."

"I hope they have a vacancy."

"Honey, thanks to Saintcrow's generosity, we can afford the best room in the place."

Holly didn't know if the suite they were given was the best or not, but at over eight hundred dollars a night, she decided the view of Times Square, the king-sized bed, enormous TV, and spacious bathroom almost made it worth the price.

Micah had no sooner put their suitcases down than there was a knock at the door.

When he opened it, a bellboy handed him a large gift basket containing a bottle of chilled champagne and a pair of crystal flutes.

"Compliments of the Crowne Plaza," the young man said. "And congratulations."

Micah smiled as he accepted the basket, then handed the bellboy a crisp hundred-dollar bill.

"Thank you, sir! If there's anything else you need . . ."

"We'll call you," Micah said. "Until then, would you please make sure we aren't disturbed?"

"Yessir!" the bellboy said with a knowing wink. "I'll make sure of that."

Micah closed the door, then placed the basket on the table beside the sofa.

"So, Mrs. Ravenwood, here we are, alone at last."

Holly nodded as a flush of anticipation warmed her cheeks.

"Are you ready to get out of that dress yet?" he asked, his voice a low growl of impatience.

"Would you like to help me?" she asked with a coy wink.

"Is that a trick question?"

"Micah, I don't think I can wait any longer."

"You don't have to ask me twice!"

Moving behind her, he kissed his way down her bare back to the first silk-covered button. He unfastened it slowly, his tongue stroking her skin, undoing one after another until the gown pooled at Holly's feet, leaving her clad in nothing but a lacy white bra and bikini panties.

"One of us is overdressed," Holly said as she slid his jacket over his shoulders and tossed it on a chair. In no time at all, she had him stripped to his briefs.

Murmuring, "I married a hussy," he swung her into his arms and carried her to bed. He made short work of her bra and panties, tossed his briefs on the floor, then wrapped her in his arms.

"I love you, Micah. I think I loved you from the first moment I saw you."

"No more than I love you." He kissed her brow, the tip of her nose. "I didn't want to fall in love again," he admitted. "After Shirley, I vowed the next time I fell in love, it would be with a vampire." He laughed softly as he nipped her earlobe. "And what do you know? I did."

"And I'm so glad."

His hands moved over her, working their familiar magic. They had made love before, but never like this, she thought as she surrendered to his touch. He was hers now, forever hers, as she was his.

She explored his hard, muscular body as if it were the first time, reveling in his kisses, caressing him as he caressed her, taking and giving, pledging her love with every touch, every word, until the sun stole the stars from the sky. With a last lingering kiss, she slipped into oblivion.

Chapter Thirty-Five

Saintcrow woke an hour before the setting of the sun. Pulling on a pair of jeans, he left his lair and walked up the hill to Blair House. He paused at the door, his gaze sweeping the neat rows of homes in the town below. All but Shirley's were starting to show signs of neglect—gardens filled with dead flowers, lawns that needed mowing, weeds that needed pulling. Perhaps he should just bulldoze the lot of them. Maybe level the whole damn town. Except for meeting Kadie, he had no good memories of this place. It often surprised him that the spirits of those who had died here rested in peace. Or maybe they didn't. Kadie claimed to have felt something cold and clammy near the graveyard. Micah believed he'd seen Shirley's ghost.

Saintcrow blew out a sigh. Hell, he thought as he removed the wards from the front door of the old mansion. Anything was possible.

Ethan woke in a dark room with no recollection of how he'd gotten there or where he was. Pain clawed at his vitals, threatening to rip his insides to shreds. His body felt strange, alien. Empty. Not the way it did when he was hungry. But kind of hollow, like the Tin Man.

He sat up, his gaze sweeping the room, which was empty save for the bed beneath him. There were cracks in the ceiling. The paint was peeling around the door.

Ethan frowned. How could he see minor things like that in the dark?

He ran his hand over the blanket, feeling every stitch, the tightness of the weave.

How was that possible? And how could the colors look so vibrant when the room was pitch black?

Where the hell was he? Had he been kidnapped?

He heard footsteps outside the door. Friend or foe? He scrambled to his feet, determined not to let his fear show.

A tall man stood in the doorway. His hair was inky black, his eyes like deep pools of ebony. A thin white scar ran from the outer corner of his left eye and down his cheek until it disappeared under his shirt collar.

"What am I doing here?" Ethan demanded. "If you don't let me go, I'll have you arrested for assault and kidnapping."

"Yeah? I'd like to see you try."

"I'll be leaving now."

"You think so?"

Ethan took a step toward the door. Then, seeing the warning in the man's eyes, he changed his mind. "What do you want with me?"

"Why don't you sit down? You must have questions."

Ethan sank down on the edge of the bed. "Where am I? How come I can see you so clearly when there's no light in here?"

"You were attacked last night. Do you remember that?"

Ethan frowned as he searched his memory. "Some big

guy attacked me." He lifted his hand to his throat. "He bit me!"

Saintcrow nodded. "I found you in an alley. You were unconscious, near death."

"So what am I doing here? Why didn't you take me to a hospital?"

"You were too far gone for that."

Ethan stared at the stranger, his eyes narrowing. "I don't understand."

"Do you believe in vampires?"

Ethan nodded. As a kid, he'd carried a couple of wooden stakes and a bottle of holy water in his backpack. He wished he had one of those stakes now. "Who are you?"

"Rylan Saintcrow." He let his eyes go red. "Master vampire."

"Why didn't you kill me?"

"You're Holly's kin."

"Holly!" Ethan swore. "Where is she? Is she all right?"

"She's on her honeymoon."

Ethan started to rise, then doubled over as pain splintered through him. "What's wrong with me?"

"You need to feed."

Arms wrapped around his stomach, Ethan stared at him, his eyes widening as comprehension dawned. "You turned me."

Saintcrow rested one shoulder against the doorjamb. "Like I said, you need to feed. The longer you wait, the more it'll hurt."

"And if I refuse?"

"You'll be miserable for a long time."

"What if I don't want to be a bloodsucker?"

"I think you know the answer to that."

"Go out and meet the sunrise, you mean."

"That'll do it. Or I can rip your heart out. Either way,

all your problems will be solved. So, what'll it be? Life or death?"

"I'm already dead," Ethan said bitterly. "You killed me last night."

"I'd rather think of it as saving your life, but . . ." He shrugged. "If you want to live, I'll show you how to embrace your new life. If not . . ." He shrugged again.

"Why would you help me? Your conscience bothering you?"

"Not a bit. But I know what it's like to be turned and abandoned, and I swore I'd never do that to anybody. Not even a jerk like you."

Ethan scrubbed his hands over his face. Did he want to live as a bloodsucking vampire? He gasped as pain knifed through his gut, more excruciating than before. He couldn't make any kind of rational decision now, he thought, not when all he could think of was the pain, the way his veins felt as if they were shrinking, melting.

Rising on shaky legs, he said, "What do I have to do?"

Minutes later, his head spinning, Ethan found himself standing on a street corner. "Where are we?" It was no place he'd ever been before.

"A little town in southern Wyoming. First lesson, it's not a good idea to feed where you live."

Feed. Ethan grimaced. The word had once meant meat and potatoes. Now it meant blood.

"Pay attention. You see that woman coming out of the drugstore?"

Ethan nodded.

"Call her to you."

"How the hell do I do that? I don't even know her name."

"Call her with your mind. Plant the thought in her head

that she wants to meet you. Once you feel a connection, your thoughts will overpower hers. You can do it. It's easy."

Ethan stared at the woman walking toward them. She was short and plump, probably in her mid-twenties, with shocking red hair. Without being sure of what he was doing, he did as Saintcrow had instructed.

And the woman walked right up to him, her expression blank.

Ethan glanced at Saintcrow. "Now what?"

"Take what you want. But gently," he warned. "You're a lot stronger now than you were before."

"Are you going to watch me?"

"This time, yeah. Bite her here," Saintcrow said, tapping the side of the woman's neck with his forefinger. "Not too deep. You don't want to kill her."

"Now? Here?"

"There's no one else around. It doesn't take long."

Feeling more self-conscious than he'd ever been in his life, Ethan pulled the woman into his arms. He expected to feel revulsion for what he was about to do; instead, it seemed like the most natural thing in the world to sink his fangs—where the hell had they come from?—into the soft skin of her throat and drink.

There was no way to describe it. At the first taste, the pain vanished. Power flowed through him, flooding his senses. He felt it in every cell and fiber of his being.

"That's enough."

Enough? Not until he had it all.

"I said that's enough!"

Ethan bared his fangs at the other vampire. "She's mine!"

"No, she's not." Saintcrow grabbed Ethan's shoulder, his fingers digging deep into his flesh. "Let her go."

Ethan blinked at Saintcrow as if coming out of a trance, then looked at the woman. Her eyes were blank, her face pale.

"Rule number two. You don't kill your prey. Rule number three. You don't wait until the pain is excruciating before you feed." Saintcrow trapped Ethan's gaze with his own. "Rule number four. If I find out you've killed anyone, I'll destroy you. Got it?"

Ethan nodded. He didn't doubt that the man—his sire—meant every word.

Chapter Thirty-Six

Holly woke to butterfly kisses. She smiled as she rolled onto her side and opened her eyes.

Micah smiled back at her. "Good evening, wife."

"Good evening, husband."

"What would you like to do tonight?" he asked.

"Go to a Broadway show. Have a glass of wine in a posh nightclub. Kiss a handsome man in the moonlight."

"Well, I'm not sure we can get tickets for your first choice, but I think I can fulfill the last two."

"Two out of three ain't bad," Holly said. "But first, I need a shower."

She should have known where that would lead. She had no sooner adjusted the water to just the right temperature than Micah stepped into the stall, took the soap from her hand, and gave her the most amazing experience she'd ever had while standing up covered in bubbles.

By the time he finished, she was clinging to him, laughing and breathless and more in love than ever.

The nightclub they chose was Webster Hall. It was like nothing Holly had ever seen before. Located in a building dating back to 1886, it occupied three floors and a basement, with different types of music on each level, and at least two bars on each floor.

After an hour, she was ready to leave.

By then, it was too late to see a show, at least from the beginning. But, using a little vampire compulsion, they managed to catch the second half of *Les Miserables*, which had Holly in tears.

"Maybe we can catch the beginning tomorrow night," Micah suggested as they left the theater.

"Maybe."

"Is something wrong?"

"I was just thinking about my cousin."

"Ah."

"Do you think Ethan's all right?"

Micah shrugged. "He's in good hands. Whether he's all right or not depends on how he reacts, whether he's willing to listen to Saintcrow."

Holly laughed as she pictured her cousin and Saintcrow in the same room. "I'm sure they're butting heads."

Hands fisted on his hips, Ethan watched the woman walk away. "So, that's all there is to it," he muttered. "Hypnotize some poor woman, steal her blood, erase the memory from her mind, and send her merrily on her way. And you've been doing this for how long?"

"A lot longer than you will with that attitude."

Ethan snorted. "You don't like my attitude? You know what you can do about it." He let out a startled cry as, in a move too quick for him to follow, Saintcrow curled one hand around his throat and shoved him against the side of a building.

"I can end it for you right now," Saintcrow hissed. "Won't bother me at all."

"Shit, what you doing?"

"I made a mistake bringing you across. Some people are born to be vampires. You're not one of them. You're gonna be miserable, and that doesn't bode well for the people you feed on. Better to end it now."

"No! Wait!"

"I can read your mind, fledgling. Letting you live might put Holly's life in danger. Micah's, too. They're important to me. You're not."

"Wait, dammit! I won't hurt anybody. I swear it on my mother's life."

"I'll know if you do."

Ethan swallowed hard. "Was it that easy for you to just turn your back on being human?"

"My sire turned me and deserted me. I did a lot of things I'm ashamed of, things that still haunt me. My life was a living hell for a long time until I learned *how* to be a vampire. I had to learn everything the hard way. I don't recommend it."

Ethan tugged uselessly on the hand at his throat. "You told me you'd never abandon anyone you turned."

"Right. But I didn't say I wouldn't kill you instead."

Later, back in Morgan Creek, Ethan sat on a boulder, his chin propped on his fist. He was a vampire. What did that mean for his future? He had a good job. Friends. Family. He frowned. Did Holly know what happened to him? Would she keep his secret?

He rubbed his throat. He could still feel the iron grip of Saintcrow's hand. He had no doubt his sire would have killed him without a qualm, knew Saintcrow wouldn't hesitate to destroy him if he hurt anyone.

He inhaled sharply and blew it out in a heavy sigh. He would probably have to move when he got back home. His neighbors would start to wonder why he stopped mowing his yard on Saturday morning. His buddies would question why he didn't show up for Sunday morning football sessions at the park. He might be able to make plausible excuses to his friends and neighbors, but what about his boss? The old man expected him to be at his desk at 9 AM sharp. There was no way around that.

Ethan stared into the distance. It wasn't just food and drink he had to give up, he thought ruefully. It was his whole way of life.

How long did Saintcrow intend to keep him here?

Kadie put the book she'd been reading aside when Rylan materialized in the room. "So, how did it go?"

"Let's just say his first night as a vampire was almost his last."

"That bad, huh?"

"Yeah. Some people adjust better than others. He's not one of them."

"Like you said, it's only been a day."

"Yeah. The kid may not like what he is, but he took to hunting like a duck to water."

"Then there's hope." Kadie snuggled against him. "I wonder how Holly likes New York."

New York was a great town, but after five days, Holly was ready to go home. The noise, the crowds, the constant temptation of so many beating hearts, it was all just too much.

"I'm sorry," she told Micah. "Maybe, if I wasn't a new vampire it wouldn't bother me, but . . ."

"Hey, you don't need to apologize."

She smiled up at him. "I love you."

"I know. Pack your bags, Mrs. Ravenwood, and let's go find a place to live."

Because she needed to know what had happened to Ethan, they went back to Morgan Creek. After dropping off their luggage at Shirley's house, they went to see Saintcrow and Kadie.

"Welcome home!" Kadie said. "Come on in and sit down. Did you have a good time?"

Holly nodded as she followed Kadie into the living room. "It was wonderful, but after a few days . . . it just got to be too much."

"I know what you mean. It takes awhile to adjust."

"You're looking well." Saintcrow gave her a hug, then clapped Micah on the shoulder. "Marriage seems to agree with the two of you. So what now?"

"We need to find a place to live," Micah said. "And Holly was wondering what happened to her cousin."

"He's staying in Rosemary's house for now," Saintcrow said.

"He's here?" Holly exclaimed.

"Yeah, I've been teaching him the ropes."

"Sounds like a boatload of fun," Micah muttered. "Sorry I missed it."

"How is he?" Holly asked.

"Aside from his lousy attitude? I think he'll be okay."

"I can't imagine Ethan as a vampire," Holly said. "He never liked the sight of blood or horror movies. I remember one day when I was five or six, I fell down a hill and cut my knee on a piece of glass. I swear, he turned three shades of green when he saw the blood." She shook her head. "He was always afraid of vampires. Never used to leave home without a wooden stake or a bottle of holy water."

"Seriously?" Kadie asked.

Holly nodded. "I'd like to see him."

"I'm not sure that's a good idea," Saintcrow said. "He's still pretty angry and not really in control."

"I'm not worried. You know what they say? Blood is thicker than water."

"I'm going with you," Micah said. "I'll wait outside, if you want, but you're not going down there alone."

Holly stood on the front porch of Rosemary's house. Now that she was here, she was having second thoughts. She had welcomed becoming a vampire, so her transition had been relatively easy. But waking up as a vampire had to be a shock. Saintcrow had said Ethan was angry and out of control. What if his first instinct was to attack her?

With a sigh of exasperation, she reminded herself that Micah was nearby and knocked on the door.

Ethan's eyes widened in surprise when he saw Holly standing outside. "What the hell are you doing here?"

"I live here. I mean here, in Morgan Creek," she clarified "Not in this house. Can I come in?"

"Sure."

Holly followed him into the living room.

He gestured at the sofa. "Make yourself at home."

Holly sat on the edge of the couch. He took the chair opposite her.

"How are you?" she asked.

"How the hell do you think? One day I'm just a normal guy, the next I'm a bloodsucking fiend being held by some master vampire with a God complex."

"Ethan, I'm so sorry for what happened."

"It's not your fault." He scrubbed his hands up and down his thighs, then shook his head. "I guess I'm just having a hard time accepting it. You know I've never liked blood or killing, or . . ." Eyes narrowed, nostrils flaring, he stared at her. "What the hell! *You're* a vampire!"

Holly nodded.

"How did it happen? Do your parents know? Good Lord, does Micah know?"

"Micah turned me," she said. "It was what I wanted."

He shook his head in disbelief. "You *wanted* this?"

"It was the only way we could stay together. And it's not so bad, really, if you don't fight it. Don't focus on what you can't do, but what you can. The pros make up for the cons, believe me. Once you get used to it . . ."

"I don't want to get used to it! I feel like a monster. All I can think about is the blood."

"That will pass. You'll be able to control the hunger, in time. After all, you were turned by the most powerful vampire in the world."

"Yeah?"

"Yeah. Remember how the two of us shared secrets in school? Well, now we have another one. A big one!"

He laughed and she laughed with him.

"Who knows," Holly said. "Maybe you'll find the love of your life and she'll be a vampire, too."

"Maybe," he said glumly. "I sure haven't found a human female who'll put up with me."

"I think I know one," Holly said, smiling. "I promised to introduce her to you at the reception. Her name's Sofia, and she loves vampires."

Holly was still smiling when she left Ethan. Life was funny, she mused. She hadn't seen Ethan in years. Now they were both vampires.

"Everything okay?" Micah asked, falling into step beside her.

"Couldn't be better."

"So, Mrs. Ravenwood, what do you say we get back to our honeymoon?"

"I'd like that, Mr. Ravenwood. Race you home!" she cried, and sprinted down the street, disrobing as she neared Shirley's house.

With a shake of his head, Micah lit out after her, shedding his own clothing as he went.

He caught her inside the front door, scooped her into his arms, and carried her into the bedroom, where he tossed her on the bed.

"Good thing I'm a vampire," she said, giggling as he landed none too gently on top of her.

"Did I hurt you?"

"Of course not, silly." Pulling his head down, she kissed him, her hands eagerly stroking his back as she wriggled her hips in invitation.

"What do you want, you hussy?"

"I don't know," she teased. "What have you got?"

He reared back in mock horror. "Have you forgotten already?"

Batting her eyelashes at him, she said, "Well, I guess you'll have to show me all over again."

"Tonight and every night," he growled. Scooping her

into his arms again, he claimed her lips in a long hungry kiss, his tongue plundering her mouth, his hands delving into her hair.

Holly wrapped her arms around his neck, purring with satisfaction as his body merged with hers. Was there anything more wonderful than being in his arms, hearing his voice whispering that he loved her, would always love her?

His gaze searched hers. "No regrets?"

Holly shook her head. Regrets? Hardly! How could she have regrets when she was in love with the most incredibly sweet, handsome man—human or vampire—she had ever known?

Hours later, she yawned, a familiar sense of lassitude stealing over her as the rising sun chased the moon from the sky.

Pillowing her head on Micah's shoulder, she closed her eyes and surrendered to the Dark Sleep, knowing that tomorrow night—and every night for the rest of her life—would be filled with the same love and happiness she found in Micah's arms.

Read on for a preview of Amanda Ashley's
next thrilling vampire romance,

A Fire in the Blood,

coming next summer!

Tessa shook her head. "Lisa, I am so *not* going in there. You know I don't believe in all that nonsense."

"It's just for fun," Lisa said, tugging on her hand. "Come on!"

Tessa stared at the black-and-gold striped tent. It sat a ways off from the rides and food booths. A tripod beside the entrance held a large, hand-lettered sign that read:

Madame Murga
Palms Read
Fortunes Told

Every time the carnival came to town, Tessa's cousin Lisa nagged her to get her fortune told. Even though she was only thirteen, Lisa was really big on the paranormal. She read all the young-adult books about vampires and werewolves, witches and zombies, watched all the movies, but she was too chicken to get her own fortune told. So every time the carnival came to town, she begged Tessa to do it.

She blew out a sigh, knowing Lisa would keep nagging her until she gave in. Might as well just get it over with.

"All right," Tessa said, "but just remember—you owe me big-time for this."

Grinning, Lisa pulled her toward the tent.

A small silver bell chimed when they stepped inside. The interior of the tent was appropriately dim. A small round table covered with a fringed, garish yellow cloth stood in the center of the floor. A pair of nondescript wooden chairs flanked the table.

Tessa stared at the crystal ball in the center of the table. Why had she let Lisa talk her into this?

A dark-skinned woman stepped out from behind a curtain. A bright red, purple, and blue scarf covered her long black hair. She wore a white peasant blouse over a colorful skirt. Tiny bells affixed to the hem jingled softly when she moved.

"How may I help you?" Her voice was deep, husky.

Lisa gave Tessa a little push. "My cousin's curious about where she'll find true love."

"You seem very young to be concerned about such a thing," the gypsy woman remarked dryly. "How old are you?"

"Fifteen. But if I'm too young . . ."

"Be seated."

Tessa sat on the edge of one of the wobbly wooden chairs, her hands tightly folded in her lap. Suddenly, this didn't seem like such a good idea.

"Your hand."

Tessa placed her left hand in the gypsy's, flinched when the woman's fingers curled around her own.

The woman bowed her head and closed her eyes.

A minute passed.

Two.

Tessa glanced over her shoulder at Lisa.

Lisa shrugged.

"I cannot see much of your future," the gypsy said, her voice sounding distant. "But I see a man. He is old. Very old. He will come into your life in a moment of danger. He will watch over you and protect you." The gypsy's hand gripped Tessa's tighter. "He will bring you death," she whispered, her voice like the rustle of dry leaves. "And life."

An icy chill ran down Tessa's spine. Jumping to her feet, she grabbed Lisa by the hand and ran out of the tent.

She didn't stop running until she was safely home with the door locked and bolted behind her.

Connect with

Books by Bestselling Author
Fern Michaels

___**The Jury**	0-8217-7878-1	$6.99US/$9.99CAN
___**Sweet Revenge**	0-8217-7879-X	$6.99US/$9.99CAN
___**Lethal Justice**	0-8217-7880-3	$6.99US/$9.99CAN
___**Free Fall**	0-8217-7881-1	$6.99US/$9.99CAN
___**Fool Me Once**	0-8217-8071-9	$7.99US/$10.99CAN
___**Vegas Rich**	0-8217-8112-X	$7.99US/$10.99CAN
___**Hide and Seek**	1-4201-0184-6	$6.99US/$9.99CAN
___**Hokus Pokus**	1-4201-0185-4	$6.99US/$9.99CAN
___**Fast Track**	1-4201-0186-2	$6.99US/$9.99CAN
___**Collateral Damage**	1-4201-0187-0	$6.99US/$9.99CAN
___**Final Justice**	1-4201-0188-9	$6.99US/$9.99CAN
___**Up Close and Personal**	0-8217-7956-7	$7.99US/$9.99CAN
___**Under the Radar**	1-4201-0683-X	$6.99US/$9.99CAN
___**Razor Sharp**	1-4201-0684-8	$7.99US/$10.99CAN
___**Yesterday**	1-4201-1494-8	$5.99US/$6.99CAN
___**Vanishing Act**	1-4201-0685-6	$7.99US/$10.99CAN
___**Sara's Song**	1-4201-1493-X	$5.99US/$6.99CAN
___**Deadly Deals**	1-4201-0686-4	$7.99US/$10.99CAN
___**Game Over**	1-4201-0687-2	$7.99US/$10.99CAN
___**Sins of Omission**	1-4201-1153-1	$7.99US/$10.99CAN
___**Sins of the Flesh**	1-4201-1154-X	$7.99US/$10.99CAN
___**Cross Roads**	1-4201-1192-2	$7.99US/$10.99CAN

Available Wherever Books Are Sold!
Check out our website at **www.kensingtonbooks.com**

More by Bestselling Author
Hannah Howell